# DEATH
## IN AN
# ENGLISH VILLAGE

# BOOKS BY FLISS CHESTER

# DEATH
## IN AN
# ENGLISH VILLAGE

## FLISS CHESTER

*Bookouture*

Published by Bookouture in 2025

An imprint of Storyfire Ltd.
Carmelite House
50 Victoria Embankment
London EC4Y 0DZ

www.bookouture.com

The authorised representative in the EEA is Hachette Ireland
8 Castlecourt Centre
Dublin 15 D15 XTP3
Ireland
(email: info@hbgi.ie)

ISBN: 978-1-83618-385-3
eBook ISBN: 978-1-83618-384-6

This book is a work of fiction. Whilst some characters and circumstances
portrayed by the author are based on real people and historical fact, references
to real people, events, establishments, organizations or locales are intended only
to provide a sense of authenticity and are used fictitiously. All other characters
and all incidents and dialogue are drawn from the author's imagination and are
not to be construed as real.

*To my family*
*What ho!*

Croquet was meant to be a genteel sort of sport, at least that's what the Honourable Cressida Fawcett had always thought. But as she drummed her fingers on her hips, standing on the edge of the croquet lawn of her parents' rambling Jacobean manor house, Mydenhurst Place, she could see only chaos. She caught her breath and raised a hand to her brow to shield her from the bright spring sunlight and tried once again to take stock of the scene in front of her. There were puppies everywhere. They were careering across the grass, through the hoops, tumbling over the heavy, coloured balls and pegging themselves out on the multi-striped stick in the middle of the lawn. She'd not seen such pandemonium on the croquet lawn since her cousin Jolyon had that unfortunate incident with the thirty bantam hens.

The puppies – five currently croqueting each other in front of her, though she was sure there were six in total – were the offspring of her adorable and adored pug, Ruby. Ruby had surprised Cressida at Christmas time with a bulging belly and then, at the end of January had given birth to six perfect little pups. Yes, six. She was sure of it, as she scanned the podgy balls of fur scampering across the lawn, peeling and rolling themselves through the hoops. They were porgis, or perhaps cogs, she wasn't sure what the official name might be; but she did know they were here thanks to an autumn dalliance between Ruby and one of Lord Totteridge's Welsh corgis.

'Speaking of Ruby,' Cressida murmured to herself. 'Where is she? And Suki?' She counted the small balls of energy that were rebounding off the croquet hoops. The month had been so dry, her father had asked Bob the gardener to fetch the croquet set out of the summer pavilion that was situated just to one side of the lawn, away from the house, and measure out the pitch in expectation of summer. Today, however, the only game that would be played between the hoops and pegs would be puppy catching, not croquet.

Cressida readied herself for another dash across the lawn as she called over to her mother, who was trying to keep two pups from running off into the rose bushes.

'I'm worried about Ruby and Suki. I think they went behind the pavilion, Mama.' Cressida pointed, pulling her cashmere cardigan around her. It was sunny, but there was still a chill in the air. A pair of red kites circled high above the trees behind the pavilion. *A small puppy would be the perfect morsel for them*, she thought, and shivered as a breeze tickled the back of her neck. She wished she'd thought to bring her scarf outside.

'There's not much there. Bob leaves the rotavator behind there sometimes, otherwise—'

'It's the back way down to the stream, though, isn't it?' Cressida replied, identifying another danger to the tiny pooches. She unclamped a small canine from her trouser leg and passed the pup over to Molly, one of the Mydenhurst maids, who was dressed in a smart black woollen dress with a white pinafore over it. It matched her white frilled headband, an item of her uniform that was working particularly hard today in keeping her russet curls off her lightly freckled face.

Smiling in thanks to the maid, Cressida ran over to the smartly painted, clapboard building on the far edge of the lawn. Reaching the pavilion in no time, she picked her way over the less formal ground around the side of it, glad she was in her sensible tweed slacks and brogues. Her mother, who had decided to follow her, much to the detriment of her rose beds no doubt, moved less nimbly, being in a skirt and twinset, and much smarter shoes. Cressida let her fall behind as she pushed away branches that grew up close to the wooden building and were having the annoying habit of getting caught up in her newly shingled and cut blonde bob.

She hoped the local jays and magpies could make use of the tufts of pure cashmere that she was losing to the brambles, too, but she bore on. Sure enough, she soon came to an opening in the undergrowth behind the pavilion that led through to a well-trodden woodland pathway. A haze of lilac bluebells either side of the path made her feel like Moses parting the waves, and she wished she had time to stop and pick a few for her mother as she always had as a girl. But her worries over Ruby and Suki's whereabouts were more pressing and she hurried along the pretty woodland path, calling back to her mother to let her know which way she'd gone. Then she called Ruby's name several times. Being almost three years old, Ruby had half a chance of remembering her name, though Cressida knew all too well that recall wasn't one of her strong suits.

A thought flashed across Cressida's mind; if Ruby wasn't great at coming to her name, Suki, being only six weeks old, would be one hundred times worse. Cressida hurried as she ran along the pathway, which wound its way through the small wood. She knew all the paths and all the fields, every tree and every shrub like the back of her own hand, having played among them all her childhood. She ducked under a low branch she knew instinctively would be there and as she did so, she noticed a chewed sock, one of hers, on the path and knew that she was on the right track. She'd mourned the loss of that very pair only last night as she'd seen Suki chew its partner to an untimely end in front of the fire.

'Ruby!' she called again, catching her breath as she slowed to a trot. The path had emerged in an open field full of long grasses, and Cressida knew that just beyond it was the stream. A shadow appeared overhead and Cressida looked up; the kites were still circling.

Picking up her pace again, Cressida ran along the path that now skirted the field and led down to the stream, known to the villagers as Hell's Ditch. She kept an eye on the hovering birds of prey, hoping she was the only one on the hunt for a delicious little puppy. As she saw one of the large birds swoop, she heard yapping and started to wave her hands above her head, warning off the bird as much as she could. Desperation flooded her heart. Just as it was about to hit the ground it banked and flew up past her. Cressida felt relief wash over her as she watched it fly back into the copse of trees along with its mate. But as she neared the old stone bridge that carried the path over the water, that relief turned to shock, and then to revulsion, and finally horror.

For what she saw in the stream was not what she had first feared. And, in fact, her darling dog Ruby came bounding up to her as soon as she'd cleared the long grasses, Suki in tow, yapping away. But what they'd run from, the terrible thing that must have attracted them in the first place, was a man. Lying face down in the stream, his woollen jacket floating out around him, a white, bloated hand still holding the remnants of what looked like a sandwich. A sandwich that may well have been his last meal.

For the man in the stream was most decidedly dead.

## 2

'Oh no, oh, Ruby!' Cressida scooped up her darling dog, who rewarded her with several licks to the face as she leaned down once again to pick up the much smaller Suki. Holding both dogs securely she edged closer towards the stream.

'Darling,' Lady Fawcett called, finally having emerged from the long grasses to the clearing at the edge of the water. 'Did you find Ruby and Suki? Oh... dear me!'

'Mama, stay back.' Cressida turned away from the body and rushed over to where her mother stood, wide-eyed, staring past her to the stream. 'Please, Mama, don't look any further. It's horrible,' she said, passing both dogs to her mother as if that would distract her.

'Don't be silly, darling. I'm your mother. Who is it? Are they dead?' She handed Ruby back to Cressida, keeping Suki in the nook of her arm.

Cressida shrugged. 'I haven't had a chance to see...'

'Come on then.' Lady Rosamund Fawcett showed her mettle, and all but pushed past her protective daughter, striding to the stream.

'And I wonder where I get it from,' Cressida whispered to Ruby as she caught up with her mother who had stopped just yards from the edge of the water.

Now they were closer Cressida could take in more of the scene. The body wasn't floating as such, the stream wasn't deep enough for that, but it – he – was face down in the shingle and stones, his arms splayed out beside him, his legs being buffeted by the water as it rushed over a small drop in the rocks. His feet were barely visible, being just that bit further under the shadow cast by the old stone bridge that spanned the stream. It wasn't a large bridge, but back in the day it would have been wide enough for a drover and his flock of geese or several sheep on their way to market. Now it was only used by the Fawcett family and their staff and tenant farmers.

Cressida turned to her mother, who was tutting and shaking her head. 'Do you know who it is? He looks familiar, that coat...' Cressida racked her brains.

'It's Bob Pringle. Our gardener,' Lady Fawcett said, her voice quiet and her face pale.

'Bob. Oh no.' Cressida knew why she recognised that old tweed jacket now. Bob had worn it almost every day for the last however many years. Bob, who had been their gardener and such a familiar face since she'd been a girl. A man she remembered fondly leaning on his spade as a robin made merry with the worms he dug up in the rose bed. She turned back to look at her mother, who was still shaking her head, her face blanched from its usual rosiness. Lady Fawcett pointed at the bridge and then spoke.

'Was he sitting on the bridge eating his lunch and then fell, do you think?'

Cressida looked back at the scene. Her mother's guess made sense. The way he was face down, his legs close to the bridge. His sandwich, soggy now, but made of good, solid farmhouse bread, still in his hand. Cressida looked around her at the grassy fields studded with oxeye daisies, the old drovers' path lined by a hedgerow that looked positively bridal thanks to the soft white and pink hawthorn blossom. Then there was the small but ancient woodland that protected this wilder spot from the formality of the Jacobean house and gardens. It would be a glorious spot to sit and have one's lunch, and it made perfect sense that Bob Pringle would be there, enjoying his sandwich. How tragic that one moment he might have been eating his lunch, and the next... she could barely process the thought. Cressida looked to her mother who was staring at the body in the stream.

'I should try and help him,' Cressida volunteered. 'Just in case he's not...' She couldn't quite bring herself to finish the sentence. As her mother nodded her assent, Cressida carefully put Ruby down and stepped towards the stream. She couldn't take her eyes off the bloated hand and its soggy sandwich, which she could see now had been cheese and pickle, but she forged ahead, stepping gingerly into the shallow stream, wobbling as she found her footing on a slippery stone.

'Careful, darling!' Lady Fawcett called across to her.

'I am being, Mama,' Cressida answered, concentrating on not falling over. She reached the part of the stream in which Bob lay and cautiously placed a hand on his shoulder. His tweed jacket here was still dry, the water hadn't even reached high enough over his shoulders to dampen it. Cressida laid her palm flat against the material and gently shook the gardener, while calling his name. But there was no response. *Poor Bob*, she thought, remembering the times he'd shaken a rake at her while she made mud pies in the flower beds or held his head in his hands as she'd kicked through the neat piles of leaves he swept up each autumn.

She stilled herself until all she could hear was the gentle

trickle of the water and her own heartbeat. She rested her hand on his back. There was no movement, no breath. What little skin she could see was tinged with an icy blue. Without the strength to roll him over she couldn't double-check, but she was sure – as she had been in that first moment that she'd seen him – that he was dead. Her mama was most likely right. He'd slipped and fallen face first into the stream. It wasn't deep, but a fall might have knocked him out and the couple of inches of rapid flowing water pushed into his lungs would have done the rest. Cressida gently patted his back and braced herself to navigate her return to the dry bank, her shoes now sodden and her toes quite perishingly cold because of it.

But something on the other side of Bob's body caught her eye. The soggy sandwich had been grasped in his left hand, the one closest to her, but his right hand, which had been harder to see at first, was clenched tightly shut. Balled into a fist, even.

Cressida thought it odd, since surely a man's first instinct as he fell would have been to open his hands, splaying them to brace his fall? She could understand not wanting to lose a delicious sandwich, but why ball up his right hand? Unless it was holding something. Something he hadn't wanted to let go of, come hell, or indeed, high water.

Cressida looked up at the bridge. There was no crumbling stone or loose mortar. If this was an accident, it wasn't from Bob losing his seat on the solid square edge of it. Could he have suffered a heart attack or had some sort of blackout and just fallen in?

'One more moment, Mama,' Cressida called to her mother as she shuffled herself around the half-damp body to the other side.

'What are you doing, Cressida?' Lady Fawcett asked. 'Don't risk getting yourself all wet, darling. Poor Bob, seems there's nothing we can do now except put a telephone call in to the coroner. Maybe Mr Botheridge at Downs Farm could help us. And your father, of course.'

Cressida let her mother's thoughts go unanswered as she squatted down, feeling the water of the stream drag and catch around the hems of her trousers. She took a deep breath, then examined the closed fist of the dead man. Gently prising it open she wondered at the determination that had kept it so firmly closed. It soon became clear though – as she managed to straighten out one, two, then three of his fingers, the nails of which were rimmed with dirt, as one would expect from a gardener – what he had been holding onto so tightly. She gasped and rocked back slightly in shock.

'What is it, darling?' Lady Fawcett asked, raising her voice in concern from the dry bank of the stream.

Cressida ignored her mother for a moment. There was something else, not just in Bob's hand, but written on his palm. Cressida prised the last finger open and slid the object away, keeping it safe in her own fist, and read what she could as the icy-cold water of the stream did its best to obscure the ink. The writing was large, but hard to make out. A capital 'D', then a squiggle – perhaps it was an 'e' – and another 'D'. *DeD... or perhaps dead?*

'Mama, you might need to telephone someone other than the coroner and Mr Botheridge,' Cressida called up, taking in what she'd seen. 'You might need to call the police.'

'The police? For an accident?' Lady Fawcett looked concerned. 'I know you adore DCI Andrews, darling, but I don't think we need Scotland Yard for an accident.'

'I'm not so sure this was an accident, Mama,' Cressida answered, holding the item that had been in Bob's fist aloft. 'I have a feeling this might have been murder.'

'Murder?' Lady Fawcett gripped her pearls with the hand that wasn't cradling Suki. She squinted at the glinting object that Cressida was holding up to show her and waited as her daughter splashed out of the stream and onto the bank next to her, shaking her feet one by one as she did so. Realising this was futile, Cressida shrugged and crossed the few steps it took to reach her mother's side, ignoring the squelching in her shoes.

Together they looked at the prize in Cressida's palm.

It was a beautifully clean, shining bright, solid gold coin.

## 3

With one dog each in their arms, Cressida and her mother, Lady Fawcett, picked their way back up the pathway from the stream towards the woods. Cressida's feet were wet and her woollen socks felt heavy in her leather brogues, not to mention the bottom few inches of her tweed slacks, which she wished she'd tucked into her socks before she'd checked Bob's body. She held the gold coin in her hand, unsure of whether she should have left it with the deceased as evidence.

DCI Andrews, the Scotland Yard detective who had been there during each of her murder investigations – or perhaps, to put it more accurately, *she* had been present at most of *his* recent murder investigations – was always scolding her for tampering with his evidence. But of what was it evidence? She'd rashly called it murder just now to her mother, who was quite rightly challenging her on it as they went back to the house to raise the alarm.

'I can't think how you can claim it's murder just because Bob was holding a coin,' she pointed out.

'And he had the word "dead" written on the palm of his hand,' pointed out Cressida.

'Well, that could mean anything. And you said it wasn't even spelled correctly.' She paused. 'Though his spelling wasn't the best. He once left me a note and it took me hours to work out that he was trying to spell rhododendrons. We've called them the dodos ever since. Still, just having the word "dead" written on his hand doesn't tell us much.'

'No, but it's not normal is it, Mother?' Cressida countered.

'Cressida, I know you're very detail-driven, which is wonderful when you help with everyone's decorating dilemmas. And I know this eye for design means you have an "eye for a crime", but in this case you might be seeing something that just isn't there. Bob's death, though tragic... oh dear, poor Marian will be devastated.' She paused, and closed her eyes, holding Suki close to her heart as she uttered what might have been a silent prayer, then brought her conversation back on track. 'Tragic but most likely an accident. Looking at how he fell, and knowing he ate his lunch on that bridge almost every day... he used to feed those jays, I saw him doing it once, pulling off great big chunks of his sandwich and throwing it to them. And it's not safe you know, that bridge. Do you remember he used to tell you off for playing on it when you were a young girl?'

Cressida did remember. She'd known Bob Pringle almost all her life. His wife Marian – well, widow – was their cook. They were local people, born and bred, and had been in service with the Fawcetts for years. Decades even. Marian's sister, Annie, ran the pub in the village along with her husband, Walter, and as far as Cressida knew, Bob had been well liked by them and everyone else in the village.

'Wasn't Bob always at the Royal Oak, Mama?' Cressida asked, still holding Ruby while also pushing back a low-swinging branch as they entered the small woods behind the pavilion.

'Darling, I don't think it's fair to accuse Bob of being intoxicated, not at midday on a workday,' Lady Fawcett reprimanded her daughter. 'The poor man's dead.'

'I wasn't accusing him of that, Mama.' Cressida sighed. 'I was just wondering who might be best to talk to about him. Find out what's been going on, and if this gold coin that he was grasping and the word "dead" written on his hand had any relevance to what's happened.'

Cressida almost bumped into her mother as she came to an abrupt halt in front of her.

'What is it?' Cressida asked, letting Ruby down and taking Suki from her mother, who used the opportunity to straighten her cashmere and adjust her pearl necklace. She then reached out and Cressida, knowing what she wanted, handed over the gold coin.

'Your father will want to see this,' Lady Fawcett said, turning it over and letting it catch the dappling sunlight that was filtering through the evergreen trees in the small woodland. For a moment there was no sound between them except for the trilling of the robin and the bickering of the blue tits.

'It's interesting, of course, but why do you say it like that?' Cressida asked, starting to walk again, conscious not just of the poor housemaid left in charge of the five other puppies on the croquet lawn, but also of the fact that they needed to telephone the authorities, pronto.

'Don't you remember the legend of the Mydenhurst hoard, darling?' Lady Fawcett answered her, catching up with her daughter, while picking her way over last year's dead bracken and pine needles on the woodland path. 'The gold coins left by the Romans or Saxons or what have you, and buried somewhere here in the village, but no one really knows where. Your father's new hobby is finding it, and he's become quite chummy with all sorts of other local buffs who seem to have theories about the exact whereabouts. This' – she held out the coin in front of her so that Cressida could see it again as they neared the clearing behind the pavilion – 'could well be part of that hoard.'

'You think Bob the gardener had found a centuries-old hoard of gold coins?' Cressida's interest was piqued. And her mother had sparked off a memory, long buried, but one she squinted to remember as they rounded the corner of the pavilion and were greeted by a cacophony of yapping from Suki's siblings. She put the little pup down and let her run off to join them, looking like a little jumping mushroom as she did. Ruby toddled off after her and Cressida waved a thanks to the now bedraggled, but blissfully happy-looking housemaid who had been quite overwhelmed, it seemed, by so much puppy energy.

Lady Fawcett stood beside her daughter and handed back the coin.

'Papa's been searching for the Mydenhurst hoard,' Cressida repeated what her mother had told her. 'And perhaps Bob found it... Do you think that would be enough to instil some sort of jealousy in these new chums of Papa's?'

'Perhaps, darling, and no time like the present to ask him. We need to put a telephone call through to the authorities too, and ask Mr Botheridge for help with poor Bob. And I'd better go and tell Marian.' She sighed. 'Though heaven knows how she'll take it. I do feel for her. And she'd been so excited for your visit and seeing the puppies. She's been preparing beef jelly and sardine pâté for them since last week.'

'Poor Marian,' agreed Cressida.

With Lady Fawcett braced to tell Bob's widow the terrible news, and the housemaid, though now divested of her apron, which was being carried across the lawn by three small pups, looking dishevelled if happy, Cressida headed to see her father, detouring briefly to change out of her wet things.

Despite the unseasonal warm spring sunshine she noted the

hairs standing up on her arms and she felt a shiver across the back of her neck. Cressida had a feeling that this coin was evidence of something very sinister happening in this quiet little English village. And perhaps Bob's death was only the start...

## 4

Cressida sat facing her father, Colonel Lord Sholto Fawcett, in his study. The gold coin she'd found gripped in Bob's hand was now sitting on the desk in between them, mesmerising them both. Her father had been shocked by the news of his gardener's death, and marked the news with a moment's silence from behind his desk. After that he was quick to telephone the local coroner and organise Mr Botheridge, their tenant farmer from Downs Farm, to get to the old stone bridge at Hell's Ditch with a donkey or handcart onto which he could load the body. Following his daughter's wishes he'd also put in a call to Scotland Yard to enquire if DCI Andrews could be spared from his current duties to pay a visit to Sussex and help them solve what they thought might be a murder. Now they sat either side of a large mahogany desk, looking at the gold coin, shining bright against the dark-green leather.

The first thing that surprised Cressida about the coin was its size. It was barely larger than her thumbnail, and thin too. So thin, she'd wondered if it had been worn away from use or time, though from what she remembered the Mydenhurst hoard had been buried for centuries and furthermore, despite its small size, there was quite some detailed patterning to it. Her father leaned forward in his chair and steepled his fingers, his elbows on his desk. A stranger in the room could have confidently assumed that Lord Fawcett was Cressida's father, as despite the fact she looked so similar to her mother, it was her father's blond hair she'd inherited. That and their slight frames, height and general mannerisms – Cressida echoed her father subconsciously and leaned forward, putting her elbows on the desk, too.

'It's a thrymsa, I believe,' Lord Fawcett said, then took his elbows off the desk and leaned back in his chair. This time, Cressida didn't echo him, instead leaning further forward and touching the coin with her fingertip.

'A what now?' Cressida asked.

'A thrymsa,' her father said again, then explained. 'I remember a lecture old Barney Trewitt gave on the hoard back in eighty-seven. He explained that the most likely thing would be for the hoard coins to be thrymsas, as they were minted in the seventh century, from about AD 630 to 670. But earlier ones, which I think this one would be, had a higher percentage of gold in them. By the end of the minting they were barely gold at all, but look how this one shines.'

'It's certainly shiny,' agreed Cressida. 'I can't believe it's stayed like this for all those years.'

'Centuries even,' agreed Lord Fawcett, who looked quite animated now. Her mother had been right, he had been exceedingly interested in the coin. He hadn't been able to take his eyes off it since he'd put the receiver down to Scotland Yard. Comparing him to a small boy on Christmas morning was one thing, though it was more accurate to compare him to a small boy who had had the amazing luck to come downstairs to find that every filled stocking from the village had appeared at *his* fireplace. Cressida loved seeing him like this, despite the tragedy that had unfolded to find it, and she prodded it with her finger, pushing it ever so slightly towards him.

'It's so small. So easy to miss. It could have been hidden under a pebble for millennia.'

'It possibly was. Though it begs the question; where are the rest? You know they say a curse was put on the hoard?' Lord Fawcett asked, looking keenly at his daughter.

Cressida's interest was more piqued than ever and she looked at her father as he got up from his desk and went over to where a low bookcase was built in under the leaded-light diamond-paned windows. Cressida had always loved the windows in her father's study. Set in stone frames, the windows were made with glass so old it was mottled in places and distorted the view outside. Cressida remembered sitting in this very spot when she was younger, perhaps even listening to this same legend of the Mydenhurst hoard, but staring out of the window, closing one eye and then the other in order to make the trees outside appear wobbly or grossly fat just like one's appearance in the hall of mirrors at the travelling carnivals. She also loved the stained glass that was set among the wobbly panes, showing the Fawcett coat of arms and the family motto, which she knew meant something along the lines of fortune favouring the brave, though with something tetchy against the French thrown in. Latin, sadly, had never been her best subject. Now though, her view of it was blocked as her father bent down and looked at the bookshelf under the window.

'Ah, here it is. Trewitt's *History of Midhurst: Taking in the Villages and Hamlets Nearby*. Catchy title, don't you think?'

'Very.' Cressida grinned.

'But within, local historical gems. Good old Barney. Still alive, you know? Must be over ninety by now.' He sat back down at his desk and thumbed through the pamphlet-style book, no doubt vanity-published by Barney Trewitt, by the looks of it late in the last century. Soon Lord Fawcett found the page and began to read aloud. '"The gold coins are believed to have been buried in the grounds of what is now Mydenhurst Place, in the village of Mydenhurst." That's us.' He broke off with a chuckle and then continued. '"The house is a grand Jacobean affair, with earlier sixteenth-century roots, hence one of the old spellings being Mydenhyrst with a y, but there's no need to describe it." Cheek. He could have written a few nice things about us.'

'The curse, Papa?' Cressida hurried him along. She knew all about their crumbling terracotta tiles and grand fireplaces and rather agreed with Barney Trewitt that they didn't need mentioning at this moment.

'Ah, yes, here we go. "The gold was thought to be buried in the early AD 700s due to repeated raids by rivals. Harald, the chieftain of the day, asked a local wise woman, it is said, to curse the gold, in case his caskets and chains weren't enough of a deterrent." Here it is.' Lord Fawcett held the pamphlet out in front of him and read the curse, putting just a bit of drama into his voice as he did so. '"He who digs the treasure trove should take great care, for he will eat the earth while the gold tastes fresh air."' He put the pamphlet down and looked at Cressida, who had felt the blood drain from her cheeks.

Cressida wasn't one for superstition. Only last autumn she'd unmasked a 'spectre' haunting the cathedral at Winchester. But as she thought about the coin she'd found gripped so tightly in Bob's hand – a hand that had the word 'dead' written upon it – she had to admit that the words of the wise woman echoed in her head and she felt a shiver run all the way down her spine.

Perhaps Bob's death couldn't be solved by Cressida's usual tactics: rather hot-headedly questioning suspects while spotting details everyone else missed. Could the reason for his death lie in the past, with a terrible ancient curse? Or was said curse just a convenient smokescreen for a very real, and very dangerous killer?

A killer who would do anything to get their hands on the gold that sparkled on her father's desk.

## 5

'What do you think of that, eh, Cressy?' Lord Fawcett raised an eyebrow at his daughter, and obviously not noticing her pale complexion, kept reading. '"Many fortune hunters have searched out clues to the gold's location, with scholars from the universities delving into the local priory's archives. Once upon a time there was a rumour that the hoard was found in its grounds, but the head prior died before much could be written, except this one verse from the 1500s."' He glanced at Cressida before reading on, adding just a touch more drama to his voice. '"Mydenhyrst's hoard was buried deep, Not in the stream where the fishes sleep, Not in the church, under altar or pew, Or on farmland with the valley's view. But our prior did find it, and we pen this verse, As we bury him, dead of the golden curse." Stirring stuff, but it only suggests where the gold wasn't found.'

He lowered the pamphlet again, summarising the rest of the chapter. 'Other archival material suggests a field to the edge of the priory's land, which would make sense with the prior of the time being the one to find it, but some believe that the land that now lies behind the Royal Oak pub, which used to be priory land, is where the hoard is stashed. All anyone knows is that the hoard would surely make a man rich, if he were to find it, and if he were to survive the curse...'

'It can't be real, Papa, can it? It can't be why Bob died?' They both stared at the small thrymsa sitting on Lord Fawcett's desk, looking innocent enough, though glinting tantalisingly in the spring sunlight. Cressida continued, 'All that about "eating the earth while the gold tastes fresh air", you don't believe it, do you?'

'Do I believe that Bob Pringle found the Mydenhurst hoard, had it in his grasp and was then struck down as he ate his sandwich by some centuries-old curse? No, of course I don't, poppet. But you think he was murdered, don't you? That writing you found on his hand and all that. And I take your point about him being the envy of some of the others in our little historical society, if he had found the hoard.'

'Tell me about them, Papa. Mama said some of them are quite obsessed with finding the gold. If Bob had... actually, was Bob in the society?'

Lord Fawcett looked embarrassed and shifted his weight in his seat. 'No, Bob wasn't. The society lends itself to more, how to put it, gentlemanly folk. But Bob was often in the Royal Oak when we met there to discuss our findings and theories.'

'Was he not allowed to join because he's "just" a gardener?' Cressida asked, affronted on behalf of the dead man. 'Papa, I'm shocked you'd allow that. Or be a member of a society that did. It's not what you taught me at all. All men are equal, you always said.'

'And women too,' added Lord Fawcett. 'Let's not forget that, else your mama will have my guts for garters. And there are women in our society, two in fact. But as for Bob, well it was a matter that weighed heavy on my mind, however it never came up on the society's agenda and Bob never officially asked to join. He used to sit by the bar of the Royal Oak talking to the landlord, Walter Rook, and I have to say, making a few overly loud disparaging comments at times. Of course, he always doffed his cap at me, but I don't think he thought much of what he might deem the "la-di-da nobs" who sat around the table by the pub's fireplace and talked of Iron Age hill forts and Georgian waymarkers.'

'I see.' Cressida sat back in her chair, relieved that her father hadn't lost his sense of fairness. She'd have hated for him to turn into just the sort of man he'd always railed against – one whose first thought was always of his status and class. 'So, this society?'

'Ah, yes.' Lord Fawcett sat back in his chair. 'Let me tell you about them. Firstly there's me, of course, and I'm the big cheese. Duly elected president of the Mydenhurst Historical Society. Ably aided by my second in command, Mrs Lilian Catchpole, society secretary and wife of Dr Catchpole. He has a surgery in Willowmere, but they live here in Mydenhurst.'

'Yes, I remember. Didn't Mrs Catchpole have twins?' Cressida asked.

'Yes, David and Daphne. Proper little terrors. Stole all the apples from the Whites' orchard last year. Eyebrows were raised when Dr Catchpole was found to be recommending his wife's home-made apple jelly as a vitamin booster through the winter months, at a mere three shillings per jar!'

'Gosh, poaching and privateering in Sussex! Who'd have thought it!' Cressida laughed and made a mental note to watch out for David and Daphne Catchpole, especially where her puppies were concerned. 'Carry on, Papa, who else is there?'

'Well, then there's the vicar, Reverend Theophilus Dunn.'

'Theophilus. Gosh that's a mouthful.'

'His brother is called Aurelius,' Lord Fawcett said with a certain amount of mirth, then frowned. 'I suppose I can't judge. Sholto isn't exactly run-of-the-mill. Anyway, Theo Dunn has been the vicar here for a few years now and has become very interested in the hoard and its connection with the church.'

'Those monks who wrote the sixteenth-century poem about the curse?' Cressida chipped in.

'Exactly. He thinks the church and the local priory, now in private hands, of course – some composer chap from London has it as a second home – have connections to the hoard. And if he were to find it on church property it would help the parish out of a sticky wicket.'

'How so?' Cressida was intrigued.

'The diocese is threatening to merge this parish with that of Stammer Hill and Willowmere. If that happened there would be just one vicar covering all three churches, and with Mydenhurst being the smaller of the three, the living here would be removed.'

'So, Reverend Dunn's livelihood relies on the church coming into some money, something to keep it from being subsumed into the larger local parishes?' Cressida laid it all out in her mind, like a curtain maker smoothing out her fabric.

'Exactly. And more than that, the church here, often said to have been commissioned by Mydenhurst's founder, Wynhelm, himself, is crumbling and in very bad repair. Daisy Marshall from Lower Marley Farm caught a nasty chill last October as she was constantly being dripped on while in the choir stalls.'

'Poor thing. And no doubt a willing purchaser of Mrs Catchpole's vitamin-boosting apple jelly.'

'Quite.' Lord Fawcett chuckled.

'Still, it gives the good reverend quite the motive to lay his hands on the hoard of gold, if it had been found,' Cressida stated and her father frowned.

'He's a good man though, Cressy. A man of God, no less. I can't imagine him killing someone over a few gold coins.'

Cressida shrugged. She'd seen people be murdered for a lot less over the last year.

Her father continued. 'Then there's the Whites.'

'They of the pilfered apples?'

'Yes. Madge and Percy. They own Lark's Leap, the rather nice farmhouse over the other side of the village.'

'Yes, I know. Madge and Mama lend each other hats sometimes, don't they? For the races and such?'

'Yes, yes.' Lord Fawcett looked to be on happier ground now. 'Madge and Percy are horse mad. Love the four-legged beasties so much they've dedicated their life to them.' He frowned and spoke more seriously. 'Of course, when neither of their sons came back from the war, it was a diversion for them. Once Gerald had been confirmed missing, presumed dead, they turned over all the grazing land they had to rescuing war horses. Some of those poor animals were in a horrendous state when they returned, barely able to stand. Terrible. But Madge and Percy have dedicated themselves to seeing right by them. Given over all their barns and fields. Had to fundraise a few years ago as the costs had mounted after the poor hay harvest of nineteen-twenty-one. Despite having all of this on their minds they joined the historical society. Lonely I suppose, just them and the horses. And we do have some scintillating conversations over that table at the Royal Oak. I can see why people would want to join just for the company.'

Cressida thrummed her fingers on the arms of the chair as she thought, then it came to her. 'Papa, in that leaflet you read from, didn't it say something about the hoard possibly being on farmland over the other side of the village?' She waited while her father found the right pages.

'You're right, poppet, it says here that "other archival material suggests a field to the edge of the priory's land" – that could well be them. Though don't forget it says it might be on land that now belongs to the pub, too.'

'Quite a few of the society, or the village, could lay claim to it then if they found it? Is there anyone else in the society? We've got you, Mrs Catchpole, the Whites and Reverend Dunn so far. And Bob who didn't join but listened in a lot with Walter Rook.'

'No flies on you, Cressy,' her father said with some pride. 'And there is one more person. A Mr Sebastian Reed. From Willowmere, though the other side from here, in one of those Victorian houses. His family only moved there after the war and he had no real affiliation to our village. But he's obsessed with finding the hoard. More so than anyone else really. We're all keen on it, of course, but the society wasn't formed merely to find the gold. We discuss the church a lot – it's a very fine example of a Norman nave – and of course the priory when the family open it. Willowmere's high street has many fine Georgian houses on it and I invite them to Mydenhurst Place too, and we discuss the history of it, not to mention the neolithic stone circle up in Marley Woods. But with Sebastian every meeting it's "hoard this, gold that". The young man seems obsessed.'

Cressida nodded and raised her fingers to her temples. Each member of the historical society had a reason for wanting the gold that was found in Bob's cold, dead fist. And according to her father, nobody was more obsessed with finding it than this Sebastian chap. She looked out of the window again, and found herself closing one eye, and then another, making the trees wobble through the handmade glass. And a thought came to her.

*Sometimes things aren't what they seem...*

Mr Reed might look like the most obsessed, but perhaps some other society members were rather more subtle. One thing was clear as glass; in her father's little historical society there were numerous people who would have loved nothing more than to get their hands on that gold.

## 6

A clattering in the hallway and voices from the front door brought Cressida out of her reverie. She and her father both stood up at the same time and went to the window to see what the fuss was about. Fearing it might be some government dog handlers primed to take away the chaotic anarchists currently rolling around on the lawn and in the rose beds, Cressida was relieved when she recognised the silver Rolls-Royce of the Chattertons in the driveway.

The Chattertons, in this case, referred to Lady Dorothy Chatterton – more usually known as Dotty, and Cressida's best friend – and her brother. He was also a Chatterton, of course, though he had taken on one of his father's – the Earl of Chatterton – subsidiary titles and was known as Lord Delafield. Though to Cressida he was simply Alfred. Dotty and Alfred were as dear to Cressida as people could be.

In fact, Dotty had been a star recently and helped so much with the puppies just after they were born, taking time away from planning her wedding to her new fiancé, the dashingly handsome archaeologist, George Parish. Cressida had insisted on staying in London during Ruby's confinement, and as she lived in her little pied-à-terre in Chelsea with no ladies' maid to help her, Dotty had been an angel. As had Alfred, of course, though he had mainly been responsible for making sure Cressida and Dotty were kept in constant supply of cream puffs and cherry slices from the nice patisserie on Cheyne Walk, and fetching steak and sardines from the butcher and fishmonger for Ruby and her pups.

But London – and the restrictions of her rather smart building, which was not designed for puppy rearing – had all got a bit too much for Cressida and she'd agreed when Dotty had suggested she take her mother up on the invitation of a stay at Mydenhurst for a while. Cressida smiled now, remembering the chaotic journey from Chelsea, where the pups had been born to the sound of costermongers on the river and the bells of Chelsea Old Church, to Sussex. She couldn't wait to tell Dotty all about it. Even getting them down the stairwell from her penthouse flat to the ground floor had been a fight, with wriggling bodies squirming out of the wicker hamper Cressida had borrowed from the greengrocer on the King's Road. She wasn't sure he'd want it back after the chewing that had gone on, but she glossed over that as a minor problem compared to losing Suki down the lift shaft. Suki had been fine, but Mrs Palmerston from the apartment downstairs had screamed to high heaven when the small dog had plopped down straight into the basket of custard tarts she was carefully bringing up via the elevator. Apologies had been made, puppy had been extracted from said tarts and herded back into wicker hamper and, together with Ruby, the pups had been strapped into the passenger seat of Cressida's little red Bugatti motor car.

'It looks like your friend Dotty is here, poppet,' Lord Fawcett interrupted her reminiscences, tapping a finger on the windowpane and waving to his guests.

'And Alfred,' Cressida added, feeling a blush start to prickle on her cheeks.

'Ah, Lord Delafield too.' He smiled at his daughter. 'A good thing too. Take your mind off this awful business with Bob. I'll let you know when Andrews calls back. You never know, he might want to come and take a look at the scene, even if Botheridge has carted poor old Bob off to the cottage hospital morgue in Willowmere.'

'Thank you, Papa.' Cressida reached out and touched her father's sleeve. 'Oh, can you remind him that one of Ruby's puppies is promised to that nice colleague of his I met at Christmas? He wanted it for his daughter – Beth, I think she was called. It pains me to see any of the litter go, but I did promise.'

'One fewer dog in the house is all right by me.' Lord Fawcett chuckled. 'Have you seen the state of my slippers? And you've only been here less than a day. I'm not sure Jim will approve.'

'Jim?' Cressida asked, cocking her head.

'Sir James Colston, you remember? Old pal of mine from Oxford. Due to arrive this afternoon as a guest of yours truly and the historical society. Quite a serious academic now. Strangely enough he was actually *good* at the old books rather than muggins here who scraped through.'

Cressida rolled her eyes, knowing full well that her father had graduated with first-class honours.

'I remember him now. Didn't he join us at the village pageant one year?'

'Yes, that's right. When you were knee-high to a grasshopper.'

'And dressed as one too. That costume was all I could think about all summer.' Cressida laughed. 'But I remember Sir James, he got what I now know to be "slightly squiffy" with more visits to the Royal Oak than the tea tent.'

'Quite astounding what children remember,' Lord Fawcett said as he waved at Dotty through the window. Cressida saw her wave back and waved too.

'Anyway,' she said, turning back to her father. 'It will be lovely to see Sir James again. He might shed some more light on our little coin, too.'

'Quite, quite. Now, hop to it and go and see your pals, while I wait by the telephone. And tell that Alfred of yours I'd like a word.' He wiggled his eyebrows at Cressida, who blushed, then touched her cheeks as if disbelieving of it.

'Papa!'

'Go on, off you pop.' Lord Fawcett dismissed his daughter. Cressida took a deep breath and then left him to it, checking her reflection and the flush of her cheeks in a small mirror by his study door, before heading out to find her friends.

'Cressy!' Dotty called down the hallway and then ran up and folded her in her arms. Cressida squeezed her tightly in return.

'Dot, I'm so glad you're here. You'll never guess what's happened.' Cressida pulled away and was then distracted by the sight of Alfred. He was walking into the hallway from the bright sunlight outside, and to Cressida's eyes he looked desperately misshapen and oddly formed.

Cressida blinked, hoping he hadn't suffered some terrible accident between the Rolls-Royce and the doorway and then realised that the abnormalities in his shape were down to Ruby's little cogs, or porgis... puggies even? Cressida was yet to work out what the crossbreed should be called, but seeing Alfred with puppies on his shoulders and climbing up his legs made her laugh.

'I see the pups have settled into country life,' he said, pulling one off his shoulder as it nibbled at his ear. 'I found these four in the rose bed by the driveway eating a cream scone. By which I assume there's some going for the bipedal guests as well as the four-legged ones?'

'I'm sure there is, Alf.' Cressida took the puppy from him –

the one she'd named Hercules as he was definitely the biggest in the litter – and gave Alfred a chaste kiss on the cheek as a hello. She was delighted to see him blush just a little.

'What's happened?' Dotty poked Cressida in the ribs as she asked, but before she could answer Lady Fawcett appeared at the other end of the hallway and greeted her guests. She said nothing of the morning's tragedy, yet Cressida could see her mother had gone from looking pristine, in her neat twinset, pearls and smart tweed skirt, to looking more like someone who'd not slept for days, or, if she had snuck in an hour's kip, it was under a hedge. It didn't help that she was carrying Suki, who was trying to eat her necklace. She did, however, muster the energy to let her guests and daughter know that tea was served on the lawn and that although approximately three scones had been lost to puppy marauders, there were plenty more to go round.

'And how is Marian, Mama?' Cressida asked, touching her mother's arm. She paused to let Dotty and Alfred, who were both juggling puppies, head down the wood-panelled hallway to the back door, which led to the croquet lawn. Once they'd disappeared back out to the spring sunshine she added, 'Was she terribly upset?'

'Of course,' replied Lady Fawcett, picking off a stray twig from her arm and flicking it onto the floor. She then thought better of it, and bent over to pick the twig up from the parquet wood. She twiddled it in her hand as she continued. 'Marian and Bob had been married for about the same time as your father and me. She was just sitting there at the table, pale as anything, and said all sorts of things about how she couldn't believe it, how they'd always joked that Bob would one day forget to turn up to his own funeral, and how Fate had played her hand. How her life wouldn't be the same and how the future now looked so different with him gone.'

'Poor thing.' Cressida shook her head. 'Just imagine losing

your husband like that, so suddenly.' Cressida paused. 'She didn't know anything about the thrymsa, did she?'

'The what now?'

'That's what I said.' Cressida smiled at her mother. 'Papa says the coin is called a thrymsa.'

'Of course he'd know that.' Lady Fawcett rolled her eyes. 'And no, though it's interesting that you say "so suddenly" as Marian did say something odd.'

'Which was?' Cressida looked intently at her mother.

'Well, she mentioned something about "that this is what it would lead to".'

'Perhaps "this" is the gold, do you think?' Cressida suggested, and felt her skin prickle as she remembered the curse.

'Possibly, darling, though seeing Bob's waistline grow over the years, it could just as easily be his penchant for pork pies and pasties. Marian was always coaxing him to eat healthier, she knew Walter's pies at the Royal Oak were too much of a lure, not to mention an expense. She even started getting in that pickle so that she could jazz up his cheese sandwiches, though no one else in the house can abide it. But other than that, although he was as fit as a fiddle, Bob was... well, he was on the large side.'

'You still think he had a heart attack or some sort of embolism, don't you, Mama?'

Lady Fawcett sighed and Cressida noticed once again how tired she looked.

'It's what I hope, darling,' she replied. 'A natural death is a much nicer thought than a murder.'


A few minutes later, Cressida, Dotty and Alfred, along with Lady Fawcett and Ruby, plus the Fawcetts' own ancient and somewhat smelly Labrador, Ernest, were seated around the white cast-iron table on the edge of the croquet lawn.

Molly, the Fawcetts' ever-enthusiastic maid, had fashioned a puppy pound for the runaway doglets out of some old badminton netting from the pavilion, pegged down with the croquet hoops, so the scones and jam and cream could be eaten in relative civility. Although it was inevitable that some cream and scone ended up heading under the table to the willing snuffles of Ruby and Ernest.

'We had a bit of a tragedy here this morning,' Lady Fawcett announced, once scones were laden with cream and jam and the tea was poured. 'Our gardener, Bob Pringle, was found dead.'

'Dead? Oh dear,' Dotty said, then looked at Cressida, who nodded.

'By us, actually. Mama and I were on the hunt for Ruby and Suki, who had absconded behind the pavilion, and we found poor Bob, drowned in the stream on the other side of those woods.'

Dotty and Alfred both turned around to look at the pavilion and the woods behind it, and Ernest used the opportunity to lick a blob of butter off Alfred's plate without him noticing.

'Are you all right, Cressy?' Alfred asked, once he'd turned back and, none the wiser, spread some more butter on his scone.

'Yes, we're fine, aren't we, Mama?' she answered. 'But it was a shock. Bob wasn't that old—'

'Fifty or sixty,' Lady Fawcett said. 'He'd been here "man and boy" as they say, and that had been for forty odd years. So, he was at least fifty-five, I'd say.'

'Still, no age,' Dotty commiserated. 'Was he unwell? A heart attack, perhaps?'

'He'd been a little unsteady on his feet recently,' Lady Fawcett said, taking another scone.

'How terribly sad. To just keel over,' Dotty added.

'Perhaps, though there were a few strange circumstances to it all...' Cressida led into telling her friends all about what they'd found; the gold coin in his clenched fist, the letters inked on his palm and the slightly strange thing his wife Marian had said about something 'leading' to this.

Dotty narrowed her eyes behind her tortoiseshell-framed spectacles. 'Well, it's a good thing Alfred and I are here, isn't it?'

'We do appreciate it, dear. So lovely for Cressida to have her friends around at this difficult time.' Lady Fawcett reached out and laid a hand on Dotty's sleeve. Dotty smiled back at her hostess, but shook her head.

'Well yes, of course, but if I'm right, and Cressy's thinking what I think she's thinking—'

Cressida put her teacup down and interrupted her friend. 'You are right, Dot, as usual, and you are reading my mind, as usual, too. I hope DCI Andrews will deem it necessary to come down, but there's no harm in Dotty, Alfred, and Ruby, of course, and I having a little head start. Get our ducks in a row, or our puppies in a pen. Present Andrews with our findings...'

'Our theories,' Dotty added.

'Our best guesses at the very least,' Alfred chimed in.

Cressida smiled at him, then turned back to her mother and said, 'And maybe even solve Bob Pringle's murder before he does.'

## 7

Lady Fawcett sighed and closed her eyes while Ernest eyed up her plate, but Dotty grabbed his collar before he could make a play for the blob of cream. None the wiser, when Lady Fawcett opened her eyes, she said, 'You still think it's murder? Not a terrible accident or illness?'

'Those letters inked on his palm, Mama, and the coin...' Cressida started, but Lady Fawcett raised her hand.

'Very well, but please don't upset Marian with this theory. Speaking of dear Marian, I must talk to your father about the possibility of finding both another cook *and* another gardener, assuming Marian will take some compassionate leave. Please excuse me. And do finish those scones, else Ernest will give himself bellyache.'

'Yes, Mama,' Cressida promised, while Alfred did as instructed and helped himself.

'Thank you, dear. And don't forget that among all of this, I'm still desperate for your help in the library. The colour of the walls is really quite depressing, and now with all this...' She waved her hand in the general direction of the house.

'Of course, Mama. I will,' Cressida promised. Her eye for

design was perhaps as necessary this weekend as her eye for a crime. She gave her mother a little wave as she departed, then turned back to her friends. Alfred was laying cream onto the scone, but Dotty was looking at her expectantly.

'Well, where do you want to start?'

Without her mother at the table to censor any of Cressida's more hot-headed ideas, she plunged right in. 'I think the historical society are breeches-deep in this. The fact Bob was gripping that gold coin tells me that he had discovered the legendary hoard, or at least some of it. Everyone in the society wanted to find it, in fact the word "obsessed" was used.'

Cressida continued to fill in her friends on the society members; Mrs Catchpole, Reverend Dunn, the Whites, Sebastian Reed and Walter Rook who, although not a member, was landlord of the Royal Oak and listened in to the meetings.

Alfred looked at his pocket watch, which was nestled in the pocket of his waistcoat, part of his three-piece tweed suit. Dressed for the country, he also wore brown brogues and had brought a cloth flat cap, though that had been left inside. All the better for showing off his chestnut-brown hair, thought Cressida, then tried to stop looking at him as he spoke.

'Sun's past the yard arm, what say we head to the Royal Oak?'

'I'm not sure we should be out drinking when Cressy's household is in mourning,' Dotty chastised him, with a look only a sister could give.

'No, Dot, not for drinking.' Alfred put his watch away and from another pocket pulled out his pipe. He liked to stick it between his back teeth, not to smoke, but as a sort of thinking aid. Remarkably he was still able to speak, and so continued. 'It might be the best place to find some of these society members. The landlord chap at the very least. Shake them up a bit, ask a few questions, get this show on the road.'

Cressida nodded. 'That's not a bad shout, Alfred. But I want to start somewhere closer to home.'

Dotty looked a little aghast. 'Not your own Papa?'

'No, Dot,' Cressida reassured her. 'Marian Pringle. Bob's widow.'

'But your mother just told you not to upset her,' Dotty said, pushing her glasses up her nose.

'I know, and I won't, I promise. But Marian might be able to shed some light on Bob's life recently. Something that she might not have realised has something to do with his death.'

'You don't think she did it, do you?' Dotty asked. She was a keen fan of reading whodunnits, and had amassed quite a library of them at Chatterton Court, the Chatterton family's country seat. In fact, Cressida had heard that her father, the Earl of Chatterton, had had to move some of the Latin primers and a whole set of Brontës out of the library so Dotty could fill them with her G.K. Chestertons and Freeman Wills Crofts. With all this inhalation of crime fiction had come a certain psychological insight into murderers and their motives, which almost rivalled Cressida's own instincts in how she solved cases.

'No, not Marian.' Cressida paused. Unlike Dotty, she'd not picked up a book since her final year at finishing school (and even then the books had been mostly placed on her head to help with deportment rather than academia). Instead she relied more on her instincts and her eye. She was happy to admit that she had an excellent eye when it came to interiors and was sought-after among high society to help with decorating. But it was her ability to notice when something wasn't quite right that had helped her solve the crimes she'd come across recently. She looked at Dotty again, who now had Ernest's head on her lap. 'I simply can't believe Marian would kill Bob, but there might be something I can glean from talking to her. I just think she might be a very good place to start.'

'You said she told your mother something strange, something about "leading to this",' Dotty said, nudging Ernest's head off her lap so she could remove her napkin. The old dog huffed and then creakily took himself off inside. Cressida cast her eye over to where Ruby was watching over her puppies and did a very quick, though hopefully accurate, head count. Still six. Molly's makeshift puppy prison was doing the trick. She looked back at Dot.

'Yes, it's probably nothing, as Mama suspects. More of a lamentation on Bob's unhealthy habits than anything, but I think it's worth asking her more about it.'

Alfred took his pipe out of his mouth, paused holding the stem in the air as he formed his thought then spoke. 'Not my place to interfere, old thing, and I know you're not planning on going in there and accusing her of murder, but the poor woman has just lost her husband. She might not want, at this very minute, to analyse words said in grief as she was told of his death.'

Cressida nodded. Alfred was right, of course. It would be highly improper to question poor Marian so soon, not to mention her promise to her mother not to upset her with theories of murder.

*She's just lost her husband...* Cressida had never wanted to marry. The whole idea was an anathema to her, what with the traditional notion of being a chattel to a man; his property. Why would she ever want that when she had all she needed anyway? Her freedom, her sporty little red Bugatti (which was currently covered in small bits of chewed wicker, but still...), her friends and, of course, her darling pup... the last of these now multiplied six times over.

But it was Alfred who had recently made her question all of her views. They had kissed for the first time on Christmas Eve, when Alfred had rescued her from the clutches of a killer. But marry him? He hadn't asked, of course, and all eyes were on Dotty and her engagement, so the moment hadn't arisen when she'd have to answer either way... but she imagined, just for a moment, that they'd been married for thirty-odd years, as Marian and Bob had been. Would she want someone questioning her mere hours after he'd been found dead?

No.

*But then again...* a thought occurred to her. Cressida looked at Alfred, noticing the now-familiar crinkle at the corner of his dark-brown eyes. She shrugged. 'I understand what you're saying, Alfred, I really do. But don't you think it would be better for poor Marian to come face to face with me – the same girl she fed porridge to growing up, the same girl who used to hang off her apron strings waiting for a cake bowl to be licked – rather than Andrews? Or worse, any other policeman?'

Alfred raised an eyebrow and Dotty smiled. 'I think she's got the better of you there, Alf,' she said.

Alfred merely raised his pipe, stem towards Cressida. 'Touché,' he said. And then after a pause he added something that set Cressida's heart racing. 'I think I better get used to it.'

## 8

Cressida couldn't help the blush that spread across her cheeks, just as Dotty couldn't stop from grinning. Alfred smiled at her too, which only made things worse, so Cressida did the only thing an Englishwoman knew what to do in the circumstances and stood up, placed her napkin on the table and said, 'Right.'

'Right,' said Alfred. Then, 'What's the plan?'

'Right. Well,' Cressida flustered. Then she remembered something her father had said and before she knew it had blushed further. 'Alfred, I'm afraid Papa would like a word with you. He's in his study contacting the authorities and waiting for Andrews to telephone from London. And no doubt warning his friend, Sir James Colston, that his stay with us will be a little different to the usual country house weekend, what with a dead body in the stream. He's an eminent historian and expert on Saxon hoards and whatnot apparently.'

'Right,' said Alfred again, and Cressida spotted a slight colour to his cheeks too.

Dotty, who was finding this all highly amusing, stood up too. 'Shall I come with you to see Marian, Cressy? Or stay here to dog-wrangle? And did you say Sir James Colston? Gosh. He's the bee's knees when it comes to Saxon history. Is he coming here?'

'Tonight apparently,' Cressida replied, though she was looking across at where the puppies were scrambling around in the makeshift puppy pen. Suki was on Hercules's back and getting ever closer to the top of the netting. It wouldn't be long before all of them were in on the escape plot and Molly had been called away inside, most likely to do something less physically draining than puppy care, such as a complete overhaul of the fireplaces or a month's worth of laundry.

Cressida turned back and answered Dotty properly. 'I forget sometimes what a history boffin you are, Dot. So yes, Sir James is apparently on the afternoon train. And yes, if you don't mind would you keep an eye on those boisterous balls of chaos over there? I fear those little terrors could be back in the rose bushes in no time at all, and with dear Bob gone we need to at least try and defend his good work, not let a marauding pack of puppies decimate the seedlings.'

'The way Suki keeps mounting Hercules reminds me of that time you entered the Cadogan Square piggyback race with Pongo Ramsbottom,' Dotty said.

'Oh yes, that was fun,' Cressida reminisced.

'You won third prize but Pongo's never walked straight again, thanks to that thing you did with the cocktail cherries and—'

'Dotty!' Cressida stopped her friend mid-sentence and nodded her head towards Alfred, who was paying a lot of attention to the herbaceous border.

Dotty came around to Cressida's side, giggling to herself, and squeezed her arm. 'Sorry, chum. And leave these pups with me. I'll have them learning calculus and reciting Tennyson by suppertime.'

Cressida laughed at her friend, who was quickly forgiven. 'Well good luck with that, Dot. I won't be long, I promise. As you did rightly point out, Alfred, I don't think Marian will be terribly keen to talk. And better it's just me, really, so as not to overwhelm her. I should go and give condolences anyway...'

Dotty squeezed her arm again. 'Just come back and tell me everything you find out.'

'Will do, Dot,' Cressida promised, and with Alfred by her side left Dotty to the tumbling pups and walked back into the hallway of Mydenhurst Place.

Cressida led Alfred into the house, blinking as the dark of the hallway took some time to get used to compared to the bright sunshine outside. The caws of the crows as they'd circled the red kite above the woods, not to mention the yapping of puppies and conversation of the three friends, were replaced by the quiet calm of the parquet-floored hallway. The only sound was the constant tick and swing of the grandfather clock that stood below the staircase. It had been one of Cressida's jobs, when she'd been old enough to take responsibility for it, to wind it every morning.

She briefly wondered who did it now, but mostly her thoughts were occupied by the handsome man behind her and how it felt to have him here. Alfred hadn't been to Mydenhurst Place before, though Dotty had been a frequent visitor during their school years and beyond. She wondered what the old manor looked like to his eyes. Starkly provincial, perhaps, compared to the elegant – and vast – proportions of Chatterton Court, the house he had grown up in and was set to inherit. In comparison, Mydenhurst, with its wobbly glass, moss-covered roof tiles and higgledy-piggledy ancient beams might seem rustic and unsophisticated. She shook the worries from her head and stopped outside her father's study door.

Suddenly lost for words, Cressida knocked, then blew Alfred a kiss, as she heard her father's voice bellow, 'Come in.'

Alfred wiggled his eyebrows at her and put his pipe back in his jacket pocket. She could only imagine what her father wanted to talk to Alfred about; all sorts of stuff about being honourable and all that she supposed. Maybe even *marriage*. It helped, perhaps, that the Fawcetts had known the Chattertons for years. She hoped it meant that her father would be a little gentler towards Alfred as a possible suitor – the word made her feel quite odd – than he would be if she'd just scooped someone up in a London club or Biarritz casino. She took a deep breath as the door closed behind Alfred, and leaving him to his fate, went to the kitchen. The familiar noise of four little scurrying feet was right behind her, and she grinned as she turned around. She looked down to see Ruby, now sitting and looking expectantly at her, her tongue out, panting away.

'Ruby, leaving your pups with Dot, are you? Let me guess, more interested in solving a possible murder than looking after your own children? How terribly modern. Come along then.' Cressida clicked her fingers and carried on towards the kitchen.

Unlike grander houses such as Chatterton Court, or at least those built in the Georgian and Victorian periods, there was no green baize door at Mydenhurst Place to separate the servants' quarters from the formal rooms. Instead the passage went from being wood-panelled to bare plaster, and the flagstone floor changed to courser brick slips, the mortar between them almost as dark as the earthenware tiles having had centuries of Fawcetts and their household walking over them.

The kitchen was in what the family euphemistically referred to as the east wing, but that was only because the kitchen garden – about half an acre of fruit and vegetables, herbs and cutting flowers all surrounded by high, brick walls – was placed there to catch the morning light. It was in one of the oldest parts of the house, with its origins in the sixteenth century, as shown by the large inglenook fireplace that now housed a slightly more modern range cooker. Old Welsh-style dressers lined the walls, holding the family's decorative Willow pattern blue-and-white china and copper pans and jelly and terrine moulds. The centre of the kitchen was home to a large farmhouse table, which was where Marian would do most of her preparation for the family's meals, and sit down herself, with Bob too on occasion, to eat. It was also where Cressida had enjoyed many a slice of cake, or warm bread straight from the oven. She'd sat at the well-worn table often enough when she was too old for nursery tea, yet too young to join her parents in the dining room. Doors led off the kitchen to a pantry and a scullery, but despite its location on the far side of the house, the kitchen itself truly was the beating heart of Mydenhurst Place.

Sitting at the table now was Marian. She was a slight, fair-haired woman who was no doubt once very pretty in her youth, but who had grown into her creases and wrinkles, be those on her linen apron or her brow. If the kitchen at Mydenhurst was the beating heart of the home, then she, the cook at the centre of it, appeared broken. The sight of her sitting at the table with her head in her hands, weeping, made Cressida well up with tears of her own.

Cressida pulled out one of the round-backed wooden chairs next to Marian and sat down. The noise and movement made Marian start, then wipe her eyes with her apron.

'Marian,' Cressida started, then instead of carrying on, just put her arms around her family's loyal cook and hugged her. Pulling away after a moment or two of tight squeezing, she tried again. 'I'm so sorry about Bob. It must be such a shock to you. I'm heartbroken for you, I really am.'

Marian fumbled in the pocket of her apron and pulled out a crumpled handkerchief. Dabbing at her eyes again, she replied, 'Thank you, Miss Cressida, that means a lot. He was only here this morning, eating his porridge and picking up his sandwich. And it is a shock...' Marian let the sentence hang; and remembering her mother's words about something 'leading to' Bob's death, Cressida could sense there was a 'but' brewing in Marian's mind.

'A shock, but perhaps not a surprise?' Cressida ventured, knowing it was a risk throwing such doubt over his death. She just hoped that their years' long acquaintance would balance out her brashness.

Marian didn't answer though, and stared at her hands resting on the table. Cressida looked at them too. Her nails were short, and the veins on the back of her hands were raised as the skin thinned across them. She wore a simple gold band around her wedding finger, but otherwise her hands and wrists were unadorned. Cressida could feel Ruby nudging her ankles, so she picked her up and held her on her lap. Marian reached over and petted Ruby, then spoke again.

'I'm so used to having Ernest poke his nose around here. More so now he's got too old to follow Bob or your father to the Royal Oak of an evening.' She paused again then sighed. 'Oh dear, that it's all come to this.'

'Will you stay on here? Please say you might, Marian? After you've had some time off, of course, but Mama and Papa would be devastated if they lost you too.'

Marian dabbed her eyes again. 'After I married Bob, who my parents did not look fondly upon I can tell you, I knew I'd lose any help from them. But it didn't matter as Bob and I have the cottage here, and many happy years we've had in it, despite our ups and downs. But it comes with *his* job—'

'Ah.' Cressida could see the problem. A tied cottage for the gardener, who happened to be married to the cook, giving her a home as well. But when her parents eventually advertised for a new gardener, the cottage might be lost to her and with Molly and the other housemaids already taking up the attic rooms there wasn't much else in the way of servants' quarters at Mydenhurst Place. 'I'm sure Papa would make some arrangement for you. You wouldn't be homeless, Marian. And I'm sorry that your parents didn't approve of your marriage.' She thought about how Alfred was at this very moment possibly getting a grilling from her father. 'That must have been hard for you and Bob.'

'Love can only get you so far,' Marian replied and Cressida couldn't quite work out if that meant she was for or against romantic matches. 'And thank you for your reassurances, Miss Cressida. I'm quite sure I'll be fine. I believe Bob had come into some money before he died. At least, I assumed he had as he was spending so frivolously.'

The image of the small gold coin clenched in Bob's dead hand came to Cressida's mind. 'So, he was acting as if he had come into some money, but didn't tell you?'

'Exactly. Walter told me he was ordering the good single malt whisky as a chaser after pints of the best bitter of a night. I said, "Bob, if you've got money to spend on posh liquor, we could do with that for our retirement, or the bicycle wheel that needs repairing, not boosting Walter and Annie's coffers," and he just shrugged and did that annoying thing where he flicked a brass button up in the air and caught it in his fist, then winked at me and said, "Never you mind, wife of mine, never you mind," which was when I generally hit him with a tea towel and told him to get lost.'

Marian choked over the last word and Cressida fetched a glass of water for her from the sink. Perhaps the single thrymsa that was in his grip was just one of many he'd found. Or even just a few, but enough to let him have some decent drinks and tease his wife in any case.

'Marian, would anyone else have known about him finding the... I mean, coming into some money?'

'Only everyone in the village.' She rolled her eyes. 'Walter told me that one night last week Bob bought everyone in the pub a drink. Like he was some "lord of the revels" or something.' She tutted.

'And he didn't tell you where he was getting the money from?'

Marian shrugged. 'No, but he would have. He was like that. Keeping a little secret here and there. More often than not he'd have a bit too much to drink one night and tell me what was what. Not that we had many secrets, you understand, but if he was planning a treat for our days off or what have you. I'm sure he would have told me sooner or later.'

Cressida nodded. 'Marian, I'm sorry to ask again, but I got the impression that perhaps you weren't that surprised by Bob's death, even though it was a shock, of course.'

This time Marian looked Cressida straight in the eye. 'You're a perceptive one, Miss Cressida. And you're right. Whether it was this money or something else, Bob had been up to something recently. Like I said, he could have his little secrets, but he'd been making trips to London, with your father's grace, leaving just as the spring gardening was needing doing. Not telling a soul who he had been seeing or what he had been doing.'

'Not usual behaviour then?' Cressida asked, and Marian shook her head vigorously.

'As I say, a few secrets here or there, yes. But taking a train to town and not saying why? No, that wasn't usual at all.' She wiped her eyes again on her handkerchief.

'So, he'd usually tell you everything in the end?' Cressida pushed further, still wondering why Marian knew nothing of her husband's fortunate find, except hearing about his grandiose generosity in the pub.

'Hmm.' She looked dreamily into the middle distance and then dabbed the corners of her eyes again. 'Bob and I were very happy but... well, it is what it is. Or perhaps it was what it was.'

Cressida sat back, still holding Ruby on her lap and she looked at Marian. A face aged through years of work, looking forward to retirement. Then not only does her husband start disappearing off to London, acting oddly and secretively, but he dies suddenly.

Marian seemed to be speaking in grief-laced riddles, but it was clear that just before he died, Bob had been keeping a secret, most likely the whereabouts of the legendary local gold. He obviously hadn't confided in his long-suffering wife, but the question was, had he told anyone else about it?

## 9

Cressida gave Marian another hug and then left the kitchen deep in thought. So deep in fact that she almost bumped into Alfred in the passageway near her father's study.

'What ho, old thing,' Alfred said, and Cressida was pleased to see that he looked well enough and not like a chap who'd just been hauled over the proverbial hot coals. She tentatively raised her hands to the lapels of his jacket, and then acted as if she merely intended to straighten them and brush off some non-existent lint.

'Did Papa say anything too awkward? Was he a menace?' Concern was wrought across her face. 'He can get quite *soldierly* when he's in paternal mode. I remember once poor Timmy Maltravers from the other side of Willowmere got hauled up in front of him and told to quick march back home in the thunderous tones of a sergeant major because he'd dared to climb up the drainpipe outside my bedroom.' Alfred frowned then smiled again as she clarified, 'And we were only eight. If Papa had known what he'd done to my pigtails the day before, I'm sure the poor chap would have been sent to the firing squad.'

Alfred chuckled. 'No, he was utterly charming, if slightly eccentric, as usual. Spent quite a lot of time telling me about the breeding pair of doves down by the stream, then rhapsodised on his wonderful, long and wholeheartedly faithful marriage to your mother and then asked if I was a member of any decent clubs—'

'Oh dear,' Cressida said, pulling away and crossing her arms. 'You told him about the Mutton Pie Club, didn't you?'

Alfred cleared his throat. 'Well, yes. Of course.'

'And he was...?' Cressida half closed her eyes. She wasn't sure this particular gentlemen's dining club was the sort of thing her military-minded, erudite and disciplined father would condone. The Mutton Pie Club was formed merely so that its members could dine on what was sometimes a seven- or eight-course meal, consisting entirely of pies, from hot smoked salmon to apple and blackberry. There was no cultural significance to it, no allegiance to a regiment or smart public school. No point whatsoever, but to see who could be the one to dribble gravy down their pastry-coloured, pasty-frilled waistcoats first. To her relief, Alfred beamed at her.

'Member himself in ninety-eight! Left after a disagreement between the Scottish and English factions over whether maca-roni pie was in fact a pie, or merely a tart. Dark times for the club, dark times.'

Cressida sighed in relief and reached out to touch Alfred again. 'So, you think you passed the test then?'

'If there was one, I wasn't aware of it,' Alfred said softly. 'But I'd take any test if it meant pleasing you.'

Cressida looked into his dark-brown eyes, losing herself for a moment in them. She slipped her fingers under his lapels and pulled him just a little closer, and while doing so, felt his head bow down to meet hers. Just as their lips were about to meet, a scuffle down the corridor pulled them up short. Yapping and growling came from a few yards away.

'Ruby? Ruby, is that you?' Cressida dashed away from Alfred's embrace and followed the sounds of the growling, only to feel relief once again as she saw Ruby, standing proud on her four dinky legs, yapping at her offspring. And Ernest. Though he wasn't the subject of her ire – it was the six porgis who were hanging off the faithful old Labrador, or in Hercules's case, sitting astride him, as if riding the aged hound into battle.

'Oh, Ernest.' Cressida leaned down and nuzzled her family's old dog. 'Did Dotty leave you alone with the pups? You are the most adorable nanny, old thing, but this won't do.' She carefully pulled the puppies off the old Lab and handed them one by one to Alfred, who managed four in his arms before saying, 'No more!'

'Hercules, Fortnum, Mason and Dusty,' she counted off the ones in his arms, then held up the two in her hands. 'Suki and Lulu. That's our lot.'

A door opened down the corridor and Cressida and Alfred, and eight canine heads, all turned to see who it was.

'What's all this?' Lord Fawcett said, stepping out of his study onto the long kilim that stretched the length of the passageway. 'Ah,' he said, looking at the scene before him, then, 'that explains it all. Cressy?' He looked at his daughter, who tried her best to look as innocent as possible. 'That was Andrews on the blower. Says he'll come down on the afternoon train. And said something about your eyes having designs or something, but thought he should pop down and have a look. He'll go and see poor Bob first at the hospital morgue in Willowmere, and then come on up to the house and stay until we get this all sorted.'

'That's wonderful news, Papa. Always smashing to see Andrews.'

'Better make sure it doesn't look too much like a mad house around here, Cressy. Sir James is most likely on the same train and I would like it if he could arrive to a scene less like one of Dante's circles of hell.'

Cressida stifled a giggle. Poor Ernest had flopped down on the woven rug now and was happily panting away, but a few minutes earlier he had looked like some gruesome multi-headed, demon-plagued fiend from a Hieronymus Bosch painting. She nodded to her father and gestured for Alfred to follow her outside, where hopefully whatever breach in the puppy pen had been mended.

As Cressida and Alfred headed outside, juggling the six puppies between them, they could see Dotty and Molly hard at work fixing the pen. Ernest had creakingly got up from the rug and was walking stiffly alongside them. Cressida called over to Dotty, who looked up and then pushed herself off the lawn to standing, brushing down her woollen skirt as she did so.

'What news from the kitchen?' she asked, once Cressida and Alfred were close enough so that they could talk conspiratorially together. They all knew, that as vital as they were to the running of great houses, maids such as Molly were very often the eyes and ears of the place, as well as the much-needed hands. It paid not to speak too candidly within eavesdropping distance, so once Cressida and Alfred had de-pupped, they surreptitiously moved away from the pen towards the terrace. Once they were safely out of hearing distance, Cressida answered her.

'Not much really. She's awfully upset and, to top it all off, she made the point that Papa might have to chuck her out of the Garden Cottage once he finds a new gardener.' Cressida crossed her arms. 'Poor Marian. Imagine having to think of all the practical things while also mourning your husband.'

'I can't bear to think of it.' Dotty shook her head. 'It was bad enough at Christmas when George was threatened so horribly at the Mayfair Hotel. All the blood rushed to my head, my heart skipped several beats. I thought my world was ending.'

'Oh, Dot.' Cressida rested a comforting hand on her arm. 'I still think of that evening sometimes and how frightened you must have been.' She glanced at Alfred. 'So much happened that night.'

It was Dotty who carried on though, answering Cressida.

'It did. And I must say it was with a very heavy heart that I bid George goodbye last month for another of his expeditions. Of course, I know he'll be back in time for the wedding and it's different now I know he wants to marry me, but losing him again, albeit to Ancient Egypt, not a psychopath... well, it was hard.' She wrapped her arms around herself and shuddered with the thought of it.

'I can imagine, chum, I can imagine.' Cressida squeezed her friend's arm, then released her. 'And Marian looked genuinely distraught, she really did. But still, there was something that wasn't quite black and white about it all.'

Alfred, who'd taken his pipe out of his pocket and was busy knocking out old tobacco onto the grass, chipped in. 'Life seldom is, I suppose. And grief can come across in all sorts of different ways.'

'Yes, do you remember Leopold Von Goldsplatt's funeral?' Dotty added. 'His wife wore purple and danced until three in the morning, drinking nothing but Dom Pérignon all night. Everyone thought she was terribly uncouth, then she locked herself in a darkened room and didn't come out for a month.'

'Poor Shirley Von Goldsplatt.' Cressida nodded.

'Didn't you go to that funeral, Cressy?' Dotty asked. 'Wasn't it the night you found those antlers in the coat cupboard and did that thing with the Meissen china bowl and the bananas?'

'Yes.' Cressida blushed and glanced at Alfred, who luckily

seemed to be grinning. 'Just proves that people all react differ-
ently to a loved one's death.' She sighed. 'And, of course,
Leopold Von Goldsplatt died in the most natural of circumstances. But Bob, I'm sure of it, did not...'

## 10

'You really think it is murder then?' Dotty asked Cressida, her brow furrowed, causing her glasses to slip down the bridge of her nose.

'Yes, I do, more than ever. Marian said that Bob had been acting strangely. He'd been known to keep the odd secret from her, but he usually got round to spilling the beans, yet he hadn't mentioned anything to her about where he had suddenly got some money from, or the hoard. And I'm sure he must have found it as he was taking himself up to London just when he was most needed in the garden, and spending a lot of money on expensive drinks at the pub. Speaking of which, I think I might take you up on that offer of a snifter in the Royal Oak, you know, Alfred.'

'Right-o.' Alfred saluted her. The three of them waved to Molly, who was still corralling the puppies in the makeshift pen, and were about to head off when Cressida noticed Ruby staring up at her, her globe-like eyes wide.

'Fancy a few hours away from the little ones too, eh? I don't blame you.' Cressida leaned down and picked up her dog. 'What do you say?'

'If we take the Rolls,' Dotty piped up, 'I can come too. More than just the two seats, you see? And much more room for Ruby.'

Cressida shared a brief look with Alfred before smiling at her. 'Of course. Good plan, Dot. I think we could all do with a change of scene, and a quick run into the village would help you two get an idea of the layout of things, in relation to streams and churches and priories and hoards of gold and all that.'

'Super idea. It's been a little while since I was here last' – Dotty counted on her fingers – 'six months at least.'

'And dare I say it,' Alfred chipped in, 'not entirely sober either?' His sister elbowed him in the ribs.

'He's not wrong, you know, Dotty. You did spend that weekend sure that George had forgotten you and it took several gin and lemons to convince you otherwise.' Cressida grinned at her friend, and Alfred too, who smiled back, while Dotty rolled her eyes and shook her head.

The decision was made and once more the care of the six puppies was left to Molly, with a slightly shaky Ernest. Cressida and her friends fetched coats and hats from indoors, called out to her parents that they were off, and got into the Chattertons' silver Rolls-Royce.

Alfred would have no doubt preferred to have driven down in his natty Crossley two-seater, but Dotty had wanted to come too when he said he was weekending with the Fawcetts. It was a long-running family joke that Dotty did not travel light. In fact, one valise still remained on the back seat of the Rolls-Royce and Cressida and Dotty squeezed in next to it, letting Alfred sit up front alone, as if he were their chauffeur. After some rearranging, the valise made its way to the spacious footwell, and Cressida and Dotty were more comfortably seated on the red velvet seats.

'Ready now, you two?' Alfred had asked, as Cressida positioned Ruby on her lap and settled in. With a nod from her,

Alfred let the throttle go and they were gliding down the driveway of Mydenhurst Place and heading down the leaf-canopied lane towards the village.

Cressida looked out of the car and took in the familiar hedgerows and fields. Daffodils coloured the high-sided banks, and Cressida imagined their bright yellow trumpets heralding their journey as they motored on. She raised her voice above the noise of the engine and pointed out various places of interest.

'Down there's the way to the priory, but Papa told me it's barely lived in anymore, the weekend home to some composer chap, I think.'

'It's quite the "in" thing, isn't it? Having somewhere rather eccentric as one's weekend house. Do you remember when we were girls and we thought it a marvellous ruse to creep around it at dusk? Quite scared ourselves silly. I've had an aversion to the gothic ever since!' Dotty laughed. 'Except in novels, of course. I think I devoured *The Mysteries of Udolpho* afterwards.'

'You did!' Cressida nudged her in the ribs. 'Mrs Critchlow was over the moon that at least one of us showed the slightest interest in reading outside of the curriculum.'

'Am I missing something interesting?' Alfred called from the front seat and Cressida leaned forward.

'No, but for your information, and you might not remember this, Dot, but the priory's land meets up with the back fields of Lark's Leap, where the Whites live. They're in the historical society too.'

'Yes, I remember you saying. Mrs Catchpole's twins pilfered all their apples,' remarked Dotty.

'That's right,' Cressida agreed and then pointed out of the other window. 'And that way is the church, it's just down a little lane in the oldest part of the village. The rest of the village, the pub and the houses around the green, are about half a century younger, though still five hundred years old!'

'Lovely,' admired Dotty as they pulled to a stop outside the

Royal Oak. It was a whitewashed building with a low roofline. The terracotta roof tiles were covered in moss and the white of the outside was tinged with green from years of wet winters and climbing plants finding their way up between the diamond-paned windows. A sign outside had the familiar imagery of a grand old English oak tree, the crown of England held safely in its branches to represent the sanctuary given to the fleeing future King Charles II as he escaped the Roundheads in the seventeenth century.

'Grandfather tried to change the name to the Fawcett Inn back in the 1870s. I'm glad the villagers persuaded him not to, though.' Cressida squinted up at the sign, as the sun made a reappearance again, then back at Dotty who was now standing next to her, Ruby in her arms. 'Sounds a bit painful, doesn't it? Fawcett Inn.'

Dotty laughed and Cressida smiled at her, then waited as Alfred cut off the engine and climbed out of the stately car.

'Still drives like a beaut,' he said, giving the old Rolls-Royce an admiring pat on the bonnet.

'Sounds like a traction engine though.' Dotty shifted Ruby's weight in her arms. 'How lovely to be able to hear the birdsong again!'

'Closed I'm afraid, ladies and gent,' a voice came from behind them and Cressida turned back towards the pub and saw a man leaning over the bottom half of the stable-style door at its entrance. 'Laws and all. Closed between lunch trade and evening. But there's a tea room in Willowmere, which is only a mile or so away and no distance for a motor such as yours, sir. You'll find something there if you've travelled far.'

Cressida could see the man eyeing up the Rolls-Royce as he spoke, and the chance to make a penny or two, perhaps, and before they knew it, he'd changed his mind. 'Though I could stretch to a lemonade, if you don't mind sitting outside?' He nodded at one of the wooden trestle tables with benches on the grassy patch to the front of the building and Cressida smiled back at him.

'Yes, please, if you don't mind. We don't fancy trudging into Willowmere, not yet anyway, so that would be smashing.'

'Are you sure?' Dotty called out just to check, but the man's head and shoulders had already disappeared back into the dark of the pub.

Once the three friends had seated themselves at the table, Cressida whispered her thoughts to them.

'I think that's Walter Rook, the landlord. His wife, Annie, is Marian's sister.'

'Marian your cook?' asked Dotty.

'Recently widowed?' added Alfred.

'The very same,' confirmed Cressida. 'I'm going to take it as a compliment that he didn't recognise me. I think I've grown up a bit since he last saw me. He and Annie used to come and see Marian. She'd give them excess produce from our kitchen garden I think and Walter would whip them up into specials for the pub. Anyway, apparently Bob and Walter used to stand either side of the bar in there' – she gestured towards the half-open door of the pub – 'and listen in to the historical society. I'd be interested to see what Walter says, whether he picked up on anything.'

'And if he corroborates what Marian said about Bob spending more money recently, buying the village drinks and all that,' added Dotty.

Cressida nodded as there was a clunk and slide as the bolt was drawn from the bottom half of the stable door. Walter emerged with a tray and three glasses, plus two jugs; one of water and one that looked cloudy.

'Apple juice, I'm afraid. Not the season for lemons, of course,' the landlord said. 'But apples last all year and the last ones from autumn we juice or make into pies, pickles and the like.'

'Delicious,' murmured Alfred at the word pie. Cressida rolled her eyes at him, then looked at the landlord.

'Thank you. It's Walter Rook, isn't it? I'm Cressida Fawcett, from up the road.' She stuck her hand out and he shook it, a look of realisation appearing as he did.

'Ah, Lord and Lady Fawcett's daughter?' He let her hand go. 'Terrible accident this morning over by your stream. It must have been a shock to you all.'

'Yes.' Cressida accepted the kindness, but replied, 'Though it should be us offering our condolences to you. Bob Pringle was your brother-in-law, I believe? And a friend too? I hear he was a regular here at the Royal Oak?'

'Yes, yes, he was that.' Walter stood with his hands on his hips. He evidently wasn't going to go so far as to pour the drinks from the jugs, so Dotty took over and played mother.

'You say "accident", do you think Bob fell? You see, it was me who found him.' Cressida looked at Ruby, who was sitting patiently on the bench next to her, her face raised to the spring sunshine and her eyes closed. 'Or at least my dog did.'

'Did you now?' Walter asked. He shifted his weight and fixed her with a look. 'You don't think it was an accident?'

Cressida silently cursed. She didn't want to reveal the fact she'd found a gold coin in his hand. She felt this was a trump card she wanted to play a little later. But how to answer him?

Luckily Dotty did it for her.

'How could anyone tell? From what it sounds like, he fell, but who could say if he was pushed or had some sort of fit or sudden palsy?'

Cressida nodded. 'Quite. Still, poor Marian. She's devastated, of course.'

'Hmm.' Walter nodded.

'You knew Bob well, Mr Rook. Do you think it's an accident? Mama said Bob had been unsteady on his feet recently, she thinks he had an embolism.'

Before Walter Rook could answer, Alfred spoke: 'But DCI Andrews is coming down from Scotland Yard. And he wouldn't be if he didn't have a hunch.'

The pub landlord cleared his throat. 'I wouldn't like to disagree with her ladyship, but it could be Bob was in a spot of bother.'

Cressida looked at Walter, intrigued. 'A spot of bother? Could this be to do with the money he had come into? I heard he'd been splashing it around a bit, buying drinks for the village and all that.'

'Aye, that he did. And as grateful as the punters were, we were doubly so behind the bar. It's hard business these days. I says to him, "Bob, where'd you get that money from?" and he just taps his nose and nods over to the table where that society sit and says, "Don't tell the posh nobs," your father excusing, of course, Miss Fawcett, but he says, "Don't tell them, but I've found what they're looking for. And they'll be spitting feathers when they find out."'

A quick look between Cressida and her friends assured her of their silence. She didn't necessarily want Walter to know that they knew about the hoard. But what he said next made the blonde hairs on her arms stand on end.

'I wouldn't be surprised if someone in that fancy society of your father's killed Bob. He weren't beyond a bit of gentle taunting. Didn't just buy drinks for the village, did he? Made sure he did it on a night the society were at their usual table. He took great pleasure in placing those dry sherries down in front of Mrs Catchpole and Mrs White, and the beers he bought for the gents. Said he owed them. Now, if you say a detective from Scotland Yard is coming, then maybe something wrong happened to Bob. And if you ask me, if there's found to be foul play, it'll be someone who was sitting at that table.'

'Killed just for buying them all a drink?' Alfred looked a little perplexed but Cressida knew what Walter was saying.

Between the lines, unsaid... by buying them all drinks, Bob had been telling the historical society that he'd found the gold. That he'd overheard enough of their conversations and pieced it together for himself without telling any of them how he'd done it. And the members were no doubt fuming that a simple gardener, a non-member even, had managed it.

Cressida watched as Walter took the empty tray back into the dark interior of the Royal Oak. His friend, his brother-in-law even, had found a substantial amount of money.

Perhaps it wasn't just the historical society who were fuming that the good fortune hadn't fallen to them?

## 11

'Papa will be devastated if someone in his historical society is a murderer.' Cressida stared into her apple juice.

'On the plus side, at least future historical society members can talk about the time when Mr So-and-so from the 1920s committed a murder most horrid here in their very own village,' Dotty ventured.

'*My* very own village,' Cressida all but squealed.

'Sorry, Cressy.' Dotty rested her hand on Cressida's arm. 'That was cruel of me. I've obviously been reading too many of those silly books. Trivialising murder.'

'We don't yet *know* it's murder,' Alfred added, fetching his pipe from his jacket pocket and ramming it between his molars. Clenching his jaw, he carried on. 'Not for certain anyway, despite that Walter chap there leaping onto your theory too.'

'Yes, he was rather quick to suggest that Bob might have been dispatched by one of the regulars. I wonder if he knows more than he's letting on?' Cressida then sat upright in a flash as something pinged against her glass. In a moment, Dotty had the same look of shock on her face as a similar projectile ricocheted off her own glass and plopped into Alfred's.

This feat of aerial acrobatics was accompanied by the unmistakable sound of children giggling and Cressida let out the breath she'd been holding. Keeping a protective grip on Ruby, she turned around on the bench and sought out their attackers.

Not far from the grass in front of the pub was the village green with cricket pitch, and in front of that, just the other side of the road was the newly erected war memorial. It bore the names of villagers who died in the Great War of 1914 to 1918, including Gerald and Frank White, the sons of Percy and Madge from the historical society, and behind it, grinning from ear to ear, were two ruddy-looking faces. One boy and one girl, both with mousey-brown hair; his short and hers in plaits that dangled down her shoulders tied with red ribbons. She had her hand over her mouth, hiding her laughing, but he, the little boy, was focused on pulling back the sling of his bright red catapult.

'Watch out,' called out Cressida just as another hazelnut pinged across the table, skittering across the wood and rolling to a stop next to Alfred's glass.

'Oi, young man!' Alfred called, getting up from the bench.

This show of machismo was merely met with more giggles and a kerfuffle behind the war memorial as the children ran off across the village green, ribbons and catapult bright spots of red against their grey flannelled clothing.

'Little blighters,' said Alfred as he sat back down at the table and took a swig of apple juice. His look of disappointment when he remembered it wasn't beer was so obvious that Cressida almost laughed at him. And again, as he slurped and realised he still had a hazelnut bobbing around in his glass.

'Let me guess,' said Dotty, who was staring at the retreating figures. 'David and Daphne Catchpole?'

'That makes sense,' Cressida said, picking up the nut that had rolled across the table, as Alfred tried to fish out the one in his glass. 'They were described to me as little terrors. Pilfering the Whites' apples. I haven't seen them since they were very small, but they look familiar.'

'Got to admire their spirit,' said Alfred gamely, once his drink was nut-free.

'But it doesn't get us any further on what happened to poor Bob,' Cressida brought the conversation back on track. 'I'd like to get to Willowmere if possible, see if the mortuary has any information yet. Find out once and for all if this was murder. That strange writing on Bob's hand, it's still niggling at me, like a loose thread or a wonky curtain hem.'

'Andrews will let us know, surely, as soon as he's arrived and made enquiries,' Dotty suggested, but Cressida merely raised an eyebrow at her.

'And when will that be? Hours away, possibly. I have no idea what time the "afternoon train" actually gets in.'

'The joys of one's own motor car,' Dotty said wistfully and Cressida nodded.

'Exactly. And as discussed, wouldn't it be marvellous if we could be just that touch ahead of Andrews in the investigation stakes?'

Alfred pulled his watch chain out of his pocket and flipped open the silver case. 'Agreed. And we might not have that long. As it happens, I do know the times of the trains and the afternoon one from London will be getting into Willowmere at four thirty. I remember looking at the timetable when we were discussing how to get here, Dot,' he clarified as his sister had given him a look. 'You're not the only one au fait with Bradshaw you know, sis.'

'I'm impressed, Alf,' Dotty said, knowing full well the size and structure of the inches-thick guide to the railways, a book she'd insisted on buying at Inverness station last summer, and which had helped immeasurably during their investigation of murder on the Scotland Express. She frowned, though, when

Alfred muttered something about excessive baggage costs and some poor porter's back the last time they travelled by train.

'I'm impressed too, Alfred,' Cressida said, with just a tint more rosiness to her cheeks than a few minutes earlier. Having Alfred be so game for her adventures was hugely gratifying. Then she looked at her own wristwatch. 'It's past four o'clock now. If we can get to Willowmere before Andrews, we might be able to find out what really happened to Bob. If it was murder, we can impress Andrews with our findings and if the patholo-gist has ruled natural causes, well, then we can welcome Andrews in for a snifter before supper and invite him to stay the night. He and Papa can catch up on Boer War stories like the battered old soldiers they are.' Cressida was about to get up from the table when a voice shrilled across the cricket pitch at the friends.

'Excuse me! Cooeee!'

Cressida looked around again, but this time coming from behind the war memorial was a very primly dressed woman, who looked to be in her early thirties. Her skirt was floral and finished well below the knee, and she wore a lemon-yellow woollen twinset with a single-row pearl necklace. Her hair was neatly tied back and Cressida couldn't help but notice that it was the same colour as the two mini assailants who had been bombarding them with hazelnuts just a few moments ago. She looked familiar too, and Cressida was sure she had met her at one of her parents' drinks parties or perhaps the village fete, held each year here on the village green and cricket pitch. Her suspicions that this woman might be the troublesome twins' mother was confirmed as she had gripped in one hand a small red hair bow.

'Good afternoon,' Cressida called out to her as she approached.

'Good afternoon, and I'm sorry for interrupting you all,' the woman said, then introduced herself. 'Mrs Lilian Catchpole.'

'Cressida Fawcett, I think we've met? And this is Dotty and Alfred,' Cressida made the introductions. 'And Ruby too, my pug.'

'Oh, Lord Fawcett's daughter? Yes, of course. Down from London? How wonderful. We hear all about you at the historical society. Sounds like you have such adventures.'

Dotty and Alfred shared a look, but Cressida ignored them and took the opportunity to quiz Lilian.

'I do, we all do... but it sounds like there's been quite some goings-on here recently, too. A hoard of gold found, perhaps?'

'Oh really? Found?' Lilian looked both excited and disappointed. 'Has it? Was it Bob?'

'Bob Pringle?' Cressida confirmed. 'Why Bob?'

'He's been acting very strangely recently. Spending money I must say I had no idea he had. He's just – well, he's your gardener. And if you pay him that well, I might see if Edward fancies a change of career. Edward's my husband you see, and a doctor. Our local general practitioner, in fact. Have you met him? I feel sure you might have done?' Cressida smiled and shrugged. She had perhaps met him, but with no face to put to the name she couldn't be sure. Mrs Catchpole continued. 'But even he would shudder at buying drinks for everyone here at the Royal Oak of an evening!'

'When did Bob do that?' Cressida knew the answer, but was interested to see what Mrs Catchpole said.

'Oh, just the other night. What are we now? Friday? And the society meets on Thursdays so it must have been last Thursday night.'

'That was generous of him.' Cressida kept the conversation light, knowing that she really should tell Mrs Catchpole of his recent demise. But the fact that she didn't know – *or at least was acting as if she didn't know* – seemed important... Cressida carried on. 'Gosh, imagine finding the hidden hoard. Papa says everyone's very interested in it.'

'Oh yes, some of the society are literally obsessed.' Mrs Catchpole swept a strand of loose hair out of her face. 'Gold this, gold that.'

'Who in particular?' Cressida pushed.

'Well, the reverend is more interested in material goods than one might assume of a vicar. Man of the cloth and all that, but he definitely prefers silks to sacking, if you know what I mean. Of course, you didn't hear that from me. And there's that young Sebastian chap from Willowmere who talks of nothing else. I was thinking of tabling a motion to have him removed, in fact, as it's quite dull for the rest of us who care about all things historical, not just gold.'

'So, you wouldn't fancy finding the hoard then?' Cressida asked.

'Oh, well, of course it would come in useful,' Mrs Catchpole conceded. 'But I don't much fancy getting on the bad side of that curse. I know I'm married to a man of science, but it made me shiver when we read Barney Trewitt's book and the curse was mentioned. Wise women were the doctors of their day and, while it's amazing what Edward can do with pills and injections these days, we shouldn't underestimate those wise women of old.'

Cressida found herself agreeing with Lilian Catchpole up to a point. Curses notwithstanding, there was a case to answer that wise women were horribly overlooked in the pages of history. But she had to tell Mrs Catchpole now about Bob; it was becoming rude that she hadn't.

'Mrs Catchpole, I'm sorry, as I now realise that you might not know, but I'm afraid Bob was found dead earlier this afternoon. In Hell's Ditch – you know, the stream that runs through our estate.'

Lilian Catchpole instantly paled. 'Dead?' She raised a hand to her throat and laced her fingers over and under her pearls. 'Dead?' she repeated.

'Yes, I'm sorry. I should have told you before we got onto talk of curses and all that.'

'Dead…' Mrs Catchpole shook her head. Then apropos of nothing she asked, 'Have you seen my children?' She held up the red ribbon she'd been gripping in her hand. Cressida noted the sudden change in subject, but answered her nonetheless.

'Funnily enough,' Cressida replied, holding up a hazelnut, 'yes. A boy and a girl?'

'That's right, David and Daphne. David's got a catapult' – she eyed up the hazelnut – 'and Daphne has plaits.'

'They went that way.' Cressida pointed to the other side of the green, where she was sure she could see a flash of red disappearing behind an old stone wall of a garden.

'Ah, they've made their way home then it seems. Thank you,' Mrs Catchpole said. 'Nice to see you again, Miss Fawcett. And you too.' She nodded to Dotty and Alfred. Then she left, the look of shock and confusion still very much on her face.

'Well,' Cressida said, turning back to her friends when Mrs Catchpole was out of earshot, 'that was interesting.'

'Certainly was. Seems news of Bob's death hasn't travelled much beyond the family yet,' Dotty agreed.

Cressida nodded. 'I should imagine the wheels of the gossip cart will be in motion now though. And speaking of travelling, what say we head to Willowmere quick smart? Andrews won't be far behind us if Alf's right about the train times.'

'But how are we going to get into a mortuary? We're not with the police. We're just three amateurs with our nosy noble old noses,' Dotty pointed out.

Cressida shrugged as she took the last swig from her glass. Picking up Ruby she said, 'Not sure, Dot. But we have a two-mile drive and three noble old brains, too. We'll work something out!'

## 12

Willowmere was one of those English market towns that are peppered around the country; the lifeblood of those who live in it or close to it, but of little importance to anyone who lived more than thirty-odd miles away. It had a station that connected it to London and the south coast and a high street, which bustled on market day, but was otherwise relatively quiet. The road was wide, with plenty of room for carts and motor cars to stop or park up in front of the Victorian, Georgian and even older buildings that lined each side of it.

Willowmere had been an important stop between the bustling ports of the south coast and London, and was graced with a couple of grand Georgian coaching inns, their columned porches stretching out on the pavement, as well as the usual array of shops in the medieval and Victorian buildings, such as bakers and grocers, plus a gentlemen's outfitter and several ladies' boutiques. But most importantly for Cressida and her friends, at one end of the high street, down a laurel-lined lane, there was a cottage hospital, one of the largest in the area, and within it, the local morgue.

'I don't much like the idea of actually going into a mortuary,' said Dotty as they got out of the Rolls-Royce in front of the hospital. She held the door open, allowing Ruby to jump out. 'But I did see a rather charming bookshop on the high street. Do you mind if I go and see if they have a book by that namesake of mine, Dorothy L. Sayers? I've heard good things and, as she's a Dorothy too, I thought we should stick together.'

'Of course, Dot. It's just along the way there, past the museum and butcher. You never know, your namesake might give us some ideas. And speaking of ideas, as much as I hate to be parted from her, do you mind taking Ruby? She might not be the best behaved in bookshops, but better that than misbehaving in a morgue...'

'Point taken!' Dotty nodded, and once she'd scooped up Ruby she didn't hang about by the foreboding door in front of them, with the sign above it that said MORTUARY – AUTHO-RISED STAFF ONLY in rather austere black capital letters.

'No time like the present, eh, Cressy,' said Alfred, once his sister had left them to it. Then with a raised eyebrow he contin-ued, 'After you...' He pushed open the door, which swung open all too easily.

'Unlocked and everything. Practically inviting us in, I'd say.' Cressida justified their actions as best she could. She walked in under Alfred's arm, which was keeping the weighted and sprung door open. Once he was in behind her, he let it go. As it slammed shut, the passageway they found themselves in was suddenly in darkness and Cressida ran a hand along the wall hoping to find a light switch.

That electric lights had been fitted was a blessing indeed, and in a moment two high-hung bulbs along the corridor illumi-nated and showed them the pristine, if dull, corridor. With a shared look and slight shrug, they walked along the passageway, heeding signs on doors and dismissing those rooms – caretaker, office, stores – as of no use to them.

Cressida crept along turning a corner, Alfred just behind

her, until she abruptly came to a stop as she caught sight of movement on the other side of a door, glazed with a panel of frosted glass. Etched onto the frosted glass was the word 'Mortuary' and she could hear voices coming from within, thanks to the door being slightly ajar. She turned to Alfred and pressed a finger to her lips. He nodded, understanding, and even more stealthily than before they both edged towards the door.

'What does this tell us, then, Dr North?' The voice was a familiar one. Cressida turned to Alfred and pulled a face. He smiled at her and rolled his eyes. Then guided them both up against the wall next to a wheeled trolley of surgical instruments, close to the door but out of sight of anyone in the room.

'Most simple explanation is poison, Chief Inspector,' a second voice said. 'Most likely *atropa belladonna* I should imagine.'

'Deadly nightshade,' the familiar voice of DCI Andrews translated from the Latin. 'How can you tell?'

'We can't until the tests are back from London, of course, but look here, you see how his fist is gripped? Atropine poisoning, for that's what nightshade is, causes seizures. And here, around his lips, you see this rash? Touching the plant can cause irritation. I would hazard that he ate some form of the plant, ingested it, and within twenty or thirty minutes was going into cardiac arrest, convulsing enough to fall off the bridge you say he'd been sitting on, and then suffer a nasty combination of drowning and organ failure. A horrid, sudden and violent death. Not nice at all.'

'But you're sure there's no way this could have been a natural death?' Andrews asked.

'Well, it depends what you call natural. There was nothing synthetic going on. However, for your purposes, Chief Inspector, I assume you mean "pathological". And I'd have to say no. This death was brought about by ingestion of poison. Whether that be by this man's own hand, on purpose or by accident, or by persons wishing him ill – very ill – I can't say. But poison it was. The laboratory tests will confirm it, I'm sure.'

'Speaking of hands, you said there was writing on his palm?'

'Yes, though it's unreadable now. I don't think there's much to suspect about the ink though, if that's what you're thinking. There's no rash or irritation where it was, indicating it wasn't a topical means of poisoning him. No, he ingested that poison, and then died because of it. I'm certain of it.'

'Anything else of interest?'

'Not really. Bruising that would fit with the fall at the point of death, though there are some more acute bruises on his neck. Hard to work out what they might be, though I'd hazard it was some sort of projectile. Small, red and purple blemishes you see, here and here.'

'I see,' Andrews said and Cressida heard some 'hmmms' as he obviously took in the small bruises. Dr North spoke again.

'Those wouldn't have had a bearing on his death though, some are a few days old at least and the newer ones of little consequence.'

'Thank you, Dr North,' Andrews said and Cressida could hear an audible sigh she recognised all too well. She, and Alfred, also heard the footsteps come closer to the door, and in their haste to make themselves scarce they forgot about the trolley of surgical instruments that was just behind them and with an almighty crash they both fell into it. Losing her balance, Cressida was the first of them to fall to the ground and while Alfred had tried to be gentlemanly and offer her a hand, that had only made matters worse and he'd skidded along with the trolley for a moment, then tripped over Cressida's leg, bringing himself and the trolley – and all of its surgical instruments – down to the tiled floor too.

Syringes, scalpel handles and metal instruments were scattered all around them, but what was worse was that two gruff-looking faces were staring down at them. The bald, egg-shaped man with horn-rimmed glasses and bright red braces showing under his white laboratory coat must have been Dr North, the pathologist. While the bearded man in the three-piece tweed suit, with grey flecks now showing in his brown hair and grizzled beard, and a look of exasperation on his face, well that was DCI Andrews.

'Miss Fawcett,' he said, then looked at Alfred, 'and Lord Delafield. Can I even begin to ask what you're doing here?'

'You know these people?' the egg-shaped pathologist asked. 'This is a restricted area. You shouldn't be here. Does Mrs Grayshott know?'

Cressida, who had no idea who Mrs Grayshott was, shook her head and raised a hand, which Andrews reached down and took, pulling her up to standing. She brushed herself down, removing a few cotton swabs from her hair, as Andrews did the same for Alfred. Then the policeman spoke for them.

'Yes, Dr North, I do know them. And although that doesn't excuse their trespassing, it does at least explain it. Can I introduce you to Lord Fawcett's daughter, the Honourable Cressida and her friend, Lord Delafield.'

'Good day to you both,' the doctor said, slightly mollified by their grand titles but still nonplussed at their presence in his mortuary. Andrews continued.

'Miss Fawcett here found the body.' He nodded back into the room, and not being able to help herself, Cressida craned her neck to try and see into it. All she managed was a peek at a white-sheeted form on a gurney. A glare from Andrews reminded her she was already in hot water. 'She and Lord Delafield have helped the Yard on several occasions. I'll take it from here, Dr North. And thank you for seeing to Mr Pringle so quickly. You've been a great help.'

Andrews started to herd Cressida and Alfred down the passageway as Dr North replied.

'Very well. I'll have the laboratory tests forwarded onto you as soon as I get them back. I'll stake my career on it being belladonna though.'

Andrews thanked the pathologist again and ushered the two young interlopers out of the door and back into the spring sunshine. Squinting, Cressida said, 'Thank you, Andrews. And what ho and all that. Sorry for eavesdropping—'

'Again,' the policeman said with a raise of his brow.

'Yes, it's becoming a bit of a habit, isn't it? Sorry about that. All very interesting though. Corroborated what I suspected about it being a murder. Though I never spotted the rash, but only because I couldn't see his mouth, him being face down and all that. I did spot the ink though, and before it got too washed away, I could have sworn it spelled out the word "dead" on his hand.'

'Really?' Andrews removed a notebook from his pocket and noted it down. 'Though I'd be surprised if that were some threatening message from a murderer, Miss Fawcett. Not often one gets one's hand grabbed and written upon.'

'I suppose not, but it was there all the same.' Cressida shrugged.

'More like that he would be writing himself a reminder. But it's not often one writes oneself a note to remember to die later on that day,' Andrews continued, raising an eyebrow at Cressida.

'You're laughing at me, Andrews.' Cressida squinted up at him, but her hands remained firmly at her hips. 'I'm just telling you what I noticed. And why I thought it was murder, or at least highly suspicious. And look, you see, it *is* murder. I was right.'

'Not necessarily. The poison could have been self-adminis-tered. From what I remember deadly nightshade has very tempting-looking berries. Hence why so many innocent children fall foul to it, year after year,' Andrews countered.

'Berries? It's spring, Andrews. There aren't any berries out; they come in autumn,' Cressida retorted, in a matter-of-fact way. Then she crossed her arms and thought. 'Also, Bob was a gardener. He'd know better than to eat any part of the nightshade plant. He'd grown up with these plants, he'd know them better than anyone.'

Andrews sighed. 'That's a fair point, Miss Fawcett.'

Cressida nodded, accepting the compliment. 'If only we'd kept the sandwich. Cheese and pickle, I thought. It was just a glance though.'

'If it wasn't berries, then how does one hide poisonous leaves in a cheese and pickle sandwich?' pointed out Alfred, rubbing his elbow from where he'd fallen rather hard onto the tiled floor of the mortuary corridor.

'Chopped up, minced, extracted in some way... a pickle would taste strong enough to disguise anything in it. Anything could have been chopped into that sandwich and he'd bite down, none the wiser.'

'Murdered then?' Andrews asked.

Cressida looked at him and nodded again. Then a wave of remorse came over her, remorse that she'd brought Andrews into the investigation, remorse that she'd insisted it was murder at all. She brought her hands up to her face as the realisation took hold. She felt a touch to her back, a reassuring hand and a voice in her ear.

'Cressy, what is it? What's wrong?' Alfred asked.

Cressida dropped her hands from her face and scrunched up her eyes before looking at Alfred and then Andrews. Finally she said, 'Yes, murdered. But there can only really be one suspect, can't there? If the poison was in the pickle in the sandwich, then the most likely suspect has to be whoever made that sandwich for him.'

'Ah,' Alfred said, taking a step back as he caught up with Cressida's thinking. 'The cook.'

Cressida nodded. 'Yes, the cook. Who also happens to be his wife and about to come into a lot of money now he's dead. Marian.'

## 13

Alfred and Andrews looked as ashen-faced as Cressida as they realised that her family's beloved cook, the grieving widow, was the likeliest murderer. Wordlessly they climbed into the car, Andrews sitting in the front passenger seat next to Alfred, while Cressida sat glumly on the red velvet seats in the rear. They motored down the high street just in time to catch Dotty emerging from the bookshop with several brown-paper wrapped parcels under each arm and even more held swaying tower-like in her hands.

Ruby was keeping her distance from the precarious purchases and Cressida and DCI Andrews leapt out of the Rolls-Royce in order to help Dotty as she veered one way and then the other. As DCI Andrews helped steer Dotty towards the car, Cressida held the back door open saving Dotty juggling with both books and door handles. She glanced back at the bookshop, where she saw the bookseller with a wide smile across her face. Understandable, judging by the obvious spending spree Dotty had just been on.

'Well, as Alf said, we're not taking the train home,' Dotty

explained as she deposited her parcels in the footwell of the back seats, next to her valise. Then she added, 'And what ho to you, Mr Andrews. So lovely to see you again.'

'And you, Lady Dorothy,' Andrews said, prising one of the packages away from her so she could finally move her arms again. He held one of the parcels up. 'Research?'

'Possibly. All good grist for the mental mill in any case,' Dotty answered him as she climbed into the back seat. Cressida beckoned to Ruby to jump in after her, and Andrews climbed in next to Alfred in the front again.

Alfred let the throttle go and pulled out onto the cobbled high street. Once the historic town was behind them and the houses and shops had given way to hedgerows and fields, Cressida told Dotty about their findings at the mortuary, thanks to Dr North's observations. Dotty had been as glum as Cressida at the realisation that the chief suspect simply had to be Marian Pringle, but good manners overtook bad news, and she enquired after their second-favourite policeman.

'No Sergeant Kirby this time, Andrews?' Dotty asked, her voice raised over the sound of the engine. Sergeant Kirby had attended all their investigations and was rarely not at Andrews' side with his notebook poised and his helmet strap pulled regimentally tight.

'No, not yet, though with Dr North's pronouncement on the presence of poison, I might be calling him. I must admit, I thought it might have been a false alarm and I was tempted down by an invitation from Lord Fawcett. Always good to see him and your mother, Miss Fawcett.' He paused, which didn't go unnoticed by the friends. 'And you all, of course.'


As the three friends, Ruby and DCI Andrews clattered into the main hall of Mydenhurst Place, they were met by Lady

Fawcett, who greeted Andrews as an old friend. In many ways he was, as he was a man held in the highest regard by the Fawcetts due to Lord Fawcett's belief that Andrews had saved his life during the Boer War. Of course, Andrews' version of the story was that his commanding officer, Colonel Lord Sholto Fawcett, had been the one to save his life, and so the mutual affection arose.

Cressida had grown up with a very dog-eared, but now framed, photograph of Lord Fawcett and Andrews, who had been his batman, on her father's desk and had been delighted that Andrews had been the Scotland Yard detective assigned to the first case she'd been able to solve; that of Lady Chatterton's missing diamonds – and the murder at Chatterton Court – last summer. Lady Fawcett obviously held DCI Andrews in great affection, too, and once the policeman had blushed at the kisses she bestowed upon his cheeks, they were all invited into the drawing room to meet the most recent house guest; Sir James Colston.

Cressida hadn't seen Sir James in a while, but was struck by the difference between him and her father. While Lord Fawcett endeavoured to be as fit and active as he could, maintaining his slim frame despite his war injury, his old university friend, Sir James, was short, plump, pale as an oyster and with a hint of the same sheen that one might expect from a mollusc, too. His brown hair flopped over his head and he sweated through his country tweed. Yet he looked jolly enough and greeted everyone as they were introduced. Cressida noticed Dotty looking quite shy and while her mother offered sherries, for the sun was well and truly heading towards the yard arm, if not in Mydenhurst then at least somewhere in the world, she asked her if she was all right.

'All right? Cressy, I'm star-struck!'

'Star-struck?' Cressida looked about the room, just checking in case Buster Keaton had made an appearance.

'Sir James,' Dotty hissed, pulling on Cressida's arm. 'Like I said, he's one of the most eminent historians in the country. He wrote *Time and Tide: A History of the South Coast*, and *Warrior Kings: England's Fighting Monarchs*.'

'They both sound scintillating,' Cressida said drily.

'They *are*, Cressy.' Dotty nudged her. 'He's the cat's pyjamas when it comes to Saxon history. If you want to know more about this hoard of yours, he's your man.'

Cressida perked up at this.

'Really?' She thought of the thrymsa coin she'd found in Bob's fist and the others that must have been unearthed alongside it. 'I suppose it's why Papa invited him to stay.'

'Darling,' Lady Fawcett called over to her daughter. 'Do come and talk to Sir James and tell him all about your whizzy little interiors jobs you do.'

Cressida didn't need much persuasion to go and talk to this expert on Saxon gold, and especially not the elbow in the ribs that Dotty gave her, which made her almost stumble across the room towards the outstretched hand of Sir James Colston.

'*Howjado*, Cressida,' he said, jolly as anything. 'Haven't seen you since God was a boy.'

'Hello, Sir James.' Cressida gripped his hand and smiled at him. 'And yes, it's been a fair few years. One of the village pageants, I think, but I was much younger then. This is my friend Dorothy, by the way, Dorothy Chatterton.'

Dotty squeezed past Cressida and stuck her hand out at the ageing academic. Shyness it seemed had been surpassed by a fervent admiration. 'Good day, Sir James,' she said. 'I'm a huge admirer of yours. Your essay on the unreadiness, or indeed not,' – she snorted in laughter – 'of Ethelred was a delight.'

'Thank you, Lady Dorothy.' Sir James beamed and rested his thumbs inside his lapels as he basked in the attention.

As Dotty expressed in the warmest terms that the 'lady' part of her name could definitely be dropped and how wonderful it was to meet such an esteemed historian, Cressida noticed DCI Andrews exit the room. Leaving Dotty to talk, her hands gesturing as wildly as one could imagine as she spoke on her favourite subject, she stepped towards Alfred.

'I saw it too,' he said, without Cressida needing to say a word.

'Do you think I should go to her? Or send Mama? Some support perhaps while she's being interrogated?'

'I think we both know Andrews to be the sort of stand-up chap not to throw his weight around. But, Cressy, do you think she did it?'

'Kill her husband? No. I don't... but the evidence is all pointing that way.'

Their hushed voices weren't quite quiet enough and Lady Fawcett, leaving her husband to talk to Sir James and Dotty, came over to them. All it took was for her to arch an eyebrow for Cressida to tell her what she suspected was happening in the kitchen.

'Oh dear,' Lady Fawcett said, a concerned look on her face, one hand threading its way through her long rope of pearls. 'Not that I suspect for a moment that she could be responsible, Marian wouldn't do anything like that. She can barely bring herself to pluck a pheasant, Bob or your father has to do it for her. I do hope Andrews will be gentle with her. She's insisted on staying on and cooking dinner for us all tonight. I told her she should take the rest of the day off, and as many as she needs after that too, but she said something about keeping busy.'

'Hmm, we'll see what Andrews has to say about that. At the moment she's only a suspect and as the sandwich Bob was eating must have been swept down the stream, it's still only a working theory that that's how Bob was killed. I should imagine Andrews might be raiding the pantry though for any remaining pickle,' Cressida said, frowning. 'And poor Marian. To add this to her grief too. We should probably be prepared for a sudden cook-based exodus.'

Lady Fawcett sighed, which brought the attention of the others in the room. They were swiftly filled in, and joined Lady Fawcett and Cressida in the consensus that any suspicion of Marian being the murderer was not to be borne.

'She can't even pluck a pheasant,' said Lord Fawcett.

'That's what I said, darling,' Lady Fawcett agreed. Then she turned back to her daughter. 'As you say though, darling, we'll be on stand-by with the cold cuts and leftovers' – she looked at Sir James – 'for which I can only apologise, James. I am sorry that you've come into a household racked by death.'

Sir James bowed. 'Please don't mention it, dear lady. Us historians are used to a bit of death. Our bread and butter, if you will.'

Cressida exchanged a look with Dotty, who just shrugged. Perhaps historians did always have a cavalier attitude to death? To them, deaths, however horrid, were just fodder for best-selling books and gaining doctorates. Lady Fawcett broke the slightly awkward silence, showing a level of diplomacy of which an ambassador would have been proud.

'Well, bread and butter shall wait until the morning. I believe Marian had prepared beef en croute and early beans from the greenhouse. I shall ring the bell presently. Dressed for drinks at seven?'

Everyone nodded, and Cressida couldn't help get a little thrill from the thought of seeing Alfred in a rather smart tuxedo, which she knew he'd recently had made by his tailor following the latest fashion.

'Darling,' Lord Fawcett's voice cut through the murmuring of the family and guests as they milled around the room. 'James and I are going to walk down to the stream.'

'The stream?' Lady Fawcett looked quizzically at her husband and Cressida turned to face her parents.

'Yes, to see if there's anything of Bob's down there. Reunite it with his widow and all that.'

Lady Fawcett nodded, whether it was in whole-hearted agreement with her husband or more in acquiescence, Cressida couldn't tell. She watched as her father and his friend left the room, a furtive look on their faces.

## 14

The sun had set soon after Cressida had watched her father and Sir James Colston traipse down to the stream. The rest of the household had parted ways, heading to their bedrooms to change and dress for dinner. Cressida had lurked by the door to the kitchen, but except for some faint murmurings she'd been unable to eavesdrop with much success. That was the downside of having such thick old oak-panelled doors; doors so thick the hinges were made of solid cast iron, with the braces stretching right across the solid wood. She'd cursed the adeptness of the Jacobean builders and headed up to her room, keen to be ready in time to meet Dotty and Alfred before the gong sounded for cocktails at seven o'clock. And more importantly, try and catch Andrews and see if she could wangle out of him a word-by-word account of his interview with Marian.

Cressida always insisted on living without a lady's maid – and had even updated her wardrobe accordingly with dresses that had easy-to-reach fasteners, and her bobbed and shingled hair took little more than a cursory comb to style it. She found the trend for wearing a headband helped immeasurably when one's comb didn't quite do the job. However, Molly, her mother's maid, was dutiful enough to skip from room to room, helping Cressida, Dotty and Lady Fawcett dress for dinner. Cressida had brought one of her new evening gowns from London, but she was pleased of Molly's help, adjusting the low waistband's tie and helping her position her glittering headband just so. With Alfred debuting his new tuxedo, she wanted to look just as snazzy.

What wasn't helping was the constant yapping and distraction that six – or even seven if you counted Ruby – small dogs was adding to the preparations.

'I don't know, miss,' Molly had said when Cressida had asked her whether she thought her parents would like to have one or two permanently. She thought about it as she pinned Cressida's headband in place. 'They're quite an 'andful, miss.'

'That they are!' Cressida had agreed and laughed as Suki and Hercules rolled across the Persian carpet, loose strands of the fringing in their mouths. 'Oh dear. Don't tell Mama the current fate of her second-favourite rug, Molly!'

The maid dipped a curtsy, but there was a smile on her face as she looked at Cressida through the mirror. 'Yes, miss, secret's safe with me. Though I think your mama is more concerned with poor Mrs Pringle and if she's up to the dinner tonight. Did you know your father invited some of his friends at the eleventh hour, as they say?'

'No? Did he?' Cressida turned around on the dressing-table stool and looked up at the maid. 'Who? And why, when poor Mrs P has enough on her plate without having to think about adding more to our literal ones?'

'I don't know *why*, miss, but I know *who,* as Mrs Pringle was... well, I don't mean to tell tales and say "moaning" but she was telling her sister who popped in—'

'Annie Rook from the Royal Oak?' Cressida asked, though only to clarify it in her head.

'Yes, that's right. Mrs Rook who came with a basket of

goodies just as Mr Andrews was leaving the kitchen. And she said to her, "Annie, I don't know what to do about all of this," and I assume she meant trying to get the beef to spread between another five guests.'

'Did she say anything about what she and Andrews had spoken about?' Cressida asked, hoping the guileless maid might spill the beans.

'No, miss, I didn't ask, miss.'

Cressida tried to hide her disappointment with another question. 'So, who are they? Our guests tonight?' She carefully prised the puppy she thought was Fortnum off her leg, knowing that her stockings wouldn't last more than a minute at this rate.

'Well, miss, I believe it's Doctor and Mrs Catchpole, Reverend Dunn and then Mr and Mrs White.'

'Hmm, the historical society secretary and her husband, the vicar and the Whites from Lark's Leap. Interesting.' Cressida turned back around and faced the mirror once again. She caught Molly's eye and raised eyebrow and returned the gesture with one of her own.

*Why had her father invited the key members of the historical society to dinner tonight?*

Could it be that, like her, Lord Fawcett believed the ancient hoard of gold was behind Bob's death? And that as he couldn't possibly believe that Marian had killed Bob, he wondered if one of the society members knew more than they were letting on? Either that or his excitement at having his good friend and renowned scholar, Sir James, here was just too thrilling not to share with fellow historians.

Either way, it would give her the opportunity to subtly question some of them, so despite her father's atrocious lack of empathy in piling more work onto poor Marian, she silently thanked him for it.

. . .

'Oh, delicious!' Dotty sipped the ice-chilled martini that Cressida passed her and clinked her glass with her best friend. Cressida was pleased that Dotty was down in the library first and had hastily shaken them both their favourite cocktail. While shaking and pouring Cressida had told Dotty about tonight's extra guests and the conversation Molly had overheard in the kitchen. After a few sips, Dotty returned to that very conversation.

'It's nice that her sister popped by though, isn't it?'

'Yes, I hope she was of some comfort to her. Poor Marian is obviously distressed. And I haven't been able to gauge how her interview with Andrews went.'

'Poor Marian. It's horrible enough when one's husband is found dead, not to mention everyone assuming it must be you who did it.'

'I just don't think she would. And obviously neither does Papa, as he's happy to invite even more guests tonight to be fed by her! Speaking of guests,' Cressida changed the subject, 'how's your wedding planning going?'

'Mama's in charge,' said Dotty plainly. 'Though we think our neighbours at Honeystone Manor will host as they have a picture-perfect chapel in the grounds, built by the second Lord Hawkingfold, who had travelled extensively in Egypt as part of his Grand Tour. The chapel mimics an Egyptian temple, so all in all rather apt for George and his passion for the ancients. He did write and say he could ship in some Nile crocodiles to help with the theme, but I think he was joking.' She took another sip from the martini glass and looked thoughtful. 'Yes, I think he was joking.'

'Well, Ruby volunteers herself for ring-bearing duty,' said Cressida and then smiled. 'And I have six perfect wedding presents for you, currently chewing up corners of priceless Persian rugs upstairs.'

Dotty elbowed her friend in the ribs and Cressida

pretended to be winded. Just as she was taking a restorative sip from her glass, trying not to spill the ice-cold cocktail down her dress, the door opened.

Cressida almost choked on her cocktail as Alfred entered the room looking the most suave she thought she'd ever seen a man in her life. His new tuxedo fitted him perfectly, and the smart black bow tie and sharp-as-a-knife creases in his pressed trousers were enough to make her go a little weak at the knees. She offered him a martini, then quickly turned her back on him as she measured out the liquor, hoping that he wouldn't see quite how pink her cheeks had suddenly become.

'What's that you're holding, Alf? And yes, of course he'll have one, won't you?' Luckily Dotty answered for her brother, allowing Cressida time to add a drop of vermouth to the shaker, while trying really very hard to keep her hands from trembling. She gave a silent prayer of thanks that martinis benefitted from a good shake – there was no way she could have made anything else at this very moment.

'What ho, both,' Alfred greeted them. 'And yes, please, rather. A martini would very much hit the spot. And this? Oh, something I found in the hallway. Box of chocs, I think?'

Cressida, having shaken the life out of the cocktail, poured Alfred his glass and turned around to hand it to him. She was pleased, if a bit blushingly so, to see him taking in her daring dipped neckline and long, low string of pearls that hung down her chest. The speed at which he took his first sip made her smile and she made a note to order more dresses from this particular Chelsea boutique.

'Chocs?' Dotty said, oblivious to the frisson happening between her brother and best friend. She opened the box and then screwed up her nose. 'Oh, yuck. Turkish Delight. It's simply horrid, don't you think?' She put the lid back on the box and pushed it along the sideboard away from her.

Cressida was just reaching out for the box, partial to the

floral sweet treat herself, when the drawing room door opened and her mother and father walked in, with DCI Andrews and Sir James following on behind.

'Darlings.' Lady Fawcett looked adoringly at Cressida and her friends. 'Don't you all look absolutely smashing.' She walked over and embraced them all, while accepting the offer of a pink gin from Alfred, who set about with the bitters and ice cubes. While Dotty spoke animatedly about history to the gents, Lady Fawcett pressed her hand into the crook of Cressida's elbow.

'Isn't he yummy? I do hope you'll say yes when he asks and give up this funny notion of yours about never wanting to marry.'

Cressida pulled away from her mother. She couldn't be cross with her, as she was about as cock-a-hoop over Alfred as anyone could be, but she was a bit miffed about her perfectly logical view on marriage being called a 'funny notion'. Still, in the way of daughters for centuries before her, Cressida deflected. 'He's got to ask first, Mama. Let's not jump the proverbial gun. Anyway, talk to me about your thoughts for this room. It's the colour on these panels, isn't it? What's your idea for them?'

Lady Fawcett gave Cressida a look in the way of mothers for centuries before *her*, while allowing the obvious change of subject. And Cressida had been canny in her choice of subject change as it was the panels and their colouring that her mother had particularly wanted her advice on.

The panels were two large sections of wall, each hung with paintings and etchings, that were in fact hinged so that with the correct push and tug they could be swung open like a great pair of doors. When opened they revealed a window that was deep set enough to also be decorated with framed paintings and etchings, while holding on its sill a stunning marble statue. Lady Fawcett hooked a finger from each hand on the brass rings that sat flush to the panels and pulled. Suddenly an ear-piecing shriek filled the room, disturbing the conversation among the guests and causing a few 'by Joves' from Alfred and Dotty.

Lady Fawcett apologised to her guests and once they'd resumed chatting, she whispered to Cressida. 'Well, it looks like a trip to the garden shed for some hinge oil should be my first mission, but I also feel that the wall colour needs a change. It's been this dull grey since I married your father and I know it goes with the moody skies of those J.M.W. Turners up there, and that brooding Venetian canal water courtesy of Signor Canaletto, but it also does nothing to show off poor Aletheia in there. She's such a beautiful marble and that grey does zilch for her.'

'In the daytime though?' Cressida asked, moving one of the panels backwards and forwards as she examined it, grateful that the initial metal-on-metal squealing had stopped. 'Which direction does this window face? North or east, isn't it?'

'Yes. Both. Sort of. So, still grey,' said Lady Fawcett, mournfully. 'Of course, the outer panels – and do be careful with that hinge, darling, it's looking a little perilous – are closed often enough as the northeast light is so poor. This room gets all its daylight from the window on the south side.' She pointed over to where Lord Fawcett and Sir James were standing in front of a large bay window, its floor-length curtains closed against the darkness outside. She looked back at the panels. 'What do you think? I thought a blueish tone.'

'That might chill poor Aletheia down even more. She's barely dressed as it is,' Cressida remarked.

'Yes, I see what you mean. She's the goddess of truth, you know. Though perhaps the Greeks could have had fewer goddesses of abstract muses and more practical ones. Where's the goddess of sensible underwear, eh?'

'Or the goddess of shoes that don't pinch. I could do with one of those.' Cressida smiled back at her mother. 'But seriously though, Mama, how about a soft pink. A dusky rose? It would go beautifully with the paintings on the outside of the panels, matching those large gilt frames and moody sunsets that Turner so loved, and it would give poor Aletheia just a touch of colour to her cheeks, both face and bottom, especially when the sun comes through that window.'

'Oh, darling, I knew you'd crack it!' Lady Fawcett beamed at her daughter. 'You are clever. You're quite right too. Though persuading your father that his library might be about to be painted pink...' She tailed off.

Before Cressida could reply, her mother had bustled off to greet the newcomers, for while she and Cressida had been deliberating over paint colours, two cars and a bicycle had rumbled up the gravel drive. The Reverend Dunn, the Catch-poles and the Whites had arrived.

## 15

The general murmur of conversation and clinking of cutlery filled the dining room as the Fawcett family and their guests tucked into Marian Pringle's best-ever beef en croute. The conversation was lively, despite the brief moment of silence that was held before the meal had begun. Lord Fawcett had raised a glass to absent friends, and nodded to Marian who had appeared at the door, her face ashen as she scanned the room. The conversation had only started up once she'd bustled around the sideboard, making sure the sauces and accompaniments were all in order.

Cressida had watched to see if any look had passed between her and DCI Andrews, but Marian seemed focused on the food, and Andrews was attentively raising his glass to his hosts and sipping his wine. She was annoyed that her mother's seating plan had placed Andrews so far away from her, she was keen as anything to hear about what had happened in the kitchen, but due to the fact that Marian was still a free woman, she had to assume that Andrews hadn't gleaned much from her, or found anything incriminating in the pantry. A debrief on it all would have to wait. For now, she focused on who she could talk to.

And that was the man next to her, Percy White from Lark's Leap. Once the general conversation allowed, she lost no time in asking him all about the historical society, or at least his take on the hunt for the golden hoard.

'Obsessed you say?' Percy White laughed as Cressida posed the question to him. 'I'm not sure any of us are obsessed with finding the gold. Though I won't deny, finding it has its allure.'

'Do you think Bob found it?' Cressida speared a green bean with her fork and popped it in her mouth after she'd asked. She watched Percy's reaction to her question carefully and wondered if she'd seen a flicker of wariness cross his weathered brow.

The Whites were what her mother would call among 'the great and the good' of the village, in that although they weren't from any particular aristocratic line, there had been Whites in the village for a few generations and they owned a fair amount of acres over the other side of the church and priory.

Madge enjoyed the races down at Goodwood and she and Lady Fawcett often exchanged hats so that neither would be seen wearing the same thing on consecutive days' racing. Percy sat on the parish council, served as a church warden and was of medium height and build, but fit for his years, no doubt because of the outdoor nature of tending all those poor war horses. He was in white tie, a little worn around the cuffs and lapels, but otherwise smartly turned out, though Cressida noticed a trace of dirt still under his fingernails and the slightest whiff of ammonia coming from him – she knew that for true horse lovers it wasn't unheard of for them to check in on the stables before they left the house, whatever they were wearing. So, for this practical and plain-speaking man to furrow his brow when Cressida asked him her question was intriguing. He answered as she sliced through her tender beef fillet and carried on eating.

'Now it's interesting you should ask that. What makes you think it?'

Cressida was caught out, and was pleased she had a mouthful of beef and pastry to give her just an ounce more time to work out what to say. She didn't want Percy to know about the coin she'd found in Bob's fist, only his views on Bob's actions in the pub.

Finally she swallowed and replied, 'Only that dear Marian said she thought he'd come into some money recently, and I heard from Walter Rook and Mrs Catchpole that Bob had been treating the village to free drinks in the Royal Oak. I just wondered if it meant he'd found some of the coins, or possibly the whole hoard?' Her choice to name-drop other members of the society and village was purposeful – divide and conquer and all that. And it worked. Percy looked over the table to where Lilian Catchpole was talking animatedly about the need for better health care in rural areas to Lady Fawcett, who was doing her utmost to look interested.

Percy rebuked her with his reply. 'That's quite an assumption to make. He might have had an inheritance, won a few bob on the horses, had an endowment mature...'

Cressida was cornered. She was fairly certain that their gardener wouldn't have invested in an endowment policy, and Marian hadn't mentioned an inheritance, but Percy White had a point about a possible gambling win. Something like that could be the reason why he hadn't told his wife about where the money was coming from. Perhaps now was the time to reveal what she knew about Bob's death. And so she did, much to Mr White's apparent interest.

'A coin in his hand, you say? My, my.'

'A thrymsa. Which is Saxon, of course, so it must be from the hoard.'

'You do know your history, don't you, Miss Fawcett?' Percy White said, approvingly. 'Like father, like daughter, eh?'

'Well, I took an interest, not so much in the coin itself, but the deadness of the fist clasping it,' Cressida replied. Then, after a pause and a deep breath she carried on, delivering the line that could get her into quite some hot water. 'And, of course, it makes me wonder if any of the historical society perhaps had a hand in it. A rivalry of some sort. Jealousy and greed over the gold even?'

'Well, that is quite the accusation on us all.' Percy White put his knife and fork down on his plate and reached out for his glass. Cressida could see a tremble to his hand. Had she struck gold? Or at the very least, a nerve?

'I don't mean to accuse anyone, Mr White,' Cressida soothed him. 'I'm just trying to work out what happened to poor Mr Pringle.'

'Well, it's news to me that the fellow died of anything other than natural, if tragic, causes.' Percy White frowned. 'Clasping a coin or not, it's more likely that he fell for some reason. You're suggesting he was murdered.'

Percy White's words were said as a statement, not a question. Cressida looked across to where DCI Andrews was tucking into his beef, with Dotty on one side of him making conversation about his shoulder – she'd helped nurse him through a gunshot wound sustained on one of their previous adventures, so she took an active interest in it. Cressida was glad Andrews hadn't heard what she was talking to Percy White about. She wasn't sure yet if anyone else knew Bob's death had been murder. However, she was stuck in a hole now and could do nothing to dig herself out of it except nod. Percy White took it with more equanimity than she imagined he might and he followed up her revelation with one of his own.

'And you say our friend over the table there' – he subtly nodded at Lilian Catchpole – 'and Mr Rook had both noticed Bob Pringle's sudden generosity? That is interesting.'

'Yes, I suppose I hadn't thought about it like that. *Why* they'd noticed. Enough to then still have it in mind when I spoke to them. What do you think, Mr White?'

'Well, if there's anyone more obsessed by the gold, I don't know it.'

'More than Mr Reed from Willowmere? Papa used the word "obsessed" when he was telling me about him. Said it drove you all to distraction how intent he was on finding it.'

Percy White shook his head. 'Infatuated, maybe. As a young man might be about the latest motor car or aeroplane. Youthful enthusiasm is all. But he has no *need* for the gold, save to make life easier for himself and his mother, though I believe they live comfortably enough in one of those large Victorian houses on Chestnut Avenue... I agree, it's all a bit monotonous at the meetings with him going on and on about the hoard and where it might be, whereas some of us would rather look into the original site of the village animal pound and excavate the old well, but I wouldn't call it an obsession in a sinister sense.'

'So why do you think...' – Cressida nodded subtly over the table in the direction of Lilian Catchpole – 'and Walter Rook are more likely to be the ones obsessed with finding it?'

'Why do you think?' Percy White attacked his pastry-covered fillet with gusto and looked about him, and Cressida wondered if he either wanted out of their conversation or if he was just checking to see if anyone was listening to them. Satisfied of the latter, he placed his cutlery down and chewed.

'I know this is perhaps not the sort of talk we should be having in polite society,' Cressida all but whispered, 'but please do elaborate.'

Percy swallowed and picked up his cutlery again to cut up a potato. Before putting it in his mouth he answered Cressida, his voice also lowered. 'As our reverend would tell us, the love of money is the root of all evil. And beyond love; need. And our friend over there has more on her plate than merely being the wife of the local doctor. She has a very ill sister, incumbent at a nursing home for the incurable over in Hindhead. I've heard the care she needs is round the clock and very expensive, even for well-off folk like the Catchpoles. The bills are mounting, beyond what even an affluent doctor can afford. And as for our local landlord, well, it's no secret that he's running that old place at a loss.'

Cressida remembered the fact that Walter had been keen to serve them drinks earlier, despite it being outside of licensing hours. She also remembered what Walter had said about Bob's death and that he also thought the historical society might be behind it. A member of which, she was talking to now. A member who might have motives of his own.

'I suppose overheads in running any sort of enterprise must stack up if business is sparse. And especially, if as in your case, there is no profit to be made at all.' She flickered her eyelashes at him as he coughed on some pastry.

'Excuse me?' Percy White seemed confused.

'Just that I heard that you and Mrs White do sterling work looking after those poor horses, and it can't be a cheap hobby.'

'It's not a hobby, Cressida.' Percy suddenly sounded a little cross, and she felt as if she was about to receive a ticking off rather than any useful information. 'Those horses saved boys' lives, not that many years ago. They came back as broken as the poor lads that rode them home. It's our duty now to look after them, as much a duty as any work we did during the war.'

'Of course, I agree. And you and Mrs White are marvellous for doing it. I just wondered that it must be hard to constantly find the money for the horses' upkeep, especially as they can't exactly earn their own hay.'

Percy White frowned and replied gruffly, 'Never you mind how we manage. It's just for the best that we do.' And with that he stabbed a blushingly pink piece of beef with his fork and shoved it in his mouth, turning away from her as he chewed.

Cressida took a slightly more elegant forkful from her plate and contemplated as she chewed. Percy White hadn't liked being asked about his own financial motives, and although that was understandable, it was slightly hypocritical since he'd been quick to point the accusatory finger at Walter Rook and even Lilian Catchpole. She placed her knife and fork together and before long Molly came around collecting the plates.

Perhaps she'd have more luck over pudding, where she'd be duty bound to speak to the person seated on her other side – a person who had just been mentioned by Percy White as someone who might have a very pressing financial motive for killing Bob Pringle; Dr Catchpole.

## 16

By the time pudding was served, Cressida had heard all about the estimable intelligence of young David Catchpole and the pleasing character of his sister Daphne. Dr Catchpole had shown himself to be a doting, if biased, father, but otherwise their conversation had been along those mundane lines until he surprised Cressida with a change of subject.

'I hear Bob Pringle has died,' he said, his voice more hushed than it had been when he'd been bragging about David's score on his recent preparatory school examinations. 'Lilian told me this afternoon. He was your family's gardener, was he not?'

'Yes, he was,' confirmed Cressida, once again deciding to hold back the information that he had been murdered to see what the doctor said. He was one step ahead of her, however.

'And I assume from the presence of a Scotland Yard detective here tonight, we suspect foul play?' Dr Catchpole was a handsome man and Cressida could see that he had a certain charisma, aided by his obvious wits and intelligence. He was broad and strong, with a nose that looked like it had suffered in the scrummage of a rugby football game or two, but it didn't detract much from his handsome face.

Cressida listened as she ate the strawberry bavarois that Marian had somehow whipped up for all twelve of them around the dining table. 'Lilian and I were talking about it as we motored over. Could have walked, of course, but we didn't much fancy crossing the bridge that he died under and using that pathway as our route home. Foul play though, eh? Lilian and I had thought it might be his heart or an embolism of some sort. Not a healthy man. Not that I can say much, as I never consulted on him, but from the number of evenings he spent at the Royal Oak I would have thought he was due a stroke. It was almost as if he was keeping tabs on the place, as well as running up quite the tab himself. All paid off though rather handsomely it seems with his little – or large – windfall. Foul play though, eh?' he repeated himself. 'Who'd have thought it in Mydenhurst of all places.'

Cressida felt cornered. There was no point denying that she – they – did indeed suspect foul play. 'Working theory is that he listened in on the historical society's discussions about the hoard and then either through blind luck, or using his excellent local knowledge, found it. It explains the sudden change in his fortune. But he didn't tell anyone, not even his wife, if he had. We only know that he was suddenly very generous with his bar bill.' She paused. 'And as for foul play, well yes "we" do think it was murder. He was poisoned. And it's exceptionally unlikely that it was self-inflicted.'

'And the historical society, therefore, become the natural suspects?' Dr Catchpole said, a guardedness to his voice. Cressida noticed that his eyes flickered up towards his wife.

'Yes. How could I not suspect them?'

'You? Or your Scotland Yard friend?'

This rankled Cressida. Did the doctor presume that she was passing off Andrews' theories as her own? This was the man who had praised his son's intelligence and his daughter's pleasant character after all. Still, she wanted to get as much information as possible from him, so she smiled sweetly, hoping that showing off some pleasant character of her own would endear her to him. She did, however, have the fingernails of one hand digging into her thigh as she did so.

'Yes, of course, clever DCI Andrews ascertained that it simply must have something to do with the gold. I found a gold coin near the body, you see, and—'

'Did you now?' the doctor interrupted her.

'Yes,' Cressida said rather hesitantly. She was feeling more and more as if the doctor had turned from prey to predator, and it was her who was now under his observant eye. She carried on, unable to merely stop the conversation, however preferable that might be. Still, she back-pedalled a little on the vociferousness of her assumptions. 'Hence why the current theory is that someone in the historical society might at least know something about it.'

'Someone with a penchant for poisons,' ruminated the doctor. 'A doctor's wife, perhaps?'

Cressida was taken aback and didn't quite know what to say, until the doctor laughed. 'I think not, Lilian is a top-notch wife, but bless her, she just doesn't have the brain for that sort of thing. A complete lack of cunning. Runs in her family, of course, gentlefolk by the very definition of that word. And as for the poison cupboard in the surgery, well I keep that under lock and key and I invite any police inspector to come and check my inventory. No, I don't think you can look towards the Catchpole residence for your poisoner, Miss Fawcett. No motive, no malice.' He tapped the side of his head and Cressida felt suddenly very sorry for Lilian Catchpole. If she proved to be far more capable than her husband gave her credit for, then she wouldn't wonder if it was the doctor who'd find himself on the receiving end of whichever poison Lilian may have got her hands on.

But he did leap to the conclusion that it had been a medical poison, not something like deadly nightshade. And while sadly this made it seem unlikely it was him, unless he was very good at deflecting, it didn't rule out his 'simple' wife. Lilian had shown admiration after all for the wise women of the past. Perhaps she knew more about their potions and recipes than she, or her husband, was letting on?

## 17

Cressida was just girding herself for more conversation with the chauvinistic doctor when a knife was pinged against the edge of a glass and the room came to silence.

'Dear friends,' Lord Fawcett said as he stood up. 'This isn't another toast, though I know we all thank Mrs Pringle heartily for this exquisite meal, prepared for us during a time of what must be barely imagined grief for her. Instead, I propose an introduction. Though, of course, to many around the table, our guest of honour here tonight will need no introduction at all. Professor of English Medieval History at Balliol College, he now leads the department where we were once bright young things starting out at Oxford. I'm honoured to call Sir James Colston here not just my friend, but my esteemed colleague in the passion we share for history, and not just history, but Saxon and Medieval history. As several of you will be aware, Sir James has come here to speak to our society tomorrow evening, but I couldn't help but jump the gun somewhat and invite you all here tonight to listen to him first. A preamble, as it were, to the talk he's kindly prepared on Anglo-Saxon hill forts and Wealden charcoal manufacture for tomorrow night. It's a subject, however, that has inspired quite a bit of chatter among us all recently. The Mydenhurst hoard.'

There was a hushed silence around the room, with the inhalation of breath audible, though Cressida didn't have a chance to work out who had been the most shocked as one of the sharp inhales of surprise had been her own. What was her father doing? He had claimed the gold was of little interest to the core of the society, save the one young man who wasn't here tonight. Yet here they were, indulging in a talk all about it in his absence. She looked quizzically at her father, but he was busy applauding his friend as the two of them swapped positions, with Lord Fawcett now sitting and Sir James now standing and thanking his hosts. After the appropriate words of gratitude, he started.

'It's a great pleasure to be back in Mydenhurst and I leapt at a chance of returning when Sholto and Rosamund invited me. Local boy that I am, I grew up playing in these Wealden woodlands, scampering through the fields of wheat, clambering in the hay barns, and my apologies to your late father, Percy, as I think those hay barns were at Lark's Leap.' There was a smattering of laughter and Percy White bowed his head in forgiveness. Sir James brought back everyone's attention by continuing his speech. 'Sadly my family have now moved away. It doesn't stop me from enjoying seeing some familiar faces from my youth when I return though.' He paused and Cressida was just wondering if he'd forgotten the rest of his prepared talk when he started up again. 'I'm ever intrigued by the rumours and legends that surround hoards such as the one we believe to be here somewhere in the hamlet of Mydenhurst. Why? Because unlike most legends, be they unicorns, giant worms or supernatural beings' – there was another ripple of laughter – 'there is always archival evidence for hoards of gold if one can find it. And my good friend Sholto here and I think we may have found not only more archival evidence, but also real and tangible evidence. Behold!' He plunged his hand into his pocket and brought out the thrymsa. It glinted in the light of the dinner candles and oil lamps as he twisted it through his fingertips. There were gasps from the guests and some proper clearing of throats. Madge White said, 'My, my,' while Lilian Catchpole darted her eyes from the coin to her husband and back to the coin again, as Sir James carried on. 'Discovered today, here in the land near Mydenhurst Place, we found this thrymsa.'

*I found that coin,* Cressida thought to herself as she accidentally clattered her pudding spoon on the wide-rimmed bowl the bavarois had been served in. *Or rather Bob did, and I found him...* She was annoyed, not only at the secret of the hoard being out, but that she wasn't being credited in some small way for finding at least one coin from it. *What is it with the men around this table tonight?* Then she blanched. What if Sir James *did* credit her? She'd have been proved to have been lying or hiding it from everyone she'd spoken to so far. She narrowed her eyes. Sir James and her father's oversight would be left unchallenged for now.

Sir James continued, 'So, is the hoard here? Within yards of this very dining room in which we all sit? Despite this coin being found so very close to the house, we think not. There was just this one coin, found in, shall we say, inconsistent circumstances, which leads us to believe the hoard is not here on my good friend's land.'

A shrug from her father followed. But Cressida had felt her body stiffen as Sir James had come so close to revealing the real circumstances of how the coin had been found. She'd kept her focus on him, and she was sure everyone else had too, though she also couldn't help but feel that some eyes had strayed to staring straight at her – accusatory eyes at that. She felt the hairs prickle on her arms so she sat back in her seat and crossed them. *So that was what they had been doing down by Hell's Ditch before nightfall.*

'This is where the new archival evidence comes in,' Sir James continued. 'We all know about Prior Zachary in the sixteenth century, and the poem written about him that describes him being buried due to "being dead by the golden curse". The author of that rhyme rules out the streams such as Hell's Ditch here at Mydenhurst Place, which only strengthens our view that the coin found in the stream doesn't indicate the hoard is there. He also says the hoard doesn't lie under farmland "with the valley's view", which means it's not over at Lark's Leap or in the fields behind the Royal Oak. And, of course, the church itself is mentioned with the gold not being "under altar or pew". So where is it?' He turned to look at the guests.

'I hope it's down our well,' said Madge White with a harrumph of humour. She wasn't the type of woman to giggle, far too sensible for that, instead huffing out laughter as and when it came, like a build-up of steam out of a locomotive. She was Cressida's mother's most local friend, and despite the tragedy of her sons' deaths, seemed stoical and stolid. The sort of woman English villages are made from. The first on the flower-arranging rota for the church, chairwoman of the fête committee and a dab hand at a Victoria sponge, all while mucking out horses and tending the hens.

Cressida wouldn't begrudge Madge White finding the gold in her well. Although she'd draw the line at forgiving her for killing Bob for it, she did think that Madge and Percy White deserved a bit of good fortune. Her attention was turned back to Sir James.

'Aha, no, Mrs White, I don't believe it to be down your well, though you may find several ha'pennies down there from wishes over the years.' This caused more laughter around the room, though Cressida thought she caught the briefest look of despair cross Madge White's face and supposed it was highly likely that she had made many a wish on that well, especially back in 1916 and 1918. Sir James continued, 'But I do think, thanks to comparing the poem about Prior Zachary's demise from the curse, or otherwise, and with our modern scholarship and recent findings, that we have a darn good stab at finding the gold this very week.'

Cressida looked around. The Whites, the Reverend Dunn and the Catchpoles were rapt by Sir James's words. Cressida could see how he'd gained such a great reputation as an after-dinner speaker, not to mention the lucrative teaching position at Oxford. It wasn't just in finding coins that the wealth in Saxon gold lay it would seem.

'Well, where then?' It was Mrs Catchpole who asked the question, but it was followed by a chorus of 'Hear, hear' and 'Do tell' from the other society members, and even Dotty and Alfred. Cressida shot a look over to DCI Andrews. He seemed the only other person at the table who had the same look of caution and awareness as she did. He raised an eyebrow at Cressida as Sir James continued.

'That, my dear Mrs Catchpole, will have to wait for tomorrow night. For now, all I can say is that we believe the poem was true, the archives are correct and the new survey maps of the local area have been a huge help. The gold is here in the hamlet of Mydenhurst. It is buried in one of the villagers' land. But I shall say no more, and leave the grand reveal for tomorrow evening.' He paused amid the groans of disappointment from the society members around the table and looked as if he were about to sit down, before he added, with a flourish, 'And if something should happen to me tonight and I don't live to see the morning, then I'll be in good company along with Priory Zachary in taking my knowledge of the gold's where-abouts to my grave!'

## 18

Lord Fawcett led the round of applause that rippled around the table as Sir James sat down. Cressida looked over at Dotty, who still appeared starstruck as she clapped in honour of her new favourite scholar, pausing only to push her tortoiseshell glasses up the bridge of her nose between bursts of enthusiastic applause. Alfred caught Cressida's eye and she rolled hers – and smiled too.

Lady Fawcett, with a nod to her husband, called the ladies to stand and retreat with her back to the library for coffee, allowing the men to enjoy their port and cigars in peace.

'You are a tease,' Cressida heard Lilian Catchpole say, tapping Sir James on the shoulder as she retreated along with Lady Fawcett and the other women. Madge White was just behind her and added in, 'Sure it's not down our well? We've got a bucket and rope all ready if so!' She huffed out that laugh of hers, but otherwise seemed happy to leave the men to their conversation.

'I always find this hideously outdated,' said Cressida to Dotty as she gave Alfred a little wave, smiling as he accepted a cigar from her father.

'I know,' agreed Dotty. 'And to think, they get to talk about Saxons and hill forts now. Oh and no doubt they'll touch on charcoal manufacturing in the nineteenth century, too.' She sighed.

Cressida couldn't help but laugh, with genuine warmth, of course. 'Oh, Dot. I do wish I shared just some of your passion for history. But don't despair. I feel that Mama will have some missions for us among the coffees and talk of Ascot hats. She's still not sure about the panels, I think, and it'll help us clear our heads for a bit to stare into the void that is a Turner sunset.'

Dotty elbowed her in the ribs and Cressida nudged her back. She glanced over her shoulder at the gentlemen around the table; her father, turning his nose up at the box of Turkish Delight and passing it on to Sir James, who was talking about Oxford restaurants with Dr Catchpole, who was next to Percy White, who in turn was now talking to Reverend Dunn about the drainage issues on their lower fields. DCI Andrews and Alfred were deep in conversation, with Cressida only slightly worried that they might be discussing her. Or worse, Alfred might be getting the low-down on what Marian said to Andrews when he interviewed her just before supper – before she could! The thought annoyed her more than it should; not because she begrudged Alfred the hearing of it, but she was so keen to know it herself.

So, it was with as much grace as she could muster that Cressida closed the door of the dining room and walked across the hallway to the library, where Dotty, her mother and the other ladies were already finding seats and starting new conversations. Cressida closed the door behind her and found herself a seat next to Dotty on one of the chintz sofas. Lady Fawcett had started to pour coffees out of a fancy silver coffee pot – one Cressida remembered borrowing to make potions in when she was a girl, using rose petals from the newly planted beds and fresh water from the stream. *Hell's Ditch...* The name of it made her shiver and she looked down to see goose pimples on her arms. She'd never worried herself over its name before, but now poor Bob Pringle had been killed in it, and while holding what might have been a cursed coin... Somehow now the name of the stream seemed so macabre. A reflection of light off the shining teapot reminded her of the coin she'd found in Bob's hand and how it had sparkled as she and her mother had both held it up to the sunlight on the walk back to the house. *Was that coin really cursed?* The poem Sir James had been referring to in his speech tonight, the one her father had read her that morning from Trewitt's history pamphlet, hinted as much. Another shiver crossed Cressida's shoulders as a thought occurred to her; could the curse be transferred from hand to hand? She banished the silly thought from her head as she accepted a delicate cup and saucer from her mother. She was pleased that the coffee came accompanied by questions about the panels again. Interior decorating was a much more comfortable topic than curses and murders.

'I was worried about the pink,' Lady Fawcett explained. 'Over supper, as I tucked into the rare beef I suddenly thought, "Oh no, will I think of this every time I look at the Canaletto," and I'm afraid I've quite gone off the idea. Anything else you can think of to smarten them up? Just not grey again. Do go and stand there for a bit, won't you, darling? Put that mind of yours to good use.'

Cressida had placed her coffee down, pleased that the slight shake to her hand had gone, and with Dotty's arm linked through hers she was now doing as her mother asked and was facing the folded panels, looking at the gold-framed paintings mounted upon them.

'You're lucky having those Canalettos,' Dotty remarked. 'One of my ancestors sold the Chatterton ones almost as soon as he brought them back from the Grand Tour.'

'Hmm?' Cressida asked, lost again in her own thoughts.

Then she followed it up with, 'Sorry, Dot, when were the Grand Tours again? You know I'm terrible at dates and things.'

'Never mind, Cressy. History-schmistory, let's discuss the present day,' replied Dotty, turning to face her friend. 'How far have we got with poor Mr Pringle?'

'Not that far, sadly,' admitted Cressida. 'And certainly not very far before Andrews turned up. Still, perhaps that's not a bad thing. It always helps to have his official know-how. For example, thanks to Dr North's post-mortem we know Bob was poisoned. And we assume it was murder as Bob was a long-in-the-tooth gardener so would know not to eat deadly nightshade.'

'Hence why you think it might have been in his sandwich?' Dotty asked.

'Well, the effects of belladonna, especially if you ingest enough to kill, are fairly quick, so it would make sense that it was his sandwich that did it. And since it couldn't have been concealed in the cheese and there's never a green leaf in a sandwich like that, it must have been added into the pickle,' Cressida deduced.

'So we're looking for a pickle-making murderer. Where does the local Women's Institute meet?' Dotty said, releasing her arm from Cressida's and getting another elbow in the ribs in return for her unhelpful suggestion.

'Let's not go blaming every pickle-making woman in the country, Dot.' Cressida rolled her eyes. 'But it's naturally why Andrews skipped off before supper to interview Marian. I'm just dying, if you'll excuse the turn of phrase, to know what they discussed.'

'She must have said something to convince him of her innocence, otherwise dinner would have been delayed, or...' Dotty paused and raised a hand to her throat. In all but a whisper she carried on. 'I really hope Marian *isn't* a dab hand at poisons.'

'She isn't,' Cressida said, squeezing Dotty's arm. 'I'm sure of it.'

Letting the conversation stall for a moment, Cressida and Dotty slowly opened the two panels in front of them trying to avoid the metallic squeal, allowing them to swing open to reveal the mounted etchings on the other side, the gold-framed paintings on the walls and the statue of Aletheia in the window nook. 'We know that almost every member of the historical society had a motive to get their hands on the gold, and perhaps to kill Bob for it. I believe that's a greater motive than Marian could have. Bob might not have told Marian about the coins yet, but he would have done and she would have shared in his wealth.'

'Sir James seems to think that the stream wasn't where Bob had found the coins,' mused Dotty. 'I suppose he might have had it in his pocket and have been holding it out to admire it when he died.'

'Or he realised that it was the cause of his death.' Cressida shuddered. 'You know, as he felt the effects of the poison set in. Don't forget there was that eerie word written on the palm of his hand – Ded – the same hand that was gripping the coin.'

'But from the looks and interest around the table tonight, everyone seemed to hang on Sir James's words. It doesn't sound like anyone else has found it.'

Cressida looked at Aletheia, the goddess of truth, standing naked in the windowsill, then whispered back to Dotty, 'Perhaps. Or they were doing a very good job of pretending not to.'

'Are you still thinking pink, darling?' Lady Fawcett came up behind them with the coffee pot, and Cressida gave a little jump. She turned around and saw Madge White standing next to her mother, her hands on her hips, looking askance at the panels.

'Pink, you say? I shouldn't think that would work at all,' Madge said. 'Would remind you of chopped liver.'

'That's what I said, Madge dear,' Lady Fawcett replied. 'Though I was more inspired by the rare beef at dinner.'

'Last thing you want to be reminded of when you're reading your *Horse & Hound* or sticking your nose into a Brontë.'

'Quite right, Madge. Cressida darling, pink is out of the question.'

Cressida nodded, sharing a knowing look with Dotty, as she closed the panels. She could feel a thread dangle tantalisingly in front of her. Until she could quiz Andrews or Marian again, she couldn't pull it any further, but she could make use of her present situation.

'Mrs White, how are the horses?' Cressida asked, accepting a refill of her coffee cup from her mother.

'Expensive,' answered Madge, huffing out her laugh.

'But worth it,' Cressida coaxed.

'Every shilling,' agreed Madge, sitting herself down on one of the chintz armchairs. Cressida perched on the arm of the one next to her and sipped her fresh coffee. She was just working out what angle she could take with Mrs White, when Madge herself kept talking. 'They're such healing animals, you know? Like a religion in a way. A faith at least. You can talk to a horse, confess your sins and be redeemed all in one go.' She huffed out a laugh. 'Our own reverend could learn a thing or two from them.'

'Reverend Dunn?' Cressida wondered if another thread had just dropped into her lap. She'd tried – and failed – to get much out of Percy White earlier, and instead of quizzing Madge along the same lines she could perhaps get some more local 'insights' out of her.

'The very same.' Madge sipped her coffee. 'I still think of the old reverend, Fellows, do you remember him?'

'Of course, he christened and confirmed me. He was here throughout my childhood,' Cressida answered, remembering the previous parish vicar with his wire-rimmed spectacles and low, sonorous voice. 'When did Reverend Dunn arrive?'

'Not that long ago. Reverend Fellows only retired a few years ago. I think the war shook his faith in the end.'

'And Reverend Dunn? You mentioned that your horses might be more—'

Cressida stopped as Madge White rolled her eyes. 'Yes, they probably would do a better job than him.'

'How so?' Cressida pushed, mentally pulling on the dangling thread in front of her.

'Dunn is next to useless in my book. Fellows used to preach. Put a bit of pep in his sermons. Knew the county, the landscape, the history. Added it all in, bringing the good Word to life. Dunn just mumbles at us from the pulpit.' Madge sipped her coffee, then put the cup and saucer down on the low table and conspiratorially leaned in closer to Cressida. 'Failed his history papers at Oxford, so I hear. Had to retake in order to graduate, even though he was primarily there to study theology and philosophy. Apparently, his tutor would have none of it and kept him back a year. And he's still got no grasp of history!'

'But he's in the historical society, he must have some interest in it.' Cressida wondered if an Oxford student's grasp of history could ever be called useless, especially when compared with her own.

'But it's all about the gold though,' continued Madge. 'I mean to say, he listens patiently when we talk about the old Roman road to Chichester, and perks up a bit when the Saxons are mentioned, but really only has anything to say when the hoard is mentioned.'

'And what does he say?' Cressida's interest was piqued. And the thread that had been dangling in front of her was well and truly pulled.

'That he'd known about the hoard before he moved here and had been looking into it for months. I did wonder if he'd skewed the interview process somehow with the bishop so that he could land this plum parish, as why else would we have received no other applicants after Fellows left?'

Cressida shrugged. But she took on board what Madge was saying: Reverend Dunn was as interested in the hoard as anyone else. Even her father had suggested that he needed the money to save the church and therefore his living. And if he found the hoard, he wouldn't even need a living from a parish such as Mydenhurst. Could his time at Oxford have been spent looking into Saxon hoards rather than whatever he was being examined on? While Cressida thought, Madge White pulled away and started talking to Lilian Catchpole. Cressida sipped her coffee and thought about Reverend Dunn. A failed historian who was now intent on finding the hoard. A thread indeed.

Eventually, the gentlemen entered the library and Cressida felt her cheeks redden as Alfred, his face crinkled with laughter, entered alongside her father. She caught the end of their conversation.

'So, Welly Watson-Wells misheard and opened the basket, letting all the pigeons out and that's why we no longer have pies on a Monday...'

'I knew his father you know, Watty Watson-Wells. Did the same trick, but with budgerigars, and never set foot in Hampton Court Palace again.'

Cressida shook her head. She was amazed the Mutton Pie Club was proving to be such a bonding experience and wondered why she'd never heard stories about it from her father. But then parenting rarely included telling one's offspring about chums who were banned from former royal palaces. She waved at Alfred and accepted a glass of whisky from him from one of the decanters on the sideboard.

The other gentlemen took their seats and she noticed how the Catchpoles and the Whites crowded around Sir James.

While Alfred was telling her about Dickie Trathan and an attempt he made on eating a record-beating mutton pie, she watched as Sir James batted off enquiry after enquiry about the whereabouts of the hoard. For someone who was thinking of calling a motion to ban Sebastian Reed from the club for talking about it too much, it was Lilian Catchpole who was pushing the most.

'How can you be sure you know where the hoard is? Have you dug it up already?' She looked concerned.

'I most certainly have not, madam,' Sir James replied confidently.

'Then how will we know that this big reveal of yours tomorrow night will be correct? Is it not just supposition still?'

'Well...' Sir James sounded less confident now and Cressida saw him look over to her father, a line or two appearing on his otherwise ovoid forehead as he realised Lord Fawcett was deep in conversation with his wife and there was no eye to catch.

'Now, now, Lilian.' It was Madge White who stepped in to rescue Sir James. 'Let's not harry the poor man. He says he'll tell us tomorrow. And I've got that bucket from my well ready and waiting!' She huffed out another of her laughs.

Cressida turned away, convinced that Sir James was keeping his secret to himself and the members would get nothing more out of him tonight. Her mother and father were now staring at the panels and she saw him shake his head vigorously at the mention of the word 'pink'. Alfred was popping the lid on a new jar of maraschino cherries and DCI Andrews was sitting alone, sipping his whisky and looking as if he had half an eye on the conversation around Sir James. Alfred or Andrews? Cocktails or crime? The decision was hard, but she knew who she had to speak to next.

## 19

'Andrews,' Cressida said, moving across the room and sitting down in the chair next to the detective.

'Miss Fawcett,' he replied, then took another sip from his whisky. There was a pause and then they both spoke together.

'I suppose you want...'

'I'd love to know what... I'm sorry, Andrews, you go first,' Cressida relented, though she'd caught enough of what he was going to say to know that it was just what she wanted to hear.

'I suppose you want to know why I didn't arrest Mrs Pringle this evening?'

'Indeed.' Cressida leaned forward, resting her elbows on the well-stuffed arm of the chintz armchair. 'And I'm glad you didn't. She's just cooked us all a wonderful three-course dinner, so I assumed you didn't think she was the poisoner after all?'

Andrews ran a finger around his collar and cleared his throat. 'Yes, it was in the back... well, front of my mind, to be honest. But there was no justification for arresting her, and it was your mother who insisted that Marian should stay if she wanted to, and she did.'

'I know you used to take orders from Papa, but you know

you don't have to take them from my mother, too?' Cressida glanced over to where Lady Fawcett was quite obviously telling her husband what was what about something or other and frowned. 'Though I can see that it's hard not to. If you ever wondered where I get my hot-headedness from, Andrews...'

'Quite. And apart from all of that, Mrs Pringle co-operated and acted most innocently. Except...'

'Except what?' Cressida leaned in.

'Except that she said the jar of pickle she'd used to make her husband's sandwich had been almost empty. She'd scraped what she could out of it and then rinsed and cleaned the jar. She found me a jar of what she thought was the same batch and handed it over so that I can send it to Dr North to test. But she looked devastated when I said it was the most likely cause of the poisoning.'

'Did she say where she'd bought it?'

'The full jar looks very home-made.' Andrews sighed. 'But if it's proved to contain belladonna then I will have to arrest her, or at least question her further. For now there's simply not enough actual evidence for the charge to hold. And with her co-operating so freely while not in a cell, well it seems churlish to arrest her when she could easily just be a grieving widow who's lost her husband.'

'You are as generous of spirit as I am hot of head, Andrews.' Cressida sat back and took a sip from her crystal glass tumbler. 'Although I agree with you on the not arresting Marian part. I don't suppose she said who had made the pickle, did she? Was it her?'

'No, she said she couldn't remember exactly. She had a think and then said that she often picked up a jar or two from the church porch, where good-hearted locals place spares from their pantries. There's an honesty box next to them with all donations to the church roof repair fund and all that.'

'Can we analyse the handwriting on the label? Find out who made it that way?'

'There wasn't one as far as I could see,' Andrews replied.

'Hmm, hard to trace then.' Cressida filed the thought away.

'And as far as we know, no deaths or illnesses from anyone eating the rest of that jar. We might have been wrong about the pickle being the way the belladonna was ingested, though Marian said Bob had had toast for breakfast at seven as usual and he would have had symptoms much earlier in the day if that had been the poisoned food.'

Andrews shook his head and then sipped his whisky again before carrying on. 'The other reason I didn't arrest Mrs Pringle was that although she knew he'd come into some money, she swears she doesn't know how much it was, or how he came about it. It's why she was so cross with him for squandering what he had on drinks. She thought he'd won a bob or two and that would have been much more useful being put towards the broken bicycle, she said.'

Cressida nodded. 'That's what she told me too. She was very worried that she'd lose her home, the gardener's cottage here on the estate, when Bob was first found dead. If she'd killed him for some vast sum of money she wouldn't have been worrying about a roof over her head.'

'Except that now she might be a very wealthy widow.' Andrews looked like he was starting to doubt himself.

'But she didn't know anything about the gold. Just that he had started acting oddly and was being a bit over generous to those in the Royal Oak.'

Andrews still looked pensive and shook his head. 'I feel like I'm missing something here. I'm not sure your father's whisky is helping either.' He put his glass down on the small mahogany table next to him and turned it once, then twice, with his fingers as he thought. 'Your loyalty to Mrs Pringle is admirable, Miss Fawcett, and I agree, my gut instinct is that she's innocent, but there's still something not quite right about it all.'

'Well, a man was murdered,' Cressida rather unhelpfully added. 'Stands to reason that something feels off. And I'm sure someone has a very good motive. Personally, I think someone in this historical society of Papa's has something to do with it.' She looked at Andrews who was still pensively staring at his whisky tumbler as he turned it. She had to admit that he had a point about Marian now potentially being quite wealthy if Bob had more of the coins stashed somewhere and she knew about it, but wasn't letting on. 'But I can see why any magistrate in the land would have Marian locked up by breakfast.'

'And I'll have to act on it by then too, if nothing else comes to light tonight that might help clear her name. There'll be rumours back at HQ that I'm getting soft and heaven knows what trouble I'd be in if she turns out to have done it and I've just sat here drinking your father's best whisky, with a murderer right under my nose.'

'Andrews, you sound like you're talking yourself into arresting her!' Cressida whispered with a note of alarm to her voice. 'Remember your gut instinct, same as mine, that she can't possibly have done it.'

'But as discussed, the money is a motive...' Andrews sighed. They both sat in silence again and found themselves looking towards the fireplace where Sir James was still in conversation with the Whites and the Catchpoles.

Cressida turned back to Andrews. 'Speaking of motives, and perhaps those of the society, I tried my best over supper to gauge what I could about Mr White, but I think he cottoned onto me a little too quickly—'

'Miss Fawcett.' Andrews shook his head. 'What have I said about interrogating people in this ad hoc manner of yours?'

'That I shouldn't stick my noble old nose where it's not wanted.' Cressida looked into her cut-crystal glass. 'But I just wanted to know if perhaps those dear old war horses were taking up a bit too much of the Whites' money. Anyway, for what it's worth, I don't think people who can care for animals like that are likely to be killers. Mrs White, Madge, gave me something much more interesting to chew over when we were banished here while you men did your port and cigars thing.'

'And?' Andrews urged. Cressida was relieved to see how interested he was. She was desperate to take his mind off the fact that Marian really did look as if she was the culprit, and after their discussion just now she realised she might not have that long to convince him of her innocence. She leaned forward and told him everything.

'She said Reverend Dunn was keen as anyone on finding the hoard. He knew about it before he arrived in Mydenhurst. In fact, it might have been what brought him here. Madge wondered if perhaps the gold means more to him personally than merely being a means to fixing the leaking church roof and all that.'

Andrews nodded thoughtfully and looked back out into the room. Cressida followed his gaze to where Dotty was fiddling with the gramophone player and choosing a record with Alfred. Cressida had chosen to speak to Andrews first, but with music now coming from the new brass horn and Alfred walking towards her, his hand outstretched, she knew exactly who she wanted to spend the rest of the evening with.

## 20

Sunlight broke through a chink in the curtains and Cressida yawned and stretched. She'd had a bad night's sleep, not helped by the pre-dinner martinis, the with-dinner wine and the post-dinner whisky she'd tucked into as the gramophone played late into the evening. But what really hadn't helped her with her beauty sleep were the six puppies, and one exhausted mother pup, who were sharing her room with her.

Cressida had woken at various points in the night, not just with Ruby taking up more than her fair share of the counterpane, but with Fortnum and Mason hatching an escape plan and eventually being tracked down to the back stairs, while Hercules and Suki had taken it upon themselves to make a new den in the bottom of her wardrobe. Her third-favourite cashmere cardigan would never be the same again.

So, it was with a rather large second yawn that Cressida slipped out of bed, to greet the day. And, for once, six sleeping puppies, looking like butter wouldn't melt, all curled up neatly in their box.

'You lot will be the death of me,' Cressida said, opening the curtains and looking out over the croquet lawn, its hoops now all skew-whiff and the centre peg at an impossible angle after yesterday's match between all the puppies. 'Fortnum and Mason, if I'd gone head over heels down those back stairs, you'd have had no one to fetch your sardines from the kitchen this morning. Speaking of which.'

She crept back towards her bed where her dressing gown was draped over one of the bedposts – a pale-blue silk one that matched her pyjamas – and swept it over her shoulders. As she found the sleeves and stretched her arms out into them, she reached down and patted Ruby on the head. 'It's not that I begrudge you your rest, Ruby my pup, but maybe you could have been more useful in the night.' She sighed, peeling her silk eye mask off her dog's head and placing it neatly on her pillow. 'Still, at least one of us got some decent shut-eye.'

Ruby slyly opened one eye and Cressida laughed. Tying the silk belt of her dressing gown, she opened her bedroom door and was buoyed up by the glorious smell of bacon grilling on the stove downstairs, its delicious aroma finding its way up from the kitchen. *Sardines schmardines*, she thought, hoping to be able to nip downstairs and fetch her puppies' breakfast – and perhaps an early morning rasher of bacon for herself – before any of the other guests saw her looking so underdressed.

She trotted down the winding oak staircase, her steps soft thanks to the old kilim runner that carpeted them. The house smelled of beeswax, the polished wood warmed by the pleasantly mild spring they were having. She breathed in that most familiar of scents, alongside that of the grilling bacon, and remembering the fun they'd had last night over those last couple of drinks, grinned. Despite poor Bob's death, there wasn't much she'd have changed about the last twenty-four hours. She had her darling, if mischievous pups, her beloved family, her best friend and her beau all under one roof. Bliss.

Marian was hard at work in the kitchen, keeping an eye on the bacon and stirring a pot of porridge that was sitting bubbling away on the stove. Cressida greeted her with a squeeze to the shoulder and a small hug, before heading to the refrigerator to source the sardines.

'How are you this morning, Marian?' Cressida asked, her head in the cool, new contraption.

'I'd have my head in there too, if I could,' Marian said, then explained. 'I'm afraid my sister Annie and her husband Walter stayed quite late here with me, and your father and Sir James were popping in and out too once the evening guests had gone. We had some of that whisky your friends in the Highlands recommended and I'm afraid I might have had a tot too many.'

'I would be last in line to blame you, Marian,' Cressida assured her. 'I probably had twice as much as you with barely a fig of the same reason.'

Marian added some salt and gave the porridge another stir and then stood back from the stove. 'I don't think it's sunk in yet, really. There would often be nights when Bob stayed away, you see, either in the woods lying in wait for poachers, or doing a bit of snaring himself.' She seemed to glaze over. Then as the pot bubbled and gurgled in front of her she shook herself to attention. 'I'm sure I'll wake up tomorrow morning and feel quite bereft, but for now... well, let's just say it doesn't yet feel real.'

Cressida nodded, then took the packet of sardines off the shelf and started chopping them up on the table, pushing the mush into six small bowls which Marian must have prepared for her, as they were already on a tray, ready to be carried upstairs. Cressida thought better than to badger Marian this morning, but then remembered about how close Andrews had come last night into talking himself into arresting her – and how this morning he might have to as there was simply no one else yet with a proper motive or the means of killing Bob. Her gut feeling was still that Marian was innocent and she hurried filling up the small bowls with the oily fish – she needed to dress and get on with her morning investigations before Marian was arrested. She left her diligently stirring the porridge as she took the much less appetising chopped sardines up to her puppies.

The stench of sardines was the last thing Cressida wanted in her bedroom, but about three minutes after she'd put the bowls down in her room, all six puppies had woken and ravenously eaten the sardines, heads and all. She fastened the buttons on a pretty cream silk blouse and tucked it into her tweed slacks. It was only while she tied the shoelaces on her sensible brogues, thankfully dried out now after their dip in the stream yesterday, that she heard the most awful noise.

Cressida shot a look at Ruby, whose ears were alert too.

They both knew what they'd just heard. That nightmarish sound had been a scream.

## 21

Cressida left her laces undone and dashed out of the door. A movement to her left and she saw Dotty emerge from a bedroom down the hallway. In synchronicity they bundled down the stairs – Dotty still pulling her arms through the sleeves of a bright-green cardigan – and followed the sounds of commotion into the dining room.

It was Alfred who met them at the door, his brow furrowed. He raised his hands up to slow down the two young women, who just about managed to stop before they bowled him over.

'Alf?' Cressida and Dotty both said, then Cressida took over. 'Alf, what is it? Who screamed? It sounded like Mama.'

'It was, but don't worry, Cressy.' Alfred's face softened, and he lowered his hands, placing one of them reassuringly on her arm. 'Lady Fawcett is fine. She's just had a bit of a shock.'

'Which was?' Cressida persevered.

'Which was?' Dotty echoed, her arms crossed in front of her, as if her brother was just being wilfully obstructive. He wasn't, and he stood aside and let them in.

'I'd want to save you from seeing this, both of you, but I

guess you've seen enough dead bodies now not to get too upset. Still, not nice.'

Dotty pushed past her brother first but soon came to a stop inside the room. She raised a hand to her mouth and rocked back on her heels, then leaned against the dado rail of the dining room wall for support.

Cressida shot a look at Alfred, frowned and then entered the room herself. What she saw was heartbreaking.

Her mother was in floods of tears, luckily being held and comforted by her father. DCI Andrews, just in shirtsleeves and his tweed waistcoat, was holding the wrist of Sir James Colston, measuring his pulse. The rest of Sir James was slumped across the table, face down in what looked like the remains of a bowl of porridge, the silver spoon that he'd been using still gripped in his other hand.

'Heavens, no,' Cressida said softly, taking it all in. 'Alfred, what happened? Did he choke?'

'I'm not quite sure. My back was to the table as I was helping myself to breakfast from the sideboard.' He indicated over to where three silver domes were sitting on the old oak sideboard. As in most country houses, breakfast was served this way, with domed platters put out for the guests full of the day's breakfast choices; sausages, bacon, tomatoes and the like. Cressida's eye moved from the silver domes to where her mother and father were standing, next to the sideboard and still holding each other. They were as far away from the body of their friend as it was possible to be in the room. Alfred carried on. 'I was about to spear a rasher when I heard a most awful noise coming from that end of the table, and turned around to see Sir James spluttering and gripping a hand to his throat. His face was floridly red and he was uttering nonsense, as though in a delirium. Then he collapsed forward into that bowl, and here we are.'

Cressida shook her head, then bit her lip as she thought. 'He didn't choke?' she asked, looking to Alfred for as much of an answer as he could give.

'I don't think so. It didn't sound like choking. More like gurgling and then some sort of fit or heart attack,' Alfred answered, keeping his voice low, aware that what he was saying was pretty ghastly stuff.

'Was it... poison?' Cressida asked, thinking of Bob, and how he too had fallen face first as he'd died.

Alfred shrugged his shoulders, unable to answer her. Cressida looked harder at the scene. There was no other breakfast food around Sir James. The only thing he had been eating was the porridge.

The porridge she'd seen Marian Pringle season and stir so intently only a short while ago.

It was as if DCI Andrews read her mind. And she tried not to take offence at him looking straight at her as he gave the instruction for the bowl of still-warm oats not to be touched. But... *it couldn't be Marian, could it?*

The next few moments passed in a bit of a blur. Lord Fawcett held Lady Fawcett tight as he escorted her out of the breakfast room, and Alfred patted his sister's shoulder as she sniffed into a handkerchief. Cressida was more intent on what DCI Andrews had to say about the cause of death, but annoyingly for her he'd scooted out of the breakfast room barely saying a word.

Cressida peered through the dining room door and saw him heading into her father's study, no doubt to use the telephone which was connected there. With him gone, Cressida, Dotty and Alfred were left standing by the table, Sir James Colston slumped dead in front of them.

'I think we should probably leave him in peace,' Alfred suggested. 'Poor chap.'

Dotty nodded and made to turn, but Cressida, instead of following on, moved towards the body.

'Be careful, Cressy,' Dotty warned. 'If it's poison...' She pointed towards the bowl, which was upturned, the warm porridge still oozing out of it and causing red scald marks to appear on Sir James's face, despite the pale tinge that was coming upon him.

'I won't go near the porridge, don't worry,' Cressida reassured her as she skirted around the back of his chair. 'However, Andrews didn't say I couldn't have a look at Sir James himself...' She looked at the body from the same angle that DCI Andrews had. His thick woollen tweed was pulled taut across his wide back and the stitches around the tops of the sleeves pulled with the awkward angle of his slumping. It reminded her of Bob's tweed jacket, still dry in places as the water of Hell's Ditch hadn't flowed high enough to dampen it. *Bob*... Remembering how she'd found his body, a thought came to her.

She gingerly followed the line of his taut tweed sleeve down to his fist. Andrews had been trying to find a pulse on his wrist, but the dead man's hand was still clasped shut. She gently pulled apart his fingers, aware that although they had no movement of their own, rigor mortis had not yet begun to set in. She pulled out the small object she'd guessed she might find and brought it out into the daylight. Dotty gasped as Cressida held the treasure aloft. It glinted in the sunlight coming in through the dining room windows and she recognised it immediately.

It was the gold coin, the one he'd flourished in front of the Fawcetts' guests at dinner last night. The exact same coin that Bob had been gripping in his cold, clenched hand as he had died.

At that moment, to her utmost disbelief, Cressida truly believed in the curse of the Saxon gold...

## 22

Cressida had been correct, and DCI Andrews had indeed hotfooted it into her father's study to use the telephone. He'd made a call not only to Scotland Yard to request the presence of his sergeant, Kirby, but also to the local station to ask for a few officers to attend Mydenhurst Place immediately. She'd felt bad hovering by her father's study, her ear to the door, listening in to his conversation, and almost regretted that her eavesdropping had meant she'd heard him describe Mydenhurst Place – her home – as a crime scene. Two deaths on her parents' estate in as many days... the thought brought a sudden prickle to her arms. Were her parents – and her darling friends – safe? Was she? She thought of the cursed coin, now gripped in her own fist. She allowed herself one more shiver, then vowed to stiffen her resolve. The curse was just a myth, but these deaths were very, very real. It was much more likely that there was a very earthly poisoner on the loose in Mydenhurst, and she had to find out who it was – before they struck again.

Cressida heard the familiar click of the receiver being lodged back in the cradle and stepped back from the door just in time to pretend to innocently meet Andrews out in the wood-panelled hallway. She showed him the gold coin she'd found in Sir James's hand. Andrews took it in his own fingers, then he placed it in his palm and flipped it over a couple of times, making a sort of 'mmm' sound as he did. Finally he spoke.

'Well, I'm with you on the idea that this little coin must be at the heart of the tragedy unfolding here at Mydenhurst,' he said.

'The crime scene,' Cressida couldn't help but repeat his phrase from his telephone call as she made a face.

'Indeed,' Andrews agreed, ignoring, or not noticing that she might have been listening in to him.

'I just don't think Marian would do such a thing.' Cressida crossed her arms, a frown wrought across her face.

'I'm afraid she's our most likely suspect, Miss Fawcett.' Andrews shook his head. 'Assuming the porridge was made and served by her this morning.'

Cressida closed her eyes and sighed. She'd seen Marian stir that porridge, and what's more *season it*, with her own eyes. Even she had to agree now that it was getting harder and harder to believe in Marian's innocence. Then a thought came to her. 'But why would she kill Sir James?' Cressida asked, meeting the detective's gaze with her own.

Andrews held up the coin. 'I should imagine this will have much to do with it. As I see it this coin could well be the motive behind Mr Pringle's murder. Either someone knew he had found it, and possibly others like it, such as his wife or anyone else who had heard him boasting either at the pub or here at Mydenhurst Place.' He raised his eyebrows as Cressida pulled a face. 'Well, we have to consider it, Miss Fawcett. One of the other servants might have wanted what Bob was obviously so delighted by. Or, we have the possibility that someone killed Bob to keep the location of the rest of the gold a secret. Again, that could mean Mrs Pringle, if she realised he was spending more and more and wanted him to stop before he'd considered her wishes on the matter too.' Cressida gave a sort of 'pfft' sound as he said that, but he doubled down. 'We can't rule it out. He wasn't exactly sharing with her, was he?'

'But she says she didn't know where the money was coming from. Until I found that coin on his body none of us had any idea the money he'd come into was to do with the hoard.'

'But we do, Miss Fawcett. That's what was annoying me last night, when I decided I'd had too much whisky. There is a very good reason why Mrs Pringle might have known that Bob's new money was more than just a small win on the horses. Remember his nods and winks at the society when he bought them all drinks. In front of his – and Mrs Pringle's brother-in-law – perhaps even her sister. I was thinking about it last night in bed and I fear we assumed a bit too much yesterday, believing Marian didn't know the extent of the fortune her husband had found.'

Cressida paled as she realised Andrews was right. Bob had hinted very strongly that he'd found the hoard while buying the villagers drinks. She felt like a ninny having missed that. She chastised herself as Andrews carried on.

'We'll get some more answers when I take her in for questioning.'

Cressida's frown deepened as she thought. 'You think she might have killed Sir James for a similar reason? What with him professing last night that he also knew where the hoard is buried?'

Andrews shrugged. 'I can't deny that it's a possibility.'

'But she wasn't in the room at the time he was speaking. And the historical society were... Don't you think the culprit is more likely to be one of them? They all knew – or at least had heard it hinted at strongly – that Bob had found it, and then Sir James was telling them he knew where it was and was about to reveal where it's buried. We know some of them are practically obsessed with finding the Saxon hoard.' She pointed to the thrymsa in his palm, and Andrews closed his fingers around the coin and then crossed his arms. She carried on. 'And we all saw how enthused they were last night when Sir James mentioned it. His cliffhanger of an ending too, not wanting to reveal all until the society convened tonight in the pub...'

'I'm not going to dismiss your theory, Miss Fawcett. We've worked closely enough recently for me to think twice about that, but the evidence is much more stacked towards Mrs Pringle's guilt. She could have been listening in to Sir James's speech from the hallway last night. And, of course, Bob's poison by sandwich—'

'Not yet proved,' Cressida interrupted, then more resignedly added, 'though you are probably right. If only there'd been some left in that original jar to test.'

'We'll know soon enough about the other jar though, which she said was from the same batch, though I don't hold out much hope of it being poisoned too. Come to think of it, her washing out the empty jar is awfully convenient.' He scratched his beard. 'And we'll have that porridge tested. But for now, it seems like Mrs Pringle may have poisoned her husband and then Sir James, to get her hands on this coin, and perhaps others like it. Money is always a powerful motive.'

The loud trill of the telephone receiver from the study called Andrews away and left Cressida alone in the hallway. A soft bump, bump, bump from the staircase caused her to look around and she smiled at the sight of Ruby taking one step a little jump at a time, an even slower and stiffer Ernest following on behind her.

'Come on, old thing,' Cressida said meeting her dog half-way. 'Steps are no fun after a multiple birth, are they? Speaking of which, I better see how those pups of yours are doing. Ernest old fellow, go and look after Mama, she needs you now more than ever.'

She picked up her dog and took her back upstairs, and

watched as the obedient old Ernest made his lumbering way down the rest of the stairs and headed in the direction of the sitting room. Cressida hoped that her absence wouldn't appear too rude to Alfred and Dotty, who had accompanied her mother and father, to await the police and the coroner.

Suddenly, Cressida stopped. If Mama, Papa, Alfred and Dotty were in the sitting room, and Andrews was in the study, who was with Marian?

Cressida didn't know whether to apprehend the cook or give her a nod and tell her to scarper, while she worked to clear her name. Cressida looked at Ruby, then saw movement at the top of the stairs. It was Molly, the Fawcetts' maid, starting on the bedrooms. She called up to her to ask her to look in on the puppies, and then with Ruby still in her arms she dashed back down the old oak staircase, past the lumbering Ernest still making his way to the sitting room, and made her way down the dark passageway to the oldest part of the house and the kitchen. She was still working out quite what she was going to say to Marian – whether to warn her or collar her – when she pushed the kitchen door open.

News of the death – murder – must have reached the kitchen as Cressida came upon Marian all in a dither. She was pacing up and down alongside the well-scrubbed pine table, occasionally picking up and refolding a tea towel that was slung over the back of one of the wheel-back chairs, and muttering to herself.

'Marian?' Cressida called out to her, letting Ruby down as she did so. Marian looked up at Cressida and seemed to deflate as she saw her.

'Oh, Miss Cressida,' she said, coming around the table to stand in front of her. 'Is it true? Has Sir James died?'

Cressida reached out a hand to the cook, and rested it on her arm. 'Yes. I'm afraid he has. How do you know?'

'I heard screams from the breakfast room... I was in the passageway out there, you see, carrying this platter of eggs,' – she pointed to a silver tray of perfectly scrambled eggs – 'and then I heard your mother and father leaving, her in tears and him saying something about Sir James and I... well, I just came back in here and assumed the worst.'

Cressida nodded. Whether that explanation would stand up in court she didn't know, but it seemed genuine enough to her. The large pot of porridge on the edge of the stove, with its spurtle sticking out of it, caught her eye. There was still porridge in it, and no attempt to clear it up in the moments after Sir James's death had been made. Surely if it were full of poison, it would have been the first piece of evidence to be scrubbed clean and therefore destroyed? Just like Andrews had insinuated that she'd done to the pickle jar. But what if she'd served him his bowl separately? Poisoned it somehow away from the rest of the saucepan? She thought back to the side-board in the dining room. The domes had only had sausages, bacon and tomatoes in them.

'Marian, I... I hate to ask this but was Sir James the only person who wanted porridge this morning?'

'Yes, I know he likes it. Your parents never bother with it. I don't know about your friends, of course. I remember Lady Dorothy was never fond if it though as a child. No, it was all for Sir James really.'

Cressida wasn't sure if this admission from Marian was in her favour or not. It was another example of the victim eating something only he would like, so as not to risk killing anyone else, but she was relieved that the still-full pot stood so plainly in sight. She was about to comment further when a clatter of boots in the hallway made her turn around and she saw Andrews enter the room. Usually, the sight of him bolstered her, especially when there was an investigation to be done, but she knew what he was here to do. She turned back to Marian and squeezed her arm, before letting go. She stepped back, as Andrews moved forward and made the arrest.

'Marian Pringle, I'm arresting you on the charge of murder, pertaining to Sir James Colston and also of your husband, Robert Pringle.'

'I didn't, sir, I promise you, I didn't. Miss Cressida, please...' Marian begged them both and Cressida bit her lip as the only way to bear watching their family's beloved cook being handcuffed.

'I'll do what I can to help!' Cressida called after her, as Andrews led her through the door to the kitchen garden, and from there to a waiting police car that was idling, engine running, on the driveway. Two local coppers came in and without ceremony removed the pot of porridge from the stove and carried it out to another waiting police car, spurtle and all.

Cressida was then left in the silence of the kitchen, the vast space now feeling so empty without the bustle of its cook going about her daily business. She sighed and took the few steps to where the police had left the door open to the kitchen garden. A breeze brought in the scent of spring rosemary from the kitchen garden. Closing it she turned around to see Ruby, who had somehow got herself up onto the table, delighting in being snout-first in the perfectly scrambled eggs.

## 23

'It was horrible,' Cressida said to Dotty as they sat at the garden table overlooking the croquet lawn. The sun was higher in the sky now and the three friends had retreated outside with all six puppies and Ruby, in order to allow the police and mortuary assistants free rein of the house and to get out from under her parents' feet.

'Did Andrews actually arrest her in front of you?' Dotty asked, Dusty and Lulu nestled in her arms.

'Yes, with handcuffs and everything,' Cressida replied, holding her own wrists out as she did so. She could just imagine how the cold steel of the cuffs would have felt on poor Marian as she looked down at her own slim wrists and it sent a shiver across her shoulder blades. She pulled her arms back and crossed them, hoping that might help get the image out of her mind.

Alfred, sensing her unease, passed Hercules and Suki to her from his own lap, and she reached out for them with relief at having something else to occupy her hands.

'Thank you, Alf,' she said, a smile escaping through her

misery. 'Poor Marian though. And I'm convinced this Saxon gold is at the heart of it. So is Andrews, but he thinks the buck stops with Marian, whereas I think there are other motives at play.'

'The murderer is from the historical society then?' Dotty asked.

'He, or she, must be. Just think of the number of suspects who were all also interested in it, and who attended the meetings. For example,' – she moved Hercules just a bit so she could count on her fingers – 'one, that's Lilian, two, Reverend Dunn, three and four if you count both Mr and Mrs White, five, this Sebastian Reed chap and, of course, Papa, who doesn't count. And Walter Rook from the pub as he listened in a lot.'

'But Mr Rook wasn't at dinner last night, neither was Mr Reed,' Dotty pointed out. 'They wouldn't have known Sir James was about to reveal the location of the hoard.'

Cressida thought for a moment. 'Not necessarily. When I fetched the puppies' breakfast this morning Marian was feeling a little worse for wear as her sister and Walter had stopped by, I assume to see how she was feeling after the most awful day. If she's a suspect because she might have overheard Sir James's speech, then she may well have told Annie and Walter of it too.'

'Fair point,' Dotty conceded. 'But Mr Reed in Willowmere?'

'I don't know. Not yet.' Cressida thrummed her fingers on Hercules's head, which the young dog seemed to enjoy by the looks of his short, but very waggy little tail.

'Well, the morning's bright and we're personae non gratae in the house while the police take Sir James away. Shall we go and question some of these dastardly historical buffs?' Alfred said, removing his pipe from his mouth and placing it on the table so that he could pick up Fortnum and Mason, who had started nibbling the table leg.

'If Molly can be persuaded to look after the pups, then yes.' Cressida looked more animated. She rang the little bell that had been left on the coffee tray and when Molly appeared she explained their plan.

'Oh yes, miss,' Molly said, immediately taking Suki and Hercules from her. 'I think I can prioritise the pups over the bedrooms and there's ham and some lovely new Jersey royals in the refrigerator. Mrs Pringle was so organised like that. She can't have done it, can she?'

Molly looked worried, lines crossing her furrowed brow. Cressida smiled at her, hoping it was reassuring. She was convinced that Marian was innocent, but it would be interesting to find out why Molly thought so too.

'I don't think she did it, no. We all know Mrs P to be an absolute darling. But, out of interest, apart from being a whizz at organising our lunches, why do you think she couldn't do it?'

Molly thought for a second. 'Well only that Mr and Mrs Pringle just seem part of the furniture here, don't they? You know, familiar, but also sort of quiet and practical. And never a cross word between them. You hear some folk who go off on each other over every small thing, but Mrs Pringle doesn't have a temper like that. Her sister, Mrs Rook, and her husband, well I hear they're more the bickering sort. Mr Pringle used to say so when he came home from the Royal Oak, tell Mrs P all about it. He spent quite a lot of time there.'

'Did you know Mr Pringle had recently come into some money?' Cressida pushed, wondering if she should – horror of horrors – start suspecting other members of the household too. If Molly knew Bob had been rich and if she had somehow found out the hoard's location... she stopped her mind racing as Molly answered her.

'No, miss, but I've heard a bit about it all since, miss. All I remember was Mrs P being cross with Mr Pringle as he was wasting money at the pub and not fixing the old bike. But as I said, she never really grumbled at him or nagged. And why would Mrs P want to kill some historian fella? Just doesn't make sense, does it?'

'Not to me,' Cressida said, catching both Dotty and Alfred's eyes. 'Thank you, Molly. I'm going to see what I can do about it.'

With that, the three of them got up and deposited the puppies in the makeshift badminton net pen, with Molly settled down next to them, petting them and rolling a croquet ball around for them to jump on. Ernest wobbled over from where he'd been sitting in a morning sunbeam, and as soon as he stepped over the badminton netting and flopped down on the grass, all six puppies had climbed on him, with Lulu seeming to enjoy the constant biffing that his wagging tail was giving her.

'Oh, bless you, Ernest. Ruby, are you staying or coming?' Cressida asked her little dog and laughed as Ruby took one look at the mayhem in the pen and then trotted along to Cressida's side.

'Well then,' Alfred said, 'where to first?' He checked his pocket for his car keys. Cressida noticed this and then looked up at her friends.

'Walking distance, I think. Have either of you ever been to our church? I believe historical society member Reverend Theophilus Dunn should be there this morning. And last night Mrs White was telling me all sorts of interesting things about him. Shall we start with him?'


The church of St Barnabas in Mydenhurst village was very, very old. So old, that the font had worn away at one side where every year, for the past millennia, the oxen and latterly the cows and horses of the village had been brought in to be blessed during the Sunday service closest to the feast day of St Francis of Assisi. And feet, since the eleventh century, had worn down the flagstones that led up the aisle to the most beautiful sanctuary and altar. Stained-glass windows told parables, and Cressida remembered staring at them during Sunday sermons past; the crow and the pebbles, the field of treasure, the prodigal son. It was the church in which Cressida's parents had married, and thousands of couples had before them. That only a handful had married since then was a telling sign of how the once bustling church had declined. Not that the congregation had become any less pious, but it had become smaller, as larger, newer churches had sprung up in Stammer Hill and Willowmere.

The church was located slightly away from the village, on top of a hill, with the most stunning view over the valley below. A green meadow, lightly dotted with sheep, began as the churchyard with its yew trees ended and swept down the hillside towards a row of handsome oaks that lined the lane between the church and the ancient priory.

When the south and north doors of the church were both open, an onlooker could see straight through the nave to the other side of the churchyard. In fact, if both doors were open and you happened to be standing at the lychgate to the north of the church, you'd be able to see all the way down the valley.

Cressida and her friends had hiked up the hill from Mydenhurst Place to the church, pleased that it was a nice spring day, not the height of summer. Still, early cow parsley was already appearing in the hedgerow and the bracken and ferns were unfurling their emerald-green leaves in readiness for the season ahead. Alfred had taken to swatting the long grasses with a useful stick he'd found by the wayside, the swoosh of it like a cane of an irate schoolmaster. Dotty had been as game as she could be about an outdoor excursion, though the cows they'd come across in the field they'd made a shortcut across had startled her with their bellowing. Cressida had scooped up Ruby before they could show too much interest in her and heard Dotty muttering something about cows being 'the worst' as she hopped over a steaming pat. It felt as if a collective breath was released when they climbed over the style and met the relative safety of the road up to the church.

It was a welcome sight, therefore, after their exertions, to see the black-clad figure of the vicar standing in the porch of the church's north door. He wore a wide-brimmed, domed hat made of black felt, and his cassock flowed down to the floor. As he stood upright it settled in folds around him, and at the bottom, only the toes of two shiny patent leather shoes stuck out. His face, what could be seen from under the hat, was wide and pale. Like that of the moon in that French film that she'd laughed over and delighted in as a child when the showman with the bioscope had come to Willowmere. She hadn't had a chance to speak to the reverend the evening before, but he didn't look much different now, except for the hat.

Cressida waved at him. He raised a hand in return. As she approached she could see what he'd been doing in the porch. Jars and jars, of all shapes and sizes, were lined up on the old wooden benches either side of the door. And an ink-fresh sign in front of them inviting donations for the new roof fund to be put into the honesty box on the bench.

'Good morning, Vicar,' Cressida called when she was a few feet away.

'Good morning, Miss Fawcett.' Reverend Dunn bowed, showing them the full upper side of his hat's brim. He still held the pen in his hand, and replaced the lid, slowly and carefully.

'Those look delicious.' Cressida pointed to the jars and the vicar nodded.

'Do help yourself. Anything you can donate in return would be most welcome. There's a drip, you see, over the choir stalls. The roof's in an awful state.'

Cressida picked up a jar. Marian had said the poisoned pickle had come from the church porch, if indeed that was how Bob had been murdered. She looked at the label – blackberry and apple jam made by Mrs Shelley over in Liphook. *It's not a pickle, and it's identifiably labelled, so this one should be safe enough*, she thought to herself and was a little surprised that Alfred stepped forward and slipped a coin into the honesty box on her behalf before she'd had a chance to riffle through her own pockets. She wasn't sure how she felt about it; not affronted, but not wholly on board with it either. She put that thought to one side to be analysed later, perhaps on the long drive back to London when the trip was over. Maybe even over a crumpet smothered in this home-made jam. In the meantime, she thanked Alfred and the vicar, and jam jar in hand, began her questions.

'I'm afraid all is not well at Mydenhurst Place this morning, as you might have heard?' Cressida wondered how quickly the news might have spread. The Reverend Dunn removed his hat and scratched his head, beckoning them all inside the church.

'I must admit, I heard the ringing of the bells – and, by that, I mean the ones on the police cars, not here at the church – and wondered at the reason. Though being a little out of the way here, I've seen no more of it – no felons in the back of police cars or anything. I was tidying the vestry when I remembered I had to put some sort of marker out for these jars, else they might just get picked up with no donations made and then where would we be with the roof?'

The state of the roof was obviously of pressing concern to the young vicar and once her eyes had adjusted to the dim light inside the church compared to the bright spring day outside, she looked up to the rafters and saw for herself the exposed lathes where some plaster must have fallen and the discolouring of the remainder around it. A few wasps buzzed high up in and around the beams; a nest up there would be the last thing the old building needed. She could see why the diocese was thinking about merging this old church with the newer ones in Stammer Hill and Willowmere.

'Reverend Dunn, if not enough money is ever raised, what would happen to the church?'

He sighed. 'What happens to all buildings that fall into disrepair. It would be abandoned and left to rot.'

'And the living that comes with it?' Cressida asked, trying to sound innocent enough.

The reverend exhaled another long breath. 'Gone. I'm on thin ice already, what with the amount this church costs to maintain and repair. All the diocese wants these days is money in, not money out.' He paused, tilted his head and looked at Cressida and her friends. 'We find ourselves off topic. What was happening at Mydenhurst Place this morning?'

Cressida looked over to Alfred and Dotty, who both nodded. She took a deep breath and then began. 'There was another death.' She was careful not to say murder. 'Sadly, Sir James collapsed over breakfast. He died before anyone could help him.' It wasn't an absolute lie, Cressida told herself as she remembered she was standing in a house of God, however leaking that house was.

'Now that is sad. My condolences to you and your family, Miss Fawcett. I will pay a visit to your father and mother personally. Perhaps later this afternoon once they are less in shock.' He folded his arms. 'Was it another murder?'

Cressida could only nod as his question hung heavy in the damp air of the church. She placed her hands on her hips and looked at Reverend Theophilus Dunn. He had leapt to the murder conclusion quite quickly, though she realised that after the news had got out about Bob yesterday, it would have spread around the village quicker than unset jam.

'Yes, sadly, we think it might have been. Poor Sir James.'

'Hmm, so I was right then, it was the sound of the *police* car's bell I heard. A dead man doesn't need a chiming ambulance to rush to him.'

Cressida was impressed at the reverend's power of deduction. Though perhaps she shouldn't have been so surprised, he was an Oxford man after all. He was clever, a man of logic. Clever enough to get away with murder, perhaps? And in need enough of the hoard's gold to save his beloved church...? Or as Madge White had suggested last night, just to save himself from a life of work? Whichever it was, Reverend Dunn definitely had a motive.

## 24

A sigh from behind Cressida made her turn around, only to see Dotty looking absolutely miserable. She'd forgotten in the morning's chaos that Sir James was somewhat of a hero to her history-loving friend. She gave her a sympathetic look and turned back to the reverend. 'And he left us all on rather a cliffhanger last night, don't you think?'

'You mean his reluctance to reveal where the hoard is? If there even is one...'

'You don't think there is?' Cressida asked.

The reverend shrugged. 'As with many things, perhaps only God knows. Can I ask... I mean to say, how did he die?'

'He was poisoned,' Cressida said, rolling the jam jar around in her hand as she looked him in the eye. She could detect no flicker of guilt though.

'Hmm, like Mr Pringle. How very sad. I shall say prayers and intercessions for them both, of course.'

'Thank you. I know my parents will appreciate it,' she said.

Alfred gestured for his sister to follow him as he walked around admiring the church, giving Cressida space to speak to the reverend. As they'd often discussed, the three of them together, although all perfectly pleasant and rather nice looking, could come across rather like an aristocratic press gang en masse.

Cressida gave a word of silent thanks, then spoke to the reverend again. 'Don't you believe in it? The hoard, I mean.'

'Believe in it?' The reverend scratched his head again and Cressida wondered if his heavy felt hat gave him hives. 'An odd question for someone whose life revolves around belief. Do I think the hoard exists? Well there's archival evidence for it. Whether it *still* exists, well that's less sure of course, what with the centuries that have passed and the fact that there would be many folk who *wouldn't* stop to write poems or tell the village chieftain about the fact they'd just upped and left with the gold they'd found in a field nearby. But do I *believe* in it? I believe gold has the power to twist men's minds. To damage the moral compass more surely than if it were made of pure iron.'

'It sounds like you've put quite a bit of thought into it,' Cressida couldn't help but say.

'I have.' The reverend crossed his arms and his forehead wrinkled in thought. 'I suppose I have, yes.'

'Are you interested in finding it?' Cressida pressed on, bringing the discussion back from the philosophical to the practical.

'From a historian's viewpoint? Of course. I studied history alongside theology at Oxford. But for the fortune and glory of finding treasure? No.'

'Was Sir James one of your tutors? Papa mentioned in his introduction last night that Sir James was still teaching at Oxford.'

'Indeed. Our paths crossed, though, as I say, I studied both history and theology, and of course the latter took up most of my time.'

'He wasn't the tutor that failed you then?' Cressida asked,

knowing it could derail their conversation. The reverend's eyes narrowed just for a moment but he shook his head.

'No, not him. It was a pleasure to see him last night. And to have him be so interested in our little village here.'

'Interested in the gold at least. Which you really have no interest in finding? Not even if it could save this church and therefore your job here at St Barnabas?'

The reverend rubbed a hand over his head again. 'True, true. But only if the gold was found on church land would that be the case. Finding it anywhere else in the village would have no effect on the coffers of this church, unless the treasure hunter or landowner decided to indulge us.'

This was undeniably true. Though the reverend, perhaps proving himself to be of a pure kind of heart, was forgetting that anyone obsessed with finding the gold would no doubt just steal it from whoever's land it was on.

'Miss Fawcett, if you'll excuse me, I must get on. There'll be a funeral to organise, of course, and I must visit Mrs Pringle to make arrangements.'

'Ah,' Cressida said, rather stopping him in his tracks. 'You might have a problem there. Marian has just been arrested.'

'For her husband's murder?' Reverend Dunn looked intrigued.

'And that of Sir James,' Cressida confirmed. 'You think that strange?'

The reverend shrugged. 'Perhaps.' It seemed to Cressida that he was once again holding something back from her. She pushed on, hoping to elicit some more from him.

'As unlikely as I find it, I can see why the police would suspect her of killing her husband. Marriages gone wrong and all that. Sadly, it happens all the time.'

'I do hope not,' Reverend Dunn said and mouthed a small prayer up to the rafters.

'But to kill a complete stranger? A guest in her employer's household? That doesn't make sense to me.' Cressida shrugged.

'If he were a complete stranger, then yes...' The reverend straightened his dog collar, which sat tightly under his wobbling, pale chins.

'You think Marian and Sir James knew each other?'

'Let me show you something.' The reverend gestured for Cressida to follow him and he led her down one of the side aisles. Finally, as they'd walked past several pews, the reverend stopped in front of a stone plaque that graced one of the old stone walls of the church.

The soft limestone of it had stayed remarkably undamaged, thanks to its position on the south wall with only the faintest light beaming down on it, and not a hint of a leak in this part of the roof. Cressida read the memorial stone to herself yet was still none the wiser as to why the reverend had pointed it out to her. She did, however, notice Alfred and Dotty hovering in the pews in the nave just behind one of the large stone columns. Finally, the vicar explained himself.

'This stone was laid by the Marchmont family back in 1834. Geoffrey Marchmont was a wealthy merchant in Willowmere and bought a house out here in Mydenhurst in order to escape the ordure of the town. Alas, too late, and as you see here his wife died of cholera and soon after his daughter, but his son – Geoffrey Junior, I assume – carried on trade after his father's retirement and he too settled near Willowmere in the 1850s. I believe his son then inherited his grandfather's house in the 1860s. He flourished, though Willowmere had lost some of its coaching town wealth once the railways took freight straight from the coast to London with no need for coach and horses. Still, he had two daughters who, after a while, would inherit a few pieces of land and several properties.' Cressida looked quizzically at the reverend, then it came to her.

'Marian and Annie? They're Marchmonts? And the Royal Oak... was it their father's?'

'Indeed. And now, as Mrs Rook, Annie Marchmont is landlady of the last piece of the family's heritage, as I believe the house her grandfather had bought is currently owned by the doctor and his wife. I don't know the ins and outs, but I believe there isn't much more.'

'Marian said her family didn't approve of her marrying Bob.' Cressida looked at the stern and formal etched words on the stone. Back in the 1830s this family had had money. No wonder it had been hard for them to accept that a granddaughter of Geoffrey Marchmont would marry a gardener and work as a cook. 'They cut her off.'

'But not Mrs Rook it seems.'

'No, for some reason Annie inherited the pub. They must have liked Walter. Thought he had prospects, perhaps.' Cressida mulled the idea over as she spoke. It occurred to her that her father, and indeed her mother, must know all of this, yet they'd never spoken of it.

'Perhaps. In any case, I believe the Marchmonts, in their time, donated to a few societies, one being the Colston family charity.'

Cressida's mouth almost dropped. 'The Colston family? As in Sir James's family? He knew Marian's family?' She could feel her blood run cold. Forgetting the gold for just a moment, if Marian knew Sir James... then she might have any sort of motive to kill him after all.

'Thank you, Reverend, you've been most helpful,' Cressida said, her mind full of what she'd just found out. On cue, her friends appeared and they all made their goodbyes.

'Goodbye, do pop in again. And there's evensong tonight if you're still here. Early so that I can head along to the meeting, if it's still going ahead. Perhaps after all, it won't. And do enjoy that jam.'

Cressida eyed up the jam jar in her hands and tossed it into the air, easily catching it again, despite the terrified look on the reverend's face.

'We will, Reverend Dunn. But one last thing... apart from Mrs Shelley of Liphook, who makes these jams and pickles?'

'Oh, they're donated. Several of the villagers make a batch too many. Mrs White has an orchard of apples and a very good greenhouse full of tomatoes come the summer, and, of course, the pub has use of its kitchen. And let's not forget how Mrs Catchpole benefits from the light-fingeredness of her children when it comes to fruit scrumping...' He raised an eyebrow. Cressida nodded, annoyed that there was no smoking gun when it came to who was the chief pickle maker in the village.

Cressida and her friends left the church and emerged out into the dazzling sunshine. Ruby, who had been snoozing against a sun-warmed tombstone, shook herself awake and trotted alongside as the three friends wandered along the well-kept paths beside the ancient tombs and gravestones.

The reverend had seemed as guilty or as innocent as anyone else in the society. But he had helped her make more connections. Marian had known Sir James, as had Annie. Their former home was now lived in by the Catchpoles. The reverend himself had also known Sir James, though claimed he wasn't the tutor who had held back his studies.

And almost everyone in the historical society, nay the village, was known to make pickles. Threads, golden or otherwise, hung down in front of Cressida.

She just had to work out which was the right one to pull.

## 25

A sudden crack, like that of a whip, shattered Cressida's thoughts and the glass of the jar she was holding. She looked down at her hands and saw the red jam ooze through her fingers. Shocked, she looked up, her hands held helplessly out in front of her.

'Are you hurt?' Alfred asked, rushing to her side. Dotty protectively scooped up Ruby and looked about them, her eyes darting from gravestone to tomb, to yew tree to lychgate.

'I... I don't think so,' Cressida stammered, letting the jam drip through her fingers.

'Don't let the glass cut you,' Alfred said, gently picking out the larger pieces and placing them carefully on top of the churchyard's wall. Cressida could feel his eyes look up at her face and she hoped she wasn't blushing too much – or indeed red from shock, which he might think was blushing – as he niftily removed the broken shards from her hands. He then whipped out his handkerchief and wiped off as much of the sticky jam as he could before passing it to her. Cressida rubbed her hands with the large white pocket square while Alfred spoke to his sister.

'Any sign of anyone, Dot?'

'Yes, look, over there!' Dot shifted her hand from under Ruby and pointed to the far edge of the churchyard. 'Do you see? A flash of red under that low-hanging yew tree branch – there it is again!'

'Got it,' said Alfred, removing his jacket and rolling up his sleeves as he dashed off in the direction of the large, low-boughed tree. Dotty turned to Cressida.

'Are you all right, chum? What was it? Another hazelnut?'

'I should imagine that young David, assuming that flash of red you saw was his catapult, has upgraded to ball bearings.'

'He could have had your eye out, Cressy! Lordy be, are children to be worse than cows these days? You know, in the danger-in-the-countryside stakes?'

'Children are the worst,' Cressida echoed the earlier sentiment, but an idea had come to her. Ball bearings fired so hard that they could crack glass... or perhaps cause a nasty bruise. Dr North's post-mortem pronouncement echoed in her mind as Alfred returned, a young David Catchpole held by the collar and his rather more sheepish sister, Daphne, following on behind.

'Found our assailant,' Alfred announced, letting David go in front of Cressida. 'And now, young Master Catchpole, I think an apology is in order.'

David looked from Cressida to Alfred. 'I'm sorry you're such a prig.'

'Oi,' Alfred exclaimed, shocked at the precociousness of the young lad.

Cressida bit her lip as she tried not to laugh, but felt her shoulders shaking. Dotty was no better and suddenly burst into riotous laughter. David thought this all very satisfactory and said it again, but by this time the three adults – if one could really call them that – were looking at him again in all seriousness.

'Now look here, young man, that's not on,' Alfred chastised him. 'You could have hurt someone.'

Cressida had begun to wonder if perhaps David, with his excellent – or perhaps just lucky – aim and love of lurking in the undergrowth, had seen anything of note around the village.

'You owe me a pot of jam,' she started and as soon as she saw the young boy's face fall at the thought of the weeks of pocket money he might have just smashed, she followed it up with, 'but we'll call it quits if you can tell me something.'

'What?' David asked, and Cressida crossed her arms to look more authoritative.

'Who else have you shot ball bearings at recently?'

'I have done nothing of the sort,' David said, scratching his chin, which was stuck up in the air.

'David,' hissed his sister, who had been quiet up until now, a furtive look to her as if she'd been weighing up whether to run and leave her brother to face the music, or be dutiful and face it with him.

'Shuttup, Daph,' he snapped back.

'But this lady knows the police,' Daph said, then shoved the end of one of her plaits, red ribbon and all, in her mouth.

'Daphne's right, I do.' Cressida raised an eyebrow at David. 'But I promise that what you tell me will only stay between us.' Her much-practised finger crossing was subtly taking place under her already-crossed arms.

'All right then.' David shot a dirty look to his sister, who just shrugged it off. 'I got a bullseye on the top half of the door of the Whites' stables, and a clear one on Mr Jenkinson's greenhouse, that was a corker—'

'And you got Mr Pringle on the neck,' urged his sister, with a look to Cressida who smiled at her.

'Oh, yeah, that was easy that one. He's like a sitting duck when he's on that bridge and I could practise on Daph when he wasn't there.' He mimed pulling back his catapult rubber and mouthing 'pow' as he shot an imaginary ball bearing at his sister.

Cressida glanced at Daphne, who was pouting and rubbing her shoulder.

'Well that's not very nice,' Cressida said to David. 'So, you did fire ball bearings at Mr Pringle?'

David scuffed his shoe on the gravelly pathway. 'Maybe.'

'Well? Did you?' Cressida pushed.

'It wouldn't do you well to lie at this point,' Dotty chipped in, and Cressida nodded.

'All right, yes. I did. He was funny. Usually he'd wave his hands around like he'd been stung by a bee. But yesterday he was just sitting there like a pudding, slumped a bit. Silly old man. Didn't notice at all, though I'm sure I got a direct hit. Pegged it off fairly smartish afterwards though. Doesn't pay to hang around and he wasn't any fun anyway. Was he ill? If he was, I didn't know that.'

Cressida looked at Dotty, the realisation that David's cata-pulted ball bearing might have been the final thing to push an already dying Bob off the bridge. Not wanting the poor boy, however beastly he seemed, to live with that knowledge for the rest of his life, Cressida changed tack. 'Did you see Mr Pringle with anyone else yesterday? Before you pinged him with your remarkable accuracy? Or indeed any other day?'

'Yes, he often saw Mr Rook from the pub.' David was warming to his theme now and all inhibitions about talking to grown-ups about his exploits were gone. 'And sometimes Mr White.'

'Anyone yesterday? Or the day before, perhaps?' Cressida quizzed the small boy.

'Yeah, he was talking to that man from Willowmere yester-day. The one who's in the historical society with Mummy. They got a bit argy-bargy.' He smiled at his loose use of the English language and Cressida could see he was enjoying himself –

away from his parents who most likely insisted on the King's received pronunciation at all times.

'Argy-bargy?' Cressida asked. 'Like a fight?'

'Hmm, more like a spat. Like this.' At that he turned around and shoved his finger right up close to his sister's face, which made her jump and then look as if she was about to cry.

'All right, all right, that's enough of that, young man.' Cressida stepped in as Dotty moved closer to Daphne, bending over to show her how sweet Ruby was, which stemmed any tears that might have been brewing.

'Not a way to treat a lady, even one's skin and blister, David,' Alfred said, who had now put his jacket back on and disposed of the broken glass somewhere.

'Quite,' Cressida agreed. 'Now, back to this spat. Just strong words and loud voices?'

'Yeah, that sort of thing,' David agreed, though the wind was slightly out of his sails, having been ticked off by a fellow gent.

'Did you hear anything in particular? Any words stand out?' Cressida urged him on, realising that the attention span of children was somewhere between 'short' and 'non-existent'. But even though David might have been getting to the end of his, he did suddenly come up with something quite important.

'Mr Pringle looked the most angry. He said something about horses.'

Cressida furrowed her brow. 'Carry on...'

'Um, and, er, the other chap said something about gold.'

'Do you think he said hoard, not horse?'

'Don't lead the witness,' Dotty whispered to her, having stood up straight again, though with Ruby relinquished to the attentive Daphne. 'It happens all the time in those detective books I read. The PI says something and the witness agrees.'

David nodded and Cressida wasn't sure if it was in agreement with her or Dotty, more or less proving Dotty's point.

Cressida sighed. 'All right, David. Thank you for talking to me. Now, off you both run. I'm sure your mother will be looking for you and wondering where you are.'

It didn't take much more encouragement for the two siblings to catch each other's eye and then dart off in the direction of the lychgate. Cressida exhaled a long breath.

'Well, that explains the bruises on Bob's neck that Dr North found, and he was right, they had nothing to do with his death.' She leaned back on the large tombstone next to the churchyard wall. A breeze caught the back of her own neck and she shivered. 'But maybe an argument, with an individual I presume is Mr Reed from Willowmere, did.'

## 26

While flashes of red ribbon disappeared off in the distance in front of them, the three friends, and Ruby, walked along the lane from the church to the centre of the village discussing what they'd found out. Dotty and Alfred, who'd not heard all the ins and outs of Cressida's discussion with Reverend Dunn – although had had their fill of the under-twelves for one morning – asked her to fill them in on what he'd told her. After she did, Dotty, naturally, had questions.

'Marian knew Sir James?' She was incredulous.

'Perhaps. Their families were connected, right up until the time her father struggled financially, and of course his daughters – Marian and Annie – made whichever marriage matches they could, or indeed wanted. But what if Sir James had been a childhood chum of Marian's? Or worse, some sort of nemesis? I've been so focused on the gold, and the obvious motive that gives, but what if there's something deeper going on?'

'We can't ask her now,' Alfred chipped in as the three of them walked along the lane back to the village. Swallows darted overhead, and the sun was high in the sky. It was a glorious spring day and the friends were heading towards the Royal Oak.

'No, we can't, but we can ask her sister. Annie will be at the Royal Oak and it wouldn't look strange if I paid her a visit. I really should anyway to show solidarity, what with her sister being arrested by a family friend of ours.'

'And Mr Reed of Willowmere?' Alfred asked. 'Will we go and see what this argy-bargy about gold and horses was about?'

'Yes, but we'll need the car for that. And I want to know why he wasn't at dinner last night. But he can wait, we're here now.' Cressida pointed at the low-slung white building the other side of the village green, beyond the war memorial.

The lane gradually widened as it met the village green, emerging from the canopy of trees that had sheltered them from the sun into the wide-open space, often used as a cricket pitch. The pub was visible across the green, with the war memorial in front of it. Cressida remembered David and Daphne running off in this direction yesterday when their mother had tried to find them.

The Catchpoles' house – formerly that of Geoffrey March-mont – must be one of these that edged the green, slightly hidden behind aged brick walls, covered in tumbling ivy and climbing roses. A beautiful spot, and no doubt a pretty penny to buy. And if Percy White was correct in what he said last night, then Lilian Catchpole had another very real need for the gold, with nursing home bills for an invalid sister. Cressida lowered her voice in case there was anyone just over the other side of the pretty garden walls and told her friends all about it.

'Sounds like everyone in the village has some sort of financial quandary,' Dotty said in reply. 'I do feel for them.'

'If not the village, then the society at least. I heard the pub wasn't doing too well either. The only person apparently with no real need for the money is the chap in Willowmere, Sebastian Reed. Though that doesn't go hand in hand with what young David Catchpole just told us. I wonder why he wasn't there last night?' Cressida mused, not wanting to suspect her father of disrespecting anyone by leaving them out.

'Ah, I can answer that one,' Alfred piped up. 'Your father mentioned it over port and cigars.'

'Oh yes?' Cressida looked at him. 'Anything else from the boy's club port-guzzlement that I should know?'

Alfred thought for a moment, then used his fingers to list what he remembered from the night before. 'Well, only that Reverend Dunn also studied with Jasper Devere, you know from the Mutton Pie Club. Percy White discussed horse racing, and from the sound of it he and Mrs W are both cock-a-hoop about the gee-gees. Sir James scoffed all the Turkish Delight, while your father told us all about how he'd sent a telegram to young Sebastian Reed but had never heard a reply.' He lowered his hands and stopped counting as he went on. 'Which he found odd as the young cove was so obsessed, as has been mentioned, with finding the gold and had been pestering your father for months about inviting Sir James to speak to the society. He said he'd made sure to invite him as he knew how devastated he'd be if he found out that there had been a preamble to tonight's talk, but that it was no bad thing he wasn't there as he was worried the young buck might have made a fool of himself and badgered Sir James further.'

'Right,' Cressida said, taking it all in as Alfred popped his pipe stem between his molars, punctuating his sentence. She was pleased that her father had invited the less popular member of the group after all. It was much more like him, and how he'd taught her to behave. Still, he didn't turn up, or even reply.

Cressida stopped in her tracks and turned to her friends. 'I feel bad that we didn't start off with Mr Reed yesterday; we were in Willowmere too, but then Andrews caught us in the mortuary and well, we were on thin ice already. I think asking him if we could then stop off and interview someone we thought was a suspect but that he'd never heard of before... well that ice would have cracked and we all would have got a chilly dousing. It's odd though, don't you think, that he didn't even reply to Papa? I hope he's not... no, I mean, there've been two deaths. I think we might have heard about it if one of the historical society had died.'

'I'm sure we would have done,' agreed Dotty, though she sounded less sure of herself than usual. 'Unless the police in Willowmere thought it unrelated and haven't informed Andrews?'

'Now you've got me worried, Dot,' replied Cressida, biting her lip. 'I think we should look into it before going any further. Or at least split our resources. Maybe you two could head back home, pick up the car and track down Andrews. Ruby and I'll pop into the Royal Oak and see what Annie makes of the Sir James connection. If you get a whiff of Mr Reed being missing or worse, then please come back and find me. You know where I'll be!'

## 27

Dotty and Alfred walked back down the lane towards Mydenhurst Place to fetch the Rolls-Royce while Cressida, with Ruby trotting along beside her, headed on towards the pub. Sebastian Reed was still playing on her mind. Why had he not even responded to her father's invitation? She listened to the birdsong, and a few notes from a piano playing in a cottage nearby as she headed towards the old, whitewashed-walled pub next to the village green. Looking at her watch again, she nodded to herself. Of course it was closed, it being not even midday yet. *Oh, but how much had happened already today!*

Still, Cressida was determined not to be beaten by a closed door and knew the Rooks lived in the pretty cottage attached to the pub. Once upon a time the whole building would have been a row of small cottages for the field workers, no doubt employed by one of her ancestors. Sometime, perhaps during a bad spell for the wheat fields, the row of cottages had been partially knocked together, creating a larger portion of the building as the Royal Oak (and thankfully *not* the Fawcett Inn) and one remaining separate cottage at the end.

The front of the cottage looked identical to that of the Royal

Oak, but there was a low stone wall jutting out where the internal divide must be, and it encased a small front garden, with pretty wild roses clambering over the gate, which led to a brick-laid pathway that ran up to the door. Cressida found herself knocking on this door before she'd really thought about how she was going to approach the matter with Annie Rook, or indeed Walter if he answered. She was just trying to form some sort of scheme in her head when the door was opened.

The lady who opened the door gave Cressida quite a shock. If she hadn't witnessed Marian Pringle being handcuffed in front of her that very morning and led off by Andrews into an awaiting police car, she would have thought she was standing here in front of her in the doorway of this charming cottage. Cressida had met Annie Rook once or twice a few years ago, but hadn't seen her for a little while and had forgotten quite how like her sister she looked.

'Mrs Rook.' Cressida tried to hide her surprise. 'Marian Pringle's sister.'

'Yes,' Annie said guardedly. 'And you look familiar too...'

'Cressida Fawcett, I'm—' But before she could complete her introduction, Annie Rook's face had crumpled into silent anguish. She pulled the pinafore apron that was tied around her waist up to cover her face and shook her head as she wiped her eyes with the linen. 'Mrs Rook, are you all right?' Cressida leaned forward and touched the woman's upper arm with a comforting hand.

'We're going to do everything we can to clear Marian's name,' Cressida reassured her. 'Which is why I'm here. I wondered if I could ask you about Sir James and how well you both knew him?'

Annie Rook pulled the pinafore from her face and let the fabric drop, then she smoothed it down with her hands. Cressida couldn't help but notice that they looked so similar to Marian's – chapped in places from hard work, cooking and cleaning.

Annie might have inherited what was left of the family property, but it hadn't stopped her from having to work hard for a living, despite her upper-class upbringing.

'You better come in, Miss Fawcett, though I apologise for the mess. One of our lads is home from London and you'd have thought he brought an army with him, the state of the place. Twenty years old, yet can he tidy away a dish or fold a newspaper? Cushions scattered and tankards from the pub left on all my best tables with no heed for the polish.' She sighed. 'He's the youngest and maybe I indulged him.'

'You have more children?' Cressida made conversation as she weaved her way past armchairs and tables that were too grand for the proportions of the cottage's rooms. She picked up Ruby lest the small dog added to the mess by getting lost amid chair legs or rolling around on the open newspaper that was scattered across the floor.

'Two. A boy and a girl, though they're hardly that now. Our eldest, Susan, is married and living in Petworth. Of course, we lost Harry in the war.'

'I'm so sorry.' Cressida paused. There was little else one could say. So many sons had been lost in the war that an answer like Annie's was commonplace, though no less devastating for the family. Cressida decided to concentrate on the positive. 'Lovely that your daughter is so close though. Petworth's not far. Does she have children too?'

Annie Rook smiled. 'Oh yes. Walter practically had to get the shotgun out, if you know what I mean. Still, she now has little Charlie and three-month old Annabel.' The mention of her grandchildren really made Annie's eyes twinkle, especially her namesake granddaughter. Then she chuckled. 'Like mother like daughter, I suppose.'

Cressida smiled, seating herself on the chair that Annie pulled out for her in the kitchen by the well-scrubbed table. The kitchen was typical of cottages of the type; the width of the house with a door that led through from the middle room, and another on the opposite side that opened onto the cottage garden. It wasn't a large room, yet it had a stove that was already lit and warm, with bright copper pans hanging above it and a dresser lined with fine gilt-edged china. Along with the grand – and out of place – furniture in the other rooms, the china must have been an heirloom, or at least part of the inheritance from when the family had more money.

A kettle whistled on the stove and Annie poured the boiling water into a teapot. Cressida noticed glass jars lined up on a baking tray, either about to go in, or recently come out of, the oven where they'd sterilise before being used for jams... or pickles. There was no sign of a bubbling pot though and Cressida turned her gaze back to Annie Rook. Her joy in talking about her daughter and grandchildren had faded and she looked serious again as she swirled hot water in the teapot and bustled about fetching the fine bone china cups off the dresser shelf and placing one neatly in front of Cressida, along with a dainty silver spoon. Cressida picked up the spoon while Annie found a tea strainer and noticed an etched, swirly letter M on the end. Marchmont. Annie had also inherited the family silver, it seemed.

'I can't believe it,' she said, as she sat herself down opposite Cressida. 'Marian wouldn't have hurt Sir James. Nor Bob, for that matter.'

'Did she know Sir James at all? I mean from before her time working for my parents?' Cressida asked, as she checked to see where Ruby had snuffled off to. That the new mother had curled up in front of the stove rather than go on the hunt for crumbs was testament to how tired she was thanks to her offspring.

'Oh yes. We both did. You know my sister and I used to move in much grander circles than you see us in now. We were the Marchmont sisters.' She sat up straighter and pushed a strand of her curled hair out of her face. 'Quite the catch, in Willowmere and as far as Guildford.'

'I didn't realise that Sir James had been a local lad. I thought his connection with my father was only due to them studying at Oxford together.' A flash crossed her mind... her father must have been 'on the scene' with the sisters too. She wondered how it had played out when Marian had come to be their cook. No wonder her parents were always so solicitous as to her comfort and treated her more as one of the family.

'Oh yes,' Annie continued. 'The Colstons were a Willowmere family.' She paused for a moment and pursed her lips, then took a deep breath and continued. 'Sir James, who was just plain Master James then, went up to Oxford. He and your father became firm friends and shared carriage and horses and the like on the way there and back.'

'Apart from a local acquaintance, is there any other connection between your sister and Sir James?' Cressida pushed. She'd found out that much from the reverend. What she wanted to know was *how* well they knew each other. 'At the moment the police only have circumstance to go on as Marian prepared the last meal each man was eating. And, of course, there's the fact that both men seemed to know about the Mydenhurst hoard. But I just want to be prepared in case they start digging deeper for another connection.'

Annie stared into her teacup as if trying to divine an answer from it. Then she looked up at Cressida, her face pale despite the warmth in the room.

'Yes, Marian knew him,' she answered. 'She knew him from all those years ago. But she had no reason to kill him. If anyone had a reason, it was me.'

## 28

Cressida clattered her teacup into its saucer and apologised to Annie for the mistreatment of the best china and the accidental spillage of the tea. Annie shrugged it off.

'No damage done. Just a spill,' she said as she fetched a dish-cloth from the old ceramic sink.

'Annie, you said you had reason to kill Sir James?' Cressida was astonished at the revelation and had to know more. But as Annie sat back down and sighed, Cressida realised it wasn't going to be as dramatic as all that.

'Now, don't go twisting my words. I didn't say I *had* reason to kill him, just that if it was a toss-up between me and Marian, then it would be me who had *more* reason.' She took a sip of her own tea and then sat up straight again. 'I know that sounds similar, but it isn't.'

'I think I understand,' said Cressida, though she wasn't sure she did at all. 'But could you tell me why?'

'Why?' Annie puffed out her cheeks and then gently exhaled the air. 'Well, I suppose it all comes down to that summer back in 1895 or so. We were still eligible young ladies then, Marian and I, and we were attending what amounted to a season out here in Willowmere. Parties at the Georgian Hotel, dinners and carriage drives. We were genteel, if not very rich, and both attracted the eye of a good many suitors. James Colston was one of them and I had a drive or two out in his carriage with him, walks around that little arboretum over the way, and...' She paused. 'And the promise perhaps of a life together.'

'You were courting?' Cressida put her teacup down more gently this time and glanced over to check Ruby was still asleep. A glint of sunlight caught her eye as it reflected off one of the sparklingly clean pickle jars.

'In a way,' Annie agreed.

'Can I ask... what happened?' Cressida turned her attention back to Annie, who was looking quite ashen.

'Father lost what was left of the family fortune, excepting this place. James went up to Oxford and I didn't see him again. A letter from him suggested that perhaps mine and Marian's station in life was now so reduced as to be less appealing to him. He ended any expectations I might have had of becoming Lady Colston.'

'Oh dear.' Cressida could see what had happened now so clearly and she had to admit, though she was never one to think ill of the dead, the episode seemed to have been badly handled by Sir James.

'There we were now, two spinsters with little hope of a decent match.' Annie looked maudlin, as if reliving the feelings she'd had back then as a young woman.

'Just because you lacked money? You were still well educated and well connected in the town, weren't you?' Cressida couldn't quite understand the reason for Sir James's dismissal of Annie.

Annie coughed and moved her teacup and saucer away from her. 'And our looks; we were a pretty pair, Marian and I, back then. But some men are just like that. Problem was our

parents still had expectations for us. Anyway, Walter saw the
best in us, in me, and as I say, we had Susan barely nine months
after we walked down the aisle of St Barnabas.'

Cressida nodded. 'I'm sorry that Sir James treated you so ill.
But Marian, she was never courted by him, was she?'

'By him? No, no. He only made advances towards me. She'd
have borne no grudge against him, I'm sure. A fine gent he is
now, and perhaps it's a little embarrassing for her to see him as
she skivvies in the kitchen, but no more than it is to work for
your father in the first place.'

Cressida could feel her face redden. She'd always been
taught by her parents to treat any servant, be it in her own
house or when she stayed elsewhere, as equals. She knew it was
because they were decent, principled people, but having a
reminder in one's own home that one's position could so easily
change brought it all into focus just that touch more.

'When did Marian meet Bob?' Cressida asked, changing the
subject slightly. It was Bob's employment at Mydenhurst Place
that had meant Marian had applied for the job as cook and
housekeeper there. Now Cressida knew it was a house that
Marian would have once frequented as a guest she realised how
humbling it must have been for her. But did this show a character beyond reproach, and not fazed by worldly wealth? Or
one that would stop at nothing to regain the riches of her youth?
Cressida shelved that thought for later as Annie answered her.

'Soon after Walter and I had had Susan. He turned up at
Mydenhurst, recommended by Lord Egremont down at
Petworth. Marian had been living here in this cottage while
Walter and I had lodgings in town. With baby Susan with us
and another one soon on the way, it was all for the best that she
married Bob and settled into Garden Cottage. Larger than this
one even,' mused Annie, looking around her.

'But your parents didn't approve?' Cressida asked.

'No. By then Father had taken to drinking more than he

ought and with every sip he had reality faded and he thought himself grander. I'd married Walter by then and we'd made noises about taking over the running of the pub from the tenant he'd had in. Walter had a background in brewing, he's from a Somerset family who grew barley, you see. By the time poor Marian married, Papa was quite adamant that we were once again lords of the manor and there was no way his daughter should marry a gardener. The silly sod had nothing to his name, but he didn't seem to realise. Anyway, he died soon after and Marian seemed happy enough over at your place, so we didn't fight his wishes.'

Cressida thought about this. It didn't seem quite right, but the Marchmonts' family business was their own and it was not hers to say what she thought was fair or not. It seemed Marian and Annie had remained close despite the disparity in inheritance.

'Did Marian tell you anything about the money Bob had come into?' she asked after a hot sip of tea.

Annie twitched in her seat. 'I'm not sure I'd call it that,' she huffed. 'A round of drinks. Not exactly Rockefeller, was he?'

'No, but it was indicative of something, don't you think? Winking at the historical society as he did it,' Cressida pushed.

'For Marian's sake, I hoped it was. I hope she finds more of those little blighters in his pockets as she clears out his things. Wouldn't put it past him to have forgotten where he put them, mind like a leaky bucket that man. Walter said... well, never mind. All I can say is that I don't think Marian killed Bob, or Sir James. She's not like that. When Father lost our money and we had nothing to bring to a marriage except ourselves, Marian said she'd be happy with... well, she was more prepared for it than I was, what with me losing out on Sir James like that. She'd always have been happy with these simple lives of ours. But that's what life is, isn't it? Ups and downs. Now, you'll have to excuse me. I have Susan's boys coming over and I still have to tidy up after Walt Junior.'

'Thank you, Annie, I appreciate your candour in talking about the past. And I will do what I can to clear Marian's name. I don't think she's a killer either.' Cressida clicked her fingers for Ruby as she stood up.

'It'll be something to do with money, or gold, you mark my words.' Annie looked mournful, more so even than she had when discussing their troubled past. 'Walter and I could be accused of being a touch on the materialistic side, I'll admit that. But never Marian. She's a good sister. A forbearing sort of person...' She trailed off then repeated herself as she picked up a jam jar from the stove and wiped it with a tea towel. 'It's that gold. I'd stake my life on it.'

## 29

Cressida waved goodbye to Annie Rook at the gate of her cottage, and while waiting for Ruby to yawn and waddle along the pathway, glanced across the village green. A familiar silver Rolls-Royce appeared, majestically skimming the edge of the grass on its way towards her.

Less majestic was the hand enthusiastically waving out of the window and the head, complete with chestnut bobbed hair being blown in the wind, accompanying it. Cressida smiled at her friends and waved back, and waited for the elegant car to pull up in front of the pub. Once it was stopped, and Ruby had given up chasing a pretty yellow butterfly and was helped up onto the running board, Cressida leaned on the door and greeted Dotty and Alfred through the open window.

'What ho, chaps,' she said. 'Any news?'

'Not really,' replied Dotty, adjusting her glasses on her nose and smoothing down her hair. 'Andrews was jolly decent and spoke to us on the telephone from Willowmere police station, where he was with Marian. He checked and said there had been no reports of any other deaths, murder or otherwise, but that there had been a report late last night of a bicycle in a ditch—'

'Who knows if it's connected but we thought we'd go and check it out,' Alfred leaned forward past his sister and completed her sentence.

'Hop in,' said Dotty, and Cressida did just that, scooping up Ruby from the running board and opening the rear passenger door and climbing in. As Alfred revved the engine and set off once again, she leaned forward and told her friends about the conversation she'd just had with Annie.

'How funny that they were acquaintances of your father and of Sir James,' Dotty commented, then she turned more fully in the front seat to speak to Cressida. 'And, sadly, it adds even more weight to Marian's motive, don't you think? On top of the gold, there's a connection between them. She could be angry at Sir James for passing over her sister all those years ago. Remember how angry Elizabeth Bennet was in *Pride and Prejudice*? If Agatha Christie – who's really coming up with some humdingers these days – was writing that book now, instead of Jane Austen a hundred years or so ago, I should imagine Mr Darcy and Mr Bingley would have had lethal doses of arsenic placed in their punch glasses by Lizzie for what they did to Jane.'

'Glad to see your reading has gone back to the classics, Dot, and you're not just reading murder mysteries these days,' said Cressida, suddenly clutching at her friend's shoulder as Alfred apologised for an unforeseen bump in the road.

'I haven't had a chance to start any of the new ones I bought yesterday, and I rather ran out of books back at Chatterton Court. Or at least Papa put his foot down and said I couldn't have any more space in the library for my "pot-boilers" as he called them, until I'd read some more of the classics. So, I'm rereading all the Austens, imagining them as crime novels instead. Which in fact many of them are, with nefarious chaps like Wickham and Frank Churchill in them.'

'Well, literary history is no doubt relieved that Lizzie Bennet wasn't criminally minded, else Darcy would no doubt have been a goner in chapter one!' Cressida laughed and sat back down on the comfortable red velvet seats, pleased at the cushioning as the Rolls-Royce bumped over another pothole. She mulled over Dotty's theory. Marian might be very protective of her sister, but this all happened thirty years ago. It would be a strong grudge that would drive a woman to revenge after so many years. In any case, Annie had gone on to marry Walter and have three children. No, it didn't make sense that Marian would kill Sir James because of any of that old history. And it certainly wouldn't explain Bob's death. Bob didn't go back on any promises to Annie. Once more, Cressida's mind circled back to the coin and the life it could give the finder – especially if they found the whole hoard. Yet Annie had said how little Marian cared for money and her status after their father lost the family fortune. That chimed with Cressida's gut instinct that Marian wasn't the murderer, though she had to admit, she could understand why Andrews had seen the link between the murders and arrested her.

Cressida picked mindlessly at one of the upholstered buttons on the soft seats of the Rolls-Royce while Alfred smoothly navigated the country lanes between Mydenhurst and Willowmere. Cressida looked up and caught Alfred's eye in the rear-view mirror. Her tummy flipped, and not just because of the humpback bridge they'd just taken at some speed. It seemed Alfred, perhaps, wasn't paying much attention to the road either.

The three of them, with Ruby bouncing along on the seat next to Cressida, soon arrived in Willowmere and Alfred slowed the car down as they motored along the high street. Cressida churned over the motives of the historical society and still nothing – not horse food nor a new church roof – seemed as good a motive as killing one's husband for his new-found wealth that he hadn't seemed inclined to share. Perhaps they had found their murderer already? Perhaps Marian had killed Bob and Sir James, and she had been about to abscond from the kitchen at Mydenhurst when Cressida had found her this morning? But if that were the case, wouldn't she have scarpered as soon as she'd served breakfast? There had been nothing about her demeanour that had suggested she was guilty in any way.

'Did you manage to get Sebastian Reed's address?' Cressida asked, leaning forward again. She was more convinced than ever that Marian was innocent and that hunting down the man seen arguing with Bob on the morning that he died was necessary.

'Got it here,' Dotty said, waving a scrap of paper in her hand. 'Your father was awfully gracious and wrote it out for us. He had it from Mr Reed's society application. It says Elm View Villa, Chestnut Avenue, Willowmere.'

'Just a bit further on and then to the left, Alfred.' Cressida pointed onwards. 'Past the cottage hospital and round a bit further, if I'm not mistaken.'

A few minutes later and the Rolls-Royce was gliding down Chestnut Avenue. It was a smart residential road, lined with mature chestnut trees and with wide pavements either side. A nursemaid with a glossy navy-blue Silver Cross pram walked down one side of the street and nodded to the passengers of the Rolls as it pulled up outside Elm View Villa.

The house itself was a handsome, red-brick, Victorian semi-detached property, though it was well protected from its adjoining neighbour thanks to a high beech hedge. Cressida couldn't see any elm trees, but let that slide – not every house had a historical name and Elm View Villa was as nice a name as anything else, and rather suited the elegant house with its sweeping bay window and intricate stained glass around the wide, black-painted front door.

'Look, chaps, what say I just pop up to the front door and knock. You two stay here. As discussed, the three of us en masse can be a bit overwhelming. And harder to explain. At least I can act as a concerned daughter of Lord Fawcett and check in on him.'

'Right-oh,' agreed Alfred.

'Probably best not to let the whole street know what we're up to anyway,' agreed Dotty, keeping an eye on the nanny, who was hovering on the corner of the road, bouncing her charge up and down in the well-sprung pram.

'Be careful though, old thing,' Alfred added. 'Don't forget we're dealing with a murder or two here. Not saying this chap is the culprit—'

'In fact, he's more than certainly not,' butted in Dotty. 'As he wasn't there.'

'Not necessarily, sis,' Alfred disagreed. 'Chap might have received the invitation, realised Sir James would be at Mydenhurst Place, not RSVP'd but crept up to the house and administered the poison somehow, then accidentally ditched his bicycle in the dead of night as he rode home.'

'But Sir James died the next morning,' Cressida stated, and was surprised at Dotty's answer.

'Not all poisons are fast-acting. The killer may have used belladonna again, though he – or she, as poisons do tend to be a woman's tool – may have branched out and found something else hooky in the hedgerow. Or used less of it so it was slower acting.'

'This is from your books again, isn't it, Dot?' Cressida asked, brow furrowed as she realised that Dotty had a point.

'Yes. Nine times out of ten – or according to my own personal library, forty-three times out of fifty-one poisonings – are carried out by women. That's in crime fiction, of course, but these clever authors have to get their intelligence from somewhere.'

'Interesting.' Cressida would have winked at her friend, but she found winking deplorable, being that a wink was usually issued by a lascivious gent far too late into an evening. Instead, she wiggled an eyebrow at her and with that she slipped out of the Rolls and held the door open long enough for Ruby to follow her. Alfred's theory and Dotty's trivia did put a spin on whatever conversation she might have with Sebastian Reed.

Now she just had to hope he was at home.

And indeed, alive.

## 30

Cressida heard a scuffle behind the large black front door as she and Ruby stood patiently outside it. Well, not a scuffle exactly, but more of a commotion. There was definitely a crash and she caught a word that verged on the Anglo-Saxon, and there was a rhythmic clicking noise which only made sense when the large door swung inward to reveal a young man on a pair of crutches. Behind him, no doubt the cause of the crash and rather blue language, was the umbrella stand upended on the floor, umbrellas, parasols and walking sticks now splayed out on the red and black encaustic tiles of the hallway.

'Sorry about that,' the young man said, gesturing with one crutch to the mess behind him. 'Still not used to these blooming things.'

'Sebastian Reed?' Cressida asked and held out a hand, then felt bad as he had to readjust his stance, temporarily leaning one of his crutches against the glossy black door to allow him to shake it. Apart from his obvious discomfort due to the bandaged ankle, Sebastian Reed looked amiable, though his dark-brown hair was a haywire mess – long, but upright, as if he'd just had a shock from one of those new electric lamps. He wore round, thick-rimmed glasses and there was the unmistakable smell of mothballs – camphor – coming from the house behind him.

'That's right. And you are?'

'Cressida Fawcett. Lord Fawcett's daughter.' She placed a guarding foot in front of Ruby who was trying to go into the house. 'And this is my pug, Ruby.'

'Ah, Miss Fawcett. The Honourable Miss Fawcett even. Firstly, it is my pleasure to meet you.' He bowed his head a little, though it unbalanced him and he clasped his second crutch again, taking it back under his armpit from its resting place by the door. 'And secondly, do let your dog in if she wants to. She'll only come across MacTavish the cat who I'd be willing to bet weighs twice as much as her and will no doubt scare her right back into the garden. If you see something menacing and ginger, that's the fellow.'

'I see. Well, I don't want to keep you. But we, I mean my father and mother, were worried about you, so sent me, well, to check that you're all right.' Cressida crossed her fingers, which were concealed behind her back. 'After not showing up for dinner last night. But I see...'

'Ah.' Sebastian nodded. And looked down at his bandaged ankle. 'About that. Jolly painful it was too, and I was so looking forward to coming. An invitation to the great house, and an audience with Sir James, the most knowledgeable person about Saxon gold this side of Oxford, and I only go and catch a pothole, spring a puncture and end up twisted all over the place in a ditch.'

'Ouch.' Cressida could see that Sebastian was truly upset about the whole affair. 'But we hadn't even heard from you that you were coming. That's what worried Papa more, not that you didn't turn up, but that you didn't RSVP.'

'Yes, I did. By return. I was that excited.' Sebastian's staccato sentences popped out like firecrackers and his eyes widened to almost the full diameter of his thick-rimmed glasses as he continued. 'Oh dear, does your father now think me terribly rude? I did though, you see. I even paid for a telegram.'

A chill ran down Cressida's back. 'Sebastian, when did you reply?'

'As soon as I received the invitation. It's quite notable when a missive arrives from the pen of Lord Fawcett.'

'Yes, but when was that?'

'Yesterday morning.'

'Oh dear.' Cressida scratched her head and then looked down at where Ruby was making eyes at a rather large marmalade cat. 'I do apologise. I think perhaps one of the pups might have nabbed it from the hallway. Ruby here has six little ones at home, you see, and I distinctly remember fishing some sodden paper out of Dusty's mouth yesterday, at about elevenish. In fact, I remember saying that elevenses should be purely biscuit or cake based, not paper. Oh dear, I am sorry, Sebastian. One little mystery solved at least.'

'Oh well, I suppose it doesn't matter then that I didn't turn up either. Will you explain it all to your father for me? That I wasn't being rude?' Cressida nodded to reassure Sebastian, who carried on with his thoughts. 'What a shame though, to miss Sir James. Still, there's always tonight. But what's all this about another mystery you say?'

Cressida looked at Sebastian. He was either oblivious – despite his meeting with Bob on the morning of his death, which she still viewed as being highly suspicious – or an exceptionally good actor. And giving him the benefit of the doubt for a moment, and assuming he had nothing to do with Bob's death and the news of it hadn't reached him, he most certainly wouldn't have heard about the death of his hero, Sir James Colston. But benefit of the doubt wasn't good enough – she needed to press him further on what he was doing arguing with Bob just before his death. She reset her posture and smiled at him.

'Oh, just childish chitter-chatter. Quite literally. The funny thing about you sending a telegram to reply so quickly to Papa's invitation – and then it being chewed up by Dusty, and again, my apologies – is that someone said they saw you in Mydenhurst yesterday morning. About the same time that your telegram would have arrived. Odd then, that you paid for the telegram, yet then came to Mydenhurst anyway, don't you think?'

Sebastian Reed stared at his feet.

'Mr Reed? Sebastian?' she asked, hoping that she hadn't been too blunt too soon. *Still, in for a penny...* 'Papa says that many of the society were keen to find the gold. You, perhaps, more than most?'

Sebastian looked back up at Cressida. 'Gold? The Saxon hoard? Well, yes, of course, but what's that got to do with me being in Mydenhurst?'

'Were you hunting for it? Perhaps inspired by our gardener, Bob's, insinuation that he knew where the hoard was?'

'Was? Has he found it then? Lucky blighter.'

'Well... Look, I'm sorry, Sebastian, but Bob's dead. And you were seen talking to him shortly before he died. Having already paid for a telegram to tell Papa you were coming to supper, you were then yards away from my parents' house and could have RSVP'd in person.' Cressida shrugged. She'd given up on trying to be subtle. Best now to see what Sebastian Reed had to say for himself.

'I can see that looks odd.' Sebastian looked at his feet again, then back at her, meeting her gaze. 'And yes, you're right. I did think Bob Pringle knew more than he was letting on. He was a funny sod though, if you'll excuse the gardening pun. Always listening in to our society meetings at the Royal Oak. And your father asked him enough times if he wanted to join, officially you know, which I must say Lilian Catchpole and I were a little cautious about. But Mr Pringle seemed to like leaning up against the bar with Mr Rook the other side of it. As if he were more interested in Mr Rook than us. Though Rook would sometimes try and brush him off. Not that I noticed much, of course, not really being interested in that sort of thing, not when your father was doing an exceptional job of chairing the meetings.'

Cressida nodded, then asked, 'Did you arrange to meet him then?' trying to get Sebastian Reed back on track. *No wonder he hit a pothole*, she thought, *if his bicycle wheels wander as much as his train of thought.*

'Bob Pringle? Well, no, that would be a bit odd. Town folk making an assignation with a gardener, oh dear no. Not sure how I'd contact him really. But I did think he might know a bit about the gold. And you're right, I am interested in it. Stuff of dreams, isn't it?'

'I suppose so, yes—'

'I studied history, you know. I regret to say, not at the golden spires of Oxford, but I know a bit about it. But I don't care much for the dull stuff. I don't mind saying, but it did get a bit tedious at times at our meetings, what with Mrs White going on about her ancient holloways. Who cares where the animal pound once was, eh? Who wants to know where peasants used to build their stables for their old nags? Not when there's Saxon gold to talk about!' Sebastian Reed was getting quite excited now and had tried to run his hand through his wayward hair, but forgot he was holding onto crutches. When he was balanced again, he continued, 'So, when Bob Pringle bought us all drinks and hinted heavily that he'd found it, well... he suddenly became as much as an expert on its whereabouts as the great Sir James Colston. And I can tell you, that was a bit of a shock to the system.'

Cressida thought about what he was saying. Aside from the obvious, and distinctly un-charming, snobbery he was showing towards Bob, he had told her something useful; only Bob and Sir James ever claimed to know where the gold was. Could Sebastian have realised this and killed them both, either to force them to hand over the gold, or to stop them from revealing it to the whole society? Cressida felt a breeze blow through the chestnut trees and noticed a shadow cross over them as a cloud obscured the sun. She shivered, but knew she might be onto something, so pushed Sebastian further.

'If you didn't arrange to meet him, what brought you to Hell's Ditch yesterday morning?'

'That's where I was seen, eh? Who by? Never mind, doesn't matter. Nothing to hide. Oh, I know who it was!' His train of thought was as hard to cling on to as ever, but Cressida gave him what she hoped was an encouraging look. 'One of those nippers, wasn't it? One with the catapult? Pesky blighter.' Sebastian bent his head around and, balancing as best he could on one crutch, showed her the back of his neck and a small red welt on it. 'Got me with one of his ball bearings the little s—, well, excuse my French.'

'How did you know Bob would be there?' Cressida tried to keep him on track, while not landing young David Catchpole in it. She might not be a fan of the young hoodlum, but he had provided some good intel.

'No idea. Quite by chance. You see I'd sent the telegram and then, oh I don't know, it just sort of came to mind that it might be nice to go for a stroll up in Mydenhurst. One of those things where doing one thing puts the idea into one's mind. And it was a pleasant day and because I had the address forefront in the old thoughts, I decided it might be a good place to stretch the legs. And you see, if I ran into your father I could then always tell him personally that I was a big old yes to the dinner that night with Sir James and all that. So, I hoofed my way up the hill on the old bicycle and dropped it in a hedge by the church and did that walk down to the stream and that's where I saw Pringle.'

Cressida nodded. It wasn't the worst excuse she'd ever

heard for someone being somewhere. But then it wasn't the best either. Though from what she'd seen of Sebastian's wandering mind, she could well believe he might be the sort of chap who would have an idea and act on it, however odd it seemed. But so far, no mention of the argument that David witnessed.

'Did you ask Bob about the gold?' Cressida asked and Sebastian nodded enthusiastically.

'"Look here, Pringle," I said, "If you've found it, be a good chap and put us out of our misery and all that," sort of thing. I probably came over a bit grand but one has to, doesn't one, to the working classes.'

Cressida inclined her head to one side, thinking that one definitely *didn't*, but let him carry on.

'He just acted all tough guy, and told me to mind my own business, and I was about to remind him that I was a personal friend of your father, his employer no less, which is when we first got struck by that little brute and his catapult.'

'I suppose that could look like an argument,' Cressida said, more to herself, but Sebastian answered her.

'I wouldn't call it arguing, but as I said, one has to be a bit brusque with the lower classes otherwise they'll walk all over you. But we found common ground after the first few ball bearings pinged off our ears.'

'Oh, yes?'

'Lent Pringle a pen. Said he wanted to make a note to himself to have a word with someone and so I fetched my pen out of my pocket and saw as he wrote a note on his hand.'

Cressida let out an exhale. Of course... the word DeD... she knew what it meant now.

'He wanted to remind himself later to have a word with the Catchpoles?' she suggested.

'Exactly that. David and Daphne, you know with one of those squiggles in the middle for the and.'

'An ampersand,' Cressida murmured, realising that what

she'd seen and interpreted as DeD had been D&D. David and Daphne. 'So that's that mystery solved.'

'I'm rather helping you out with all this, aren't I?'

'Yes,' Cressida agreed and shot a look back towards the Rolls-Royce. There wasn't much else she thought she could glean from Sebastian Reed. He seemed to be a fairly hapless, slightly entitled, overly snobbish and incredibly unlucky sort of man. But was he a murderer? She needed to test his reaction to one last thing, so after an exhale and a deep breath, she told him that Sir James was also dead.

'Oh dear, oh dear,' Sebastian said, shaking his head. 'What he knew about Saxon burials and the kingdoms of Wessex and the weald.' He sighed. 'Such a loss.'

Cressida studied his face. Was he genuinely upset? She pushed on further, keeping a beady eye on his reactions.

'The police have arrested Bob's wife, our cook, Marian, for both the deaths.'

'Did they? Gosh. Rather glad of that pothole now.' He laughed at his own joke. 'Better a sore ankle than being poisoned over dinner, what?'

Cressida frowned, not just at the rudeness towards Marian, but because he seemed able to joke about it... almost as if the arrest of someone else meant he was in the clear. She rebuffed him firmly. 'I don't think she did it, actually.'

'Don't you? Why not? Heard somewhere that they weren't exactly love's young dream. Wife discovers husband has found a fortune, doesn't want him spending it on beer, so bumps him off.'

'And Sir James?' Cressida pushed, wondering if Sebastian's hastily formed theory extended to explain that murder, too.

'Saw something, or heard something. There's always collateral damage, isn't there? Murderer thinks they've got away with it, then someone says, "Oi, oi, I saw you with the poison bottle," and sure enough, they then get the chop too.'

'But Sir James didn't arrive until after Bob was found, that doesn't really make sense,' Cressida countered, though there had been a truth in what Sebastian had said – she had, sadly, solved murders that had been committed for that very reason.

'Well, something else then.' He leaned more heavily on one crutch so he could start counting off his fingers as he listed. 'Old rivalry, grudge against the rich, didn't want information getting out, mistaken identity, avoiding costly divorce...'

'Hmm, I'm not sure any of those apply.' Cressida frowned, though something he had said had started to pull one of those threads she tantalisingly visualised in front of her. She often felt that mysteries were like a cross stitch, with a perfectly presented front to the world but a tangled web behind. Or a frayed hem of a divine silk fabric, that once one thread was tugged, the whole piece could unravel, destroying the perfect weave. And one of those threads dangled now in front of her, yet she couldn't quite grasp it. Not yet, at any rate.

She looked back up at the man in the doorway of his mother's house. He didn't need the gold perhaps, but it's not to say he didn't *want* it. His excuse for being in Mydenhurst at the time of Bob's death was flimsy at best and he'd offered no alibi, save the twisted ankle, for where he was when Sir James might have been poisoned. Alfred was right, he might have cycled to Mydenhurst and poisoned Sir James before ditching his bicycle on the way home and causing his injury.

Cressida thanked Sebastian for his time, wished him a speedy recovery, assured him she'd send his apologies to her father and then clicked her fingers for Ruby to follow her back down the path to the road. She heard a clattering from behind the door as it closed behind her, a caterwaul-like screech and another rather fruity word. She uncrossed the fingers behind her back, hoping that the powers that be realised she did *not* wish him a speedy recovery – he deserved that swollen ankle for being such a prig with a ghastly, dated attitude to those around him in society. He may have looked up to Sir James, due to his class as much as his learning, but Cressida wouldn't be surprised if he'd considered Bob so far beneath him that bumping him off for the gold wouldn't have troubled his conscience at all.

In fact, he'd never even expressed any sorrow for Bob's death.

Cressida had to admit that Sebastian Reed had helped her work out what DeD meant on Bob's hand, but that didn't mean he didn't kill him. He, along with the other members of the historical society, was still very much a suspect in her eyes.

## 31

'Fancy some lunch? Seems like an age since our rather disrupted breakfast,' suggested Alfred as they motored back towards Mydenhurst in the smoothly gliding Rolls-Royce. Ruby had ably jumped in with Dotty in the back, but Cressida had felt the urge to sit up front with Alfred as he confidently managed the gears and acceleration of the enormous car.

'Gosh it does, doesn't it?' Cressida agreed, though she felt 'disrupted' was rather too mild a word to describe this morning's events over the breakfast table. 'How about we head to the Royal Oak? With no cook at home I feel bad expecting Mama and Papa to cater for all of us. And I hear the pub does an excellent sandwich.'

'Wait a moment.' Dotty leaned forward from her seat at the back of the Rolls, where she had been happily ensconced with Ruby on her lap. 'Isn't that Sergeant Kirby walking along the road? Pull over, Alf!'

Alfred pressed the brake pedal and the stately vehicle slowed to a stop. Cressida wound down the window and sure enough, she recognised her second-favourite policeman. Sergeant Kirby worked with DCI Andrews at Scotland Yard in

London and had been present at all of their investigations to date. In fact, it was Kirby and his note-taking that often helped Cressida get her mind in order as she filled Andrews in on her latest findings.

'Coo-eee! Kirby!' she called from the open window and the tall, red-headed officer stopped with a start.

'Oh, Miss Fawcett, good morning, or, ah, post-meridian. Good day to you in any case,' the young policeman flustered. He was wearing his helmet, the chin strap as usual looking like it was strangling him. But the buttons on his Metropolitan Police uniform glinted in the bright sunshine and he looked awfully smart as he stood by the side of the road. Cressida frowned though, noticing that the pavement had all but run out now that they were out of suburbia and the road was bordered by tall beech trees, with holly and scrub in between them. Not the safest lane to walk up, what with the blind bends and motor cars such as the Rolls whizzing past.

'We're heading back to Mydenhurst, need a lift?' Cressida gestured to the back seat of the car where Dotty was waving enthusiastically. Kirby bowed his head and waved.

'Don't mind if I do, miss, if that's all right with your chauffeur there?' Kirby said, starting to pull his helmet off his head, much to Cressida's relief at his poor garrotted throat.

'What ho, Kirby!' Alfred leaned forward over the steering wheel and waved.

'Oh, my apologies, my lord.' Kirby flustered and almost dropped his helmet, juggling it from one hand to the other as he tried to stop it from falling to the floor. With one last catch he got it firmly and then bowed his head again. 'Sorry, my lord.'

'Nothing of it, Sergeant, hop in!' Alfred said as Dotty opened the door from the back seat.

With helmet now off his head, and safely grasped, though face bordering on the beetroot, Kirby climbed in and primly sat himself down next to Dotty.

'Lady Dorothy,' he said, greeting her more formally, keeping his eyes facing forward as he did so. 'And Miss Ruby.'

Dotty laughed. 'Good spot of mine, what? Kirby, we were just heading to the pub, but where were you heading? The Fawcetts' home? Mydenhurst Place?'

'That's right, my lady,' Kirby said. 'DCI Andrews said he would be at your abode, Miss Fawcett, having left the suspect in custody at the station in Willowmere. He requested I join him, on account of it now being a double homicide within a restricted number of hours and in coincidental circumstances.'

Cressida looked across at Alfred, who was looking straight ahead at the road, but she could see the corner of his mouth turned up to reveal just the flicker of a smile. It was a little joke between them both that, when nervous, Sergeant Kirby could sound more like a thesaurus than a normal person. Cressida let herself linger just slightly longer, looking at the crinkle at the corner of Alfred's eye, then pulled herself round to address Kirby and Dotty in the back seat of the large, elegant car.

'We'll take you straight there, Kirby. Lickety-split. But tell me, what has Andrews briefed you?'

'Well, miss, I'm not sure as I should convey the chief's private missives.' Kirby stared at the top of his helmet, as if it could reveal an answer for him. Cressida felt his awkwardness and let him off.

'Not to worry, Kirby, you keep his missives to yourself. We'll all ask him together. We'll be home in a matter of minutes.'

'Come on, old girl,' Alfred said as he pushed his foot down on the accelerator and Cressida grinned at him. She knew, for once, he was talking about the car and not her.

Mydenhurst Place was quiet as the group motored back up the gravelled driveway. Cressida was so familiar with the diamond-paned windows, grand wooden front door and stone edging to the windows that she had forgotten the effect it sometimes had on newcomers. And Kirby was looking open-mouthed at ornamental roses and honeyed stone now as they pulled to a stop outside the front door.

'Here we are, home again. Bit of a mishmash, the old place,' Cressida said, getting out and then opening the back door of the car for the policeman and her dear friend – and dear pup. 'Ruby, I think you have parental duties to perform. No doubt those pups of yours will have caused yet more chaos in the interim. And I feel I may have to apologise on their behalf to Papa for the lack of young Mr Reed's RSVP.'

'Oh, is that where it went?' remarked Dotty as she climbed out behind the mushroomy dog. 'One little mystery solved.'

'That's what I said, chum.' Cressida grinned at her. 'But still one very big one to solve, sadly. I do wonder if a few more answers lie closer to home than perhaps I thought.'

'If you'll excuse me, miss,' Kirby interrupted. 'Thanks terribly for the kind convenience of the conveyance in a Rolls-Royce.' He paused briefly and Cressida wondered if he was about to stroke the car. 'But I must converse with the chief.'

'Go on in, Kirby. And I'm hot on your heels. You were awfully good and loyal not spilling the beans just then, but I'm sure Andrews won't mind me listening in as you do.'

'It being your home and all,' nodded Kirby.

'Exactly,' said Cressida with a raised eyebrow towards Dotty and Alfred. 'Coming?'

Cressida looked up at the beautiful house she called home. She couldn't bear the thought that two victims had now been killed within it and its grounds. And a much-loved family cook – family friend indeed – accused of doing it. For the sake of Mydenhurst Place, and the Fawcett family name, she had to find out what had really happened.

As the three friends and Kirby entered the house through the old oak door, Cressida could hear a murmur coming from her father's study and gestured towards it, getting to the door first and giving a brief knock before entering.

To her surprise there was no sign of her father, just DCI Andrews sitting at his desk. Cressida smiled, not just in greeting but at the oddity that for so many years it had been the other man in the framed photograph who she'd seen sitting in that spot, her father; yet here was Andrews, replacing the telephone receiver into its cradle and looking at home in the comfortable surrounds of Lord Fawcett's study.

'Ah, Miss Fawcett... and troupe, hello,' Andrews said, then, 'and Kirby, excellent. Glad you caught the early train.'

'And I was well met by Lord Delafield here as I was walking up Stammer Hill towards Mydenhurst, Chief.'

There was an awkward silence before Cressida moved forward and perched on the edge of the large mahogany desk.

'Now, Andrews, Sergeant Kirby here has been a paragon of policing virtue and hasn't breathed a word about whatever news he brings with him from London. But I rather thought, in the spirit of our usual investigations, you wouldn't mind if we sat in on your conflab and shared and shared alike.'

Andrews shook his head, but in an avuncular sort of way and gestured for the others to make themselves comfortable.

'I assume this means you have some information for me too?' he asked, and Cressida nodded.

'Yes, along with what might be classed as more local intel and gossip than cold, hard, facts, but I'll tell you what I know. But you first. Who was that on the blower?'

Once his look of exasperation had been eased off his brow by his fingers, Andrews told them.

'That was Dr North from the mortuary. The results of a full post-mortem examination on Sir James are still to be completed, however we have the initial findings.'

'I suppose one can't keep fingers crossed and hope it was merely a heart attack, can we?' asked Cressida, actually crossing her fingers in anticipation. She was to be disappointed though as Andrews answered her.

'I'm afraid not, Miss Fawcett. Sir James, as we suspected, was poisoned.'

'Oh dear, Marian really is in the soup, isn't she?'

Cressida thought Andrews would reply straight away, but he rubbed his beard and pondered a moment longer on the information he'd just been given by the pathologist. Finally he spoke, and all ears were on him.

'Possibly, though it was a different poison this time. Not belladonna, but taxine.'

Cressida looked blankly at DCI Andrews, but Dotty piped up from her perch next to the bookshelves under the window.

'Derived from the seeds and needles of the yew tree, if I'm not mistaken?' She pushed her glasses back up the bridge of her nose, then crossed her arms.

'Quite right, Lady Dorothy,' confirmed Andrews. 'Taxine is the poison derived from the yew tree. Though you don't need any fancy chemistry sets to achieve it. Just a few seeds from the berries or a handful of needles will do it.'

'But there are yews everywhere.' Cressida thought of the boughs she passed through to reach Hell's Ditch, the grand old trees of the churchyard, the graceful, needled branches of the trees near the pub... 'Which means it could have been anyone.'

'And more than that,' Andrews added. 'It's slower acting than belladonna, the poison used to kill Bob Pringle. Taxine can take hours to take effect.' He paused and looked at Cressida specifically. 'It's likely the poison wasn't in the porridge that Sir James ate this morning at breakfast. He was, in effect, murdered last night. Most likely right in front of all of us.'

## 32

Those in the study at Mydenhurst Place sat, or stood, in silence for just a moment more, taking in this new information. Finally, Cressida broke the stillness.

'How? How could he have been poisoned last night? We all ate together and I doubt Sir James would have popped out for a handful of yew needles.'

'Of course he didn't, Miss Fawcett. As for the how... I don't know yet but as with Mr Pringle, we think this must have been a purposeful poisoning.' He looked down at his notebook and carried on. 'Dr North had noted the other symptoms – his enlarged heart, for example – and I quizzed your maid Molly on Sir James's appearance and manner during the brief hours of the day before he died. She told me that he'd appeared quite out of sorts, confused as to where the breakfast room was, and looked as if he were having palpitations. She told me that he said he hadn't slept well, with a fast heart rate all night, which he'd put down to having a strong after-dinner coffee and too much sugar. However, this would all tie in with taxine poisoning.'

'I must say,' added Alfred, waving his pipe in the air as he gestured, 'I thought the poor man looked queasy and he was spouting nonsense before he collapsed. I concur with young Molly. Those do sound like his symptoms.'

'Dare I say it, a man of Sir James's age and size, well he would have succumbed to a poison that affects the heart, fairly rapidly,' continued Andrews. 'And Dr North found a seed stuck in between his teeth. He's having it tested, but he's putting money on it being a yew tree seed.'

'Gosh.' Cressida frowned, taking in all the information from DCI Andrews. 'That really does suggest he was done in. And the night before too. As you said, Andrews, under our very noses.'

'Until the full post-mortem is carried out we won't know the levels of toxicity, but it could have been anything up to twelve hours beforehand, placing the whole of last night's dinner in the frame.'

'Which would fit in with him feeling off all night, poor chap,' Alfred added, to the nods of the others.

'And perhaps exonerates Marian?' asked Cressida hopefully. 'Especially if the porridge pot does come back with no sign of poison in it?'

Andrews shrugged. 'Except that she prepared all the food the night before too. Simple enough to sprinkle some yew seeds into the plate of food destined for one person.'

'Horrible thought.' Cressida shook the idea off her. But Andrews continued, businesslike in his approach.

'And, Kirby, your news from London?'

Sergeant Kirby reached into his pocket and pulled out his notebook, carefully flicking over the pages until he found what he needed. He stood to attention and addressed his chief.

'Ah, yes, sir, so we found that Mr Pringle had indeed been into London and had visited Spink & Son, which is the nu... numis...'

'Numismatist?' Andrews helped him out.

'That's right, sir, the coin specialist on the Strand. He had delivered to their care, with receipts all in order, three gold coins, which they had identified as being of Saxon origin, from the early half of the seventh century AD.'

'That's what Papa said,' muttered Cressida, though waved an apology to Kirby and allowed him to continue.

'Said coins were evaluated and said to be worth upwards of one thousand pounds each.'

There were collective gasps from around the room and even DCI Andrews sat back in Lord Fawcett's chair and steepled his fingers in front of him.

'My, my,' he said. 'That is a fortune indeed. One thousand pounds each, you say?'

'I should imagine because of their high gold content,' Cressida explained. 'It's something Papa told me yesterday afternoon. The earlier the coin of that period, the more weight of gold it contained. And the hoard was rumoured to be coins from that era, so very valuable. Very, very valuable, it seems.'

'You could buy a house for that,' exclaimed Dotty.

'Or a whole terrace in some parts of the country,' added Cressida. Then she continued, 'And what did he do with the coins? You said there were receipts?'

Sergeant Kirby flicked a page over. 'The three coins are in the safe at Spink & Sons, with Mr Pringle apparently deciding to submit them to auction next month. A Mr Denton, who we spoke to at Spinks, said they were sending telegrams across the world to collectors inviting them to attend. The coins were going to be the headline act. They may well go for much more each.'

'The sale won't go ahead now, surely?' Dotty asked.

'Technically the coins now belong to Mrs Pringle, unless of course she's found guilty of his murder,' Andrews explained. 'And, of course, if your father can prove they were found on

Mydenhurst Place property then he has a claim to them. Anything else from the coin specialists, Kirby?'

The sergeant looked in his notebook. 'Only that Mr Denton recorded several phone calls that failed to connect, and when he checked he recognised the exchange number as being the same as the one that Mr Pringle had initially made the connection from.'

'Meaning?' Andrews prompted.

'Meaning there were calls from another number on the exchange here at Mydenhurst – the village, not Mydenhurst Place necessarily – to Spink & Son, though Mr Denton said he didn't talk to the caller. He's asking his colleagues who did.'

'Blimey,' Cressida said. 'Bob really did have a fortune. He had found more than just the one grasped in his hand.'

A clatter at the window made Dotty jump and Cressida looked over to where a jay was beating its wings against the panes of glass. In a moment it had regained control of itself again and taken off, but with the news about the value of the coins adding to that excitement, heartbeats were raised all around the room.

Andrews was the first to speak once there was an air of calm once again in the study.

'Well, this isn't looking good for Mrs Pringle, I'm afraid. A husband who suddenly came into wealth, now dead, and another man—'

'Who she knew from years ago, a man who all but left her sister at the altar,' Cressida said, begrudgingly adding fuel to Andrews' argument.

'What's this?' the chief inspector queried and Cressida told him about her visit to Annie at the Royal Oak and the history of the Marchmont sisters and their fading family fortunes. She finished off by adding, 'But I don't think it's Marian. She loved Bob, I think, and Annie wasn't hurt over Sir James's passing her over as she married Walter only a short while afterwards. I still think there's something in this gold. It is cursed in some way, even if I don't think there's an *actual* curse.'

'Sometimes all you have to do is believe in a curse, for it to work,' Dotty said sagely.

'But Bob wasn't a sentimental chap like that, from what I've heard,' Alfred countered. 'I don't think you can scare yourself to death while also accidentally eating deadly nightshade.'

'Speaking of the time and place of his death, we collared young David Catchpole earlier,' Cressida said, adding, 'because he was being a little pest and firing ball bearings at us with that catapult of his.'

'I'll inform the Yard,' Andrews said, with a raise of an eyebrow.

'Very funny, Andrews, but he led us on a bit of a wild goose chase, if that goose was a red herring... oh, you know what I mean. Catchpole Minor told us he'd seen Sebastian Reed arguing with Bob just before he died. So, we went to see Mr Reed—'

'Of course you did.' Andrews exhaled and crossed his arms in front of him.

'How could we not, Andrews?' Cressida shrugged. 'From a purely social level, we'd never received an RSVP or heard from him after he was invited here to dine.'

'Fine, fine...' Andrews mumbled, but gestured for Kirby to get his notebook out. Cressida couldn't contain her grin and let the corners of her mouth flicker upwards just a jot.

'Kirby, you can write down that I've solved the mystery of the writing on Bob's hand, and the welts on his neck that Dr North found...' She explained it all and delighted in the fact that Andrews nodded along as Kirby scribbled. She finished up with, 'So as I said, all a bit fishy in a red herring sort of way. And all explained by Mr Reed being quite eccentric, excessively snobbish and a bit of a twit.'

'Though plausibly not a murderer,' Andrews added. 'I agree

his alibi is weak and his excuse for being in Mydenhurst the morning of Mr Pringle's death is debatable in its reasoning, but there's very little chance he could have sneaked into the kitchen here while Mrs Pringle was preparing dinner and poisoned just Sir James's plate. And although he may have been near Mr Pringle at the time of his murder, if he had no way of giving him the poison then he might as well have been fifty miles away. If the poison was in the pickle, in that sandwich, then it still points to Mrs Pringle as the murderer.'

He exhaled a long breath, then looked back at Cressida, who was looking more than a bit downhearted. 'Good work though, Miss Fawcett. And I must say, the possibility of three thousand pounds is a hefty motive, whoever you are. And in more cases than most, poison is a woman's weapon of choice—'

'That's what I said,' Dotty chipped in.

'And what with Mrs Pringle being a cook, and with easy access to both nightshade and yew—'

'There's yew trees all around the churchyard,' Dotty interrupted Andrews again.

'And here in the grounds,' added Cressida glumly. 'I just don't think Marian did it. She loved Bob. There's something we're missing.' She looked out of the window, the wobbly glass making it hard to focus, though she could see what she thought was the jay that had battered the window now sitting on the lawn pecking at a worm.

'Money is quite enough motive for me,' Andrews replied.

'Only if we all believe that Marian didn't love Bob, or that she thought Bob didn't love her and would biff off with his fortune and leave her, of which we have no proof at all.'

'As much as we love Marian,' Dotty said gently to her friend, 'it does make sense that she thought Bob had found the hoard and was hiding it from her. She may well have heard from Annie or Walter about his winking at the society when he bought all those drinks. She might even have known about the coins lodged at Spink & Sons, as she said Bob had been going up to town, which was unlike him.'

'You think she was the one who put in the telephone call to them, the one that wasn't from Bob?' Cressida asked, and Dotty half shrugged and half nodded and then pushed her glasses back up the bridge of her nose. 'But if that was the case, and she knew Bob had enough gold safely stored in Spink & Son's safe, why kill Sir James?'

'As releasing more coins onto the market could devalue the three in London,' remarked Andrews. 'Flooding the market meaning the overseas collectors wouldn't have to bid so high on the ones at auction. Or, with the whole hoard discovered it could be declared national treasure and requisitioned by the British Museum on historical grounds. Either way, she was better off with the three coins heading to auction next month and no more said about Saxon hoards from a man like Sir James.'

Cressida crossed her arms and thought about it. 'Fine, well if that was true, she only overheard Sir James talking about the hoard at the table last night, so she would have had to conjure up a poison pretty quickly to then kill him. And didn't you just say that taxine is slower acting?'

'It needs no preparation though, Cressy. And it ties in with after-dinner sweets and coffees too.' Dotty tailed off, while Cressida stared out of the window again. She would have staked her life on the family's beloved cook not being a murderer. But Dotty and Andrews were right, everything was pointing towards her.

Cressida, however, remembered the woman she'd grown up with; hiding behind her skirts when the chimney sweep came with his scary bristly brushes, licking the bowl when sponge pudding was made, learning how to poach an egg so she could survive in her pied-à-terre with just the one gas ring... these weren't experiences one shared with a murderer.

'I just don't think it's Marian,' Cressida said with a sigh, turning back to face everyone. 'And I'll just have to prove it.'

## 33

'Cressy.' Alfred caught Cressida's arm as they left the study, leaving Andrews and Kirby to discuss their next moves.

'I know it sounds like I'm just not seeing sense, Alf, but—' Cressida retorted but realised that Alfred wasn't fighting her. 'What is it?'

It was Dotty, who had left the study just behind her brother, who spoke. 'It's not that we don't agree with you,' she said as Alfred gently let go of Cressida's arm. 'We really do. You know Marian better than Andrews does. And we all know that evidence – if you can call anything we have here actual evidence – can be twisted to fit whoever's narrative anyone wants.'

Cressida agreed, still feeling the warmth of where Alfred's hand had almost encircled her arm. She touched it without realising and then felt shy as she saw his eyes on her.

'Why are you all pink round the cheeks? What's wrong?' Dotty asked. 'You must be hungry, perhaps? George always tells me that I get particularly ruddy cheeked when I get hungry—'

'It's true, you do,' nodded Cressida, hoping Dotty wouldn't cotton on to the real reason she had blushed. What with everything going on she hadn't had the chance to really work out how she felt about Alfred, especially having him here with her, in her parents' house. She wanted to cosy up with Dotty in the library and dissect it all, as they would normally do over a martini or three in London. And she wanted to hear more about the gorgeous George and Dotty's wedding plans... but having a murderer in their midst, and finding out who it was, rather trumped all of that.

With that thought – of murderers – in her mind, a shiver ran down her back. She rubbed her forearms more vigorously, chilled now despite the warm weather and looked at her dearest friends.

'Call me a fool, chaps, but do you mind if I quickly check in on Mama and Papa? It must be horrible for them, having all this happen under their roof, so to speak, and now we know Marian was more of a friend than a cook, well, I would like to see them. Would you be dears and check in on the puppies? I worry that Suki and Hercules, not to mention the other little brutes, might be running amok somewhere, and if Papa catches them pawing their way through the rose beds again, there might be more untimely deaths here at Mydenhurst Place.'

'Of course, Cressy,' Dotty said and Alfred nodded.

'Just make sure you look after yourself.' He touched her on the shoulder and Cressida wanted nothing more at that moment than to lean in and have him hold her and tell her that everything would be all right. But instead with the stiffest of upper lips she nodded vigorously and bid them both goodbye, watching as they walked down the hallway, out towards the bright sunlight of the croquet lawn where six balls of porgi energy were rolling around between the hoops and balls.

Cressida shook herself back to action and took a look in the sitting room, but only a snoozing Ernest was in there. 'Avoiding your avuncular duties, eh, old boy?' she asked as she ruffled his ears, then she carried on in her search of her parents. She was sure that nothing could have happened to them, but she couldn't help but think of her father, especially, holding that cursed coin up to the light in his study. 'Stupid curse,' she muttered as she opened the door to the library. With relief she saw her mama sitting on one of the chintz armchairs, a copy of *Country Life* open on her lap as she flicked through the pages.

'The grey is still all wrong,' was the gist of her mother's conversation, though she'd hugged her daughter back as she'd wrapped her arms around her, stooping over her in her chair. Reassured her mother was all right, she kissed her goodbye, promised she'd think about the panels some more, though she muttered something about pink being the way forward, and left her to her magazine.

She next poked her head into the kitchen, but it was empty and eerie. It should have been filled with noise and bustle as Marian and perhaps Molly prepared lunch, but all she found were some cuts of ham on the cold shelf, netted against flies and most likely small dogs, and silence in the air. She was beginning to worry about the whereabouts of her father, what with the murder to daylight hour ratio in Mydenhurst at the moment, when Molly the maid told her that she'd seen Lord Fawcett head towards the pavilion with a spade and at least two puppies following him.

With perhaps less concern for her father's safety now, unless being gnawed to death by mischievous pups was next on the list of killings, she waved to her friends who were making themselves incredibly useful playing with the remaining four pups. With Ruby now at her at her ankles, relieved again it seemed for five minutes' peace away from motherhood, Cressida followed in her father's footsteps.

She remembered how yesterday she'd trod this same path, her mother behind her, looking for Ruby and Suki. She placed a bet with her dog now that Suki was behind this current escape, no doubt aided by Hercules. What her father's intention was,

was easy enough to guess. A spade, the place where Bob had been found with a thrymsa in his hand... a coin she now knew to be worth in the region of a thousand pounds... he was surely off in search of the gold, despite Sir James claiming it wasn't on Mydenhurst Place's land. The words of the curse filled her mind and Cressida tried to drown it out with more logical thoughts. But the simple warning kept repeating itself... *For he will eat the earth while the gold tastes fresh air.*

She hurried along and found herself frowning as she turned the corner of the pavilion and followed the path behind it and into the small copse of trees. She quickened her pace as she pushed her way past the odd errant branch, hurrying through the woods that hid Hell's Ditch and the fields from the formal gardens and house. She emerged into the long grass of the field and saw the old stone bridge, still standing after all these years. But there was no sign of her father.

'Papa!' Cressida called out, and Ruby even added a small yapping bark to not much effect. 'Papa!' Cressida walked up to the bridge and stepped up onto the stone flags that arched over the small stream. At the apex she stood and looked down at where Bob had fallen. A bird flew over her head, its call a pleasant distraction from memories of yesterday morning. And now another man was dead and she was still no further along in finding out who had killed them... and as another bird flew overhead she wondered if it was the same person at all.

'Ah, Cressy!' Her father's voice broke her concentration and she turned to see him, knee-deep in a hole, just the other side of the bridge. 'Thought I heard something. I'm down here.' He beckoned her over and she headed towards him, Ruby trotting along, her nose in the air locating her pups.

'Have you got two miniature dogs with you, Papa?' Cressida asked, and was relieved when he put his spade down and held up two small puppies.

'Yes, these two have been helping me,' he replied, putting

them down just as Ruby barrelled over to him. She greeted her offspring with huffs and licks and nose bumps. Cressida noted she got a less tactile welcome from her father, though he looked pleased enough to see her, and was grasping his spade with quite some passion. He was knee-deep in a rather large and damp hole, his fishing galoshes helping to keep him dry as the mud around him slipped and slid.

'What are you doing, Papa? You can't be looking for the hoard, can you?'

'The hoard? Heavens no!' Lord Fawcett looked quizzically at his daughter. 'You know James died before he could tell us any more about it.'

'Sorry, Papa, I just don't know what to think any more. And I feel an idiot saying this, but for a moment I thought the curse might have come true and... well, I'm glad I've found you. Alive and well. If quite muddy.' Cressida sat herself down on a tuft of grass next to her father in his galoshes. She crossed her legs rather than let them dangle into the hole. It did look rather muddy and she'd already ruined one pair of woollen trousers this weekend by sploshing into the stream.

'Quite so, quite so. Very much alive and well. And muddy. Well observed. And don't fret about curses. Even if we did believe in it, which enlightened folk like us don't, do we?' He raised his eyebrows at his daughter, who shook her head. 'Well, I don't have that coin. It's gone to the police station. But you're right to be concerned. All terribly hard on your mother this. No wonder she keeps going on about the panels. Something to take her mind off it all. You should go and help her again you know.'

'I will. But can I help you? Take these puppies off your hands at least?' Cressida reached out and stopped Hercules – for she had been correct in her bet with Ruby that the two errant pups had indeed been Suki and her bigger brother – from falling into the hole. 'And, Papa, what are you doing?'

'Digging, Cressida, digging.'

'Well, yes, I can see that. But why? If not gold, what are you digging for?'

Lord Fawcett stopped digging and leaned on the top of his spade. 'It was something else James said last night that reminded me...' He looked wistfully over the stream up towards the copse of trees.

'What was it, Papa?' Cressida asked, still with no clue as to why he was literally knees deep in alluvial soil.

'We were talking about our youth as old men do, you know when we came down here before dinner last night, and it reminded me of something that happened years ago. He was stepping out with Annie Rook, née Marchmont of course, did you know that?' Cressida nodded and he carried on, seemingly not interested in *how* she knew. 'Sad state of affairs how it all ended. Marian was most affected I think in the end but, anyhow, water under the bridge. But James reminded me of a time he lost his cufflink down here and of course back then, as a young buck, I thought yah-boo sad for you, but didn't put much effort into finding it for him. But now he's dead. Well, I don't know, foolish of me perhaps, but I want to find it. Send him off with it as it were. Close that period of his life.'

'Oh, Papa.' Cressida pulled Suki onto her lap and nuzzled the soft top of her head, realising the extent of her father's grief for his murdered friend. 'I hope you find it. You must think it buried quite deep...'

Lord Fawcett looked down at the hole as if seeing it for the first time. 'Oh, crêpes.'

'Oh, crêpes indeed, Papa.' Cressida smiled at him, remembering the trip to Paris her father and mother had taken her on when she was just a girl. She'd rather enthusiastically pronounced *crêpes* like *cripes* and so the family joke had begun.

'I hadn't realised I'd got quite so far.' Her father's voice brought Cressida back from the Left Bank of Paris to the here and now. 'James said he can't have been further than six feet from the edge of the stream on the north side of the bridge when he had Annie on his knee and... well, never mind. And like a treasure hunter with a map or a set of directions, I just rather leapt to it this morning and started digging. Leave me to it, won't you, poppet? I think I need to try another hole.'

Cressida pulled herself up and then leaned over and planted a kiss on her father's forehead. 'Right you are, Papa, but I'll send Mama down to find you if you're not in by teatime. And I'll take these mischievous pups out of your way too.' She scooped up Hercules to join Suki in her arms and rather trusted that Ruby would come to heel when she set off. She'd just turned around and was about to walk back to the house when she remembered the second part of her mission in coming to find him.

'Oh, Papa, I'm afraid I have some bad news too. DCI Andrews has heard from the pathologist in Willowmere. Sir James was poisoned with taxine.'

'Taxine?' Lord Fawcett leaned on his spade again. 'Yew tree berries?'

'The seeds more likely, it seems. And unless he accidentally ate them himself, it seems like it's murder again. I'm sorry.'

'Poor James. Makes you wonder if there *is* a curse surrounding that godforsaken gold after all.' He was cross and Cressida could see that he just wanted to be alone with his spade, his galoshes and his hole. She made to leave him, but then something he'd said earlier occurred to her. 'Papa, what did you mean by Marian coming out of it the worst?'

'Hmm?' Lord Fawcett looked up from his spade. 'Oh, that. Well only that Marian was disinherited when she married Bob.'

Cressida was about to shrug and leave him to it, when the golden thread that had been dangling in front of her these last couple of days showed itself again, and she questioned her father further. 'But what did Marian marrying Bob have to do with Annie being passed over by Sir James?'

'Ah, well, that's because back then, while Annie was stepping out with James, Marian had a beau of her own on the scene, and it wasn't Bob.'

'Who was it then?' Cressida asked, juggling puppies.

Lord Fawcett's answer took her quite by surprise.

'Marian was being courted by a young man from a family down in the West Country. From a brewing family, I believe. None other than our very own Walter Rook.'

## 34

With another entreaty from her father to go and help her mother, Cressida left him in his knee-deep hole on his surely futile mission to find his dead friend's lost cufflink. His words about Marian and Walter Rook were ringing in her ears.

'Walter had been Marian's beau before he was Annie's,' Cressida told the dogs in her arms and by her feet. 'But what does that mean?'

'What does *what* mean, Cressy?' Dotty asked as she rounded the corner of the pavilion, a puppy in each arm, almost bumping into Cressida.

'Oh, Dot, for a moment there I thought you were Ruby talking back to me!'

'She's a darling dog and no doubt highly talented, but I like to think I'm slightly better read,' Dotty joked and Cressida nudged her as they both walked back around the pavilion.

'Absolutely. Even with your influence I think the only paper with words written on it that Rubes is interested in is the newspaper the butcher uses to wrap up the sausages.'

'Fair point,' chuckled Dotty. 'But anyway, what were you muttering about to yourself?'

Cressida told her friend about the revelation from her slightly batty Papa.

'Hmm,' agreed Dotty. 'Most interesting. Something you'll be sharing with Andrews?'

'Of course, though I'm famished. Aren't you? And Alfred must be. He suggested lunch aeons ago and I'm afraid I rather got carried away with this whole investigation. Why don't we take the pups with us, leave Mama and Papa in peace, and head to the Royal Oak for a sandwich. We can try and put all the pieces of this whole maddening affair together and I'd quite like a word with Walter Rook, too.'

Alfred took little to no convincing that they should head to the pub in the village and with the clock hands now pointing to long past midday, it should at least be open this time. And it was. As the Rolls-Royce pulled up outside the pub and parked, several heads who were drinking pints of beer on the tables outside turned to look at such a fine motor car.

Annie Rook came out of the stable door bearing a tray of pints and only once she'd placed it on the table in front of several men did she wave. Cressida waved back.

'Be with you in just a moment,' Annie called over as Cressida and her friends found themselves a table to sit at, happy to once again be outside in the spring sunshine. Cressida pulled Ruby up onto the seat next to her, glad that enough of the greengrocer's hamper was intact from her journey down from London to house the smaller pups. It was placed, with the puppies curled up in it, and asleep for once, on the grass next to their table.

'Marian and Walter were a couple before Annie and Walter were?' Dotty clarified once they'd all made themselves comfortable, and Cressida could see the mental cogs whirring as she furrowed her brow. 'If she and Walter are still in love, it does give her another motive to kill Bob, but if that is the motive, and it's not about the gold, then why would she murder Sir James?'

Cressida shrugged. '*If* she murdered either of them. And I don't know how she might feel about Walter, or her sister now, but it's interesting that Annie over there didn't mention she'd ended up with Marian's chap when she was being so candid about their fall from society's grace and all that. She rather glossed over it, come to think of it. Just said that Walter was there to pick up the pieces after Sir James passed her off.'

Alfred placed his finger to his lips, and Cressida shushed just as Annie approached.

'Oh, look at those adorable little... what are they actually?'

'They're porgis. Or cogs. I'm not sure which really. But Ruby here is the proud mother.'

'I remember meeting *you,* dearie,' Annie said, giving an appreciative Ruby a rub on her silken head. 'Lunch?' she then asked, dusting her fingers down her apron.

The three friends nodded most vigorously and set about ordering sandwiches, though Alfred was tempted by the pie. Once Annie had taken their order – adding three pints of best bitter to it too, and cooed a bit more at the hamper of sleeping puppies, but refused Cressida's invitation to take at least two off her hands – their conversation resumed.

'I would have ordered it, the pie that is, if I had my camera on me,' said Alfred, resting his elbows on the table. 'Pinky Stapleton had the idea of starting a Mutton Pie Club newsletter with a "pie of the month" photo competition. You two would make a smashing backdrop to a picture of a good old country pie.' He leaned back and looked at Cressida and Dotty through his fingers, shaped like a camera's viewfinder.

'Honestly, Alfred, your dedication to that club is astounding.' Dotty shook her head. 'Though speaking of pie, it does remind me of that time you met the Prime Minister and called him the Pie Minister, Cressy.'

'Oh yes, poor Mr Baldwin, not my finest hour.' Cressida smiled to herself, and admired the grin that had spread across Alfred's face, then became more alert as she saw Walter Rook himself emerge from the dark interior of the pub.

'Look, what's he holding?' she whispered to her friends.

Alfred craned his neck to look past his sister and Cressida. 'Looks like a rather thick brown envelope, and he's passing it to one of those chaps who have been eyeing up the Rolls since we arrived.'

'A fellow car enthusiast, perhaps,' suggested Dotty, who had tried as subtly as possible to turn around and have a look. 'He's just got into the only other motor here.'

'Slipping that envelope into his pocket as he went,' confirmed Alfred. 'If you ask me, that chap was a leg-breaker.'

'A what?' Cressida and Dotty looked confused.

'You know, a debt collector,' Alfred said, and then as two sets of inquisitive eyes stared at him, continued. 'I've seen them at some of the joints we visit in town sometimes. It's standard practice when a business like this owes money. The collection agent will sit and have a drink, not threatening violence or legal retribution, but plain old shame and embarrassment, until the debt is paid. Did you see his jacket?'

'No, he wasn't wearing one,' pointed out Cressida.

'Exactly. Next step would have been for him to fetch it from the motor and put it on, no doubt with the words DEBT COLLECTOR sewn in large letters on the back.'

'Gosh, Alfred, you are cosmopolitan,' Dotty said in some sort of awe to her brother.

They stopped talking as Walter appeared again, this time with their sandwiches on a tray. Without mentioning the potentially embarrassing encounter they'd just witnessed, Cressida started up a conversation.

'Mr Rook, I'm so sorry about Marian.'

'It's like I told you yesterday, it'll be someone from that

society, after the gold, what did it. Not Marian.' He took the plates of sandwiches off the tray and set them down just a touch too heavy-handedly on the table, the plates clattering as he did so, before swiping the tray back under his arm. The debt collector can't have put him in a good mood, but Cressida wondered if it was talk of Marian that had caused this reaction.

'I know, I agree,' Cressida continued. Her stomach rumbled but she held off from biting down on the delicious-looking sandwich for a moment more. 'I spoke to her this morning just before she was arrested and she said you were at Mydenhurst last night. Is there anything you saw that looked suspicious? Did you see Sir James at all?'

'She did, did she?' Walter sucked his teeth, then answered. 'Suspicious? No. Annie brought a basket of bits and bobs to Marian, as you women do, though how some bread and pickle would help a woman in grief, I don't know.'

'Bread and pickle?' the voice of his wife behind him startled Walter. 'It was more than that. And I'm glad we did as we had some of that good whisky in return, didn't we, Walt?'

'What else did you bring? It's not like we...' Walter stopped himself from going further.

'Just this and that. Some flowers, some pickle as you say, a box of Turkish Delight, which Sir James and I used to tuck into with gusto back when—'

'Well enough of that.' Walter gestured for her to place the drinks she was carrying down on the table and move back inside. 'We'll add these to your father's tab.' He nodded at Cressida and then left the friends to it.

'Well, that was awkward,' Dotty said, having swallowed a bite of her sandwich and washed it down with a ladylike sip of beer. 'Walter must think Annie still holds a candle for Sir James.'

Cressida nodded. She was listening, but she was also thinking. And the thread was dangling now in front of her, so close she could almost catch it.

'Annie brought the Turkish Delight for Sir James... but she would have had no truck with Bob...'

'It still makes no sense.' Dotty sipped her beer and held her hand in front of her mouth as she burped. 'Oh, pardon me. Very unlike me. I'm so glad George isn't here to see that!'

'He'd love you all the same,' Cressida said, though her mind was elsewhere.

'You're thinking, aren't you, Cressy?' Alfred said, picking at the crumbs left on his plate having inhaled his sandwich the fastest of the lot. Helped, of course, by Ruby who had been present for some of the errant pieces of ham that had fallen out.

Cressida nodded and took a sip of her beer. She was thinking. The gold was such an obvious link between the two deaths. Was it maybe too obvious?

She couldn't doubt the motive some might have over that much money, but she felt there was something else going on. Something from a much more recent past than gold buried from marauders centuries ago. And something, perhaps, much more personal.

## 35

Once the sandwiches had been eaten and puppies recovered from under several picnic tables, thanks to a newly gnawed hole in the wicker hamper, the three friends returned to Mydenhurst Place. DCI Andrews and Kirby had apparently left to interview Marian, and the house was quiet. Cressida wondered if her father was still knee-deep in mud down by the stream, but her thoughts became more occupied by a small escapee – Fortnum, she thought – who was currently bounding off towards the rose beds. Luckily Alfred had seen him too, and with a chirpy salute to Cressida, ran off after the little blighter.

'Have you thought about what to do with them all?' Dotty asked, peeling a rather over-affectionate Dusty off her woollen jumper which had been nibbled mercilessly, but with adoration, by the young pup.

'Wedding present or two, chum?' Cressida asked and was almost surprised when Dotty didn't say no automatically.

'George suggested cats, of course, as he's so used to seeing them in Egypt, but we'll have to find somewhere to live first. Chelsea is lovely, isn't it?'

'Oh yes.' Cressida's heart leapt at the thought of her best

friend living so close to her. She'd always rather assumed she'd lose Dotty to some rambling estate in Northamptonshire or somewhere equally far from civilisation, but to have her in London would be an absolute treat. 'That would be splendid if you and George could get a place in Chelsea. Or Kensington. Though will you often be on digs, do you think?'

'I should imagine so,' Dotty said, though she didn't sound hugely excited. 'It's not that I don't want to be with George, of course I do. But Egypt... and he's talking about the Emirate of Transjordan too, and Petra.'

'How romantic.' Cressida sighed, imagining the rust-red stone and desert sands as she watched the pale, watery sun start to sink over the chimneys of Mydenhurst Place.

'Promise you'd come?' Dotty said. 'Both of you?'

Cressida looked over to Alfred, who had returned to the makeshift puppy pen with Fortnum and was now sitting there on the lawn with Ernest's muzzle on one thigh and several puppies snoozing in the crook of his arm. He looked at her and smiled. Adventures and independence it seemed could happen, even with a chap on one's arm. Cressida smiled back at him and answered her friend.

'Oh, we promise. Don't we, Alfred?'

Cressida and Dotty spent a little while talking more of her wedding and in which part of London she and George should find a cosy mews house or mansion house apartment. They stretched their legs, walking while talking, keeping an eye on the tearaway pups on the lawn, and laughing at Alfred who'd decided to take a nap on one of the old deckchairs he'd found in the pavilion, his handkerchief over his face to cut out the low evening sunlight.

As their promenade progressed around the edge of the lawn they found themselves by the library and while mid-sentence explaining the reason behind her love for the new range of fabrics at Liberty, a sharp rat-a-tat-tat on the window made Cressida jump. Cressida looked, and saw her mother waving at them both from inside, gesturing them to come in, while also miming drinking a cup of tea. With a final glance over to a snoozing Alfred, Ernest at his feet, and six small puffballs of pups lying on and around him, Cressida, Dotty and Ruby headed inside to take tea with Lady Fawcett.

Tea had indeed been offered, but with no cook and a rather exhausted maid, Cressida had found herself back in the kitchen, searching out the tea caddy and warming the pot. Molly had taken over once she'd brought the pups in from the garden and settled them all in front of the range, which was pumping out heat, much to the puppies' delight. Cressida saw to their supper of sardines and beef jelly and followed Molly through to the library, where Dotty was sitting with Lady Fawcett, Ruby on her lap, in front of the fire.

Cressida could have sworn she'd caught the tail end of their hastily concluded conversation and she was sure she'd heard both her name and Alfred's, but with other things – such as murder – on her mind, she let it go. Once tea was poured and biscuits handed round, Cressida told her mother all about the day's events and wasn't surprised that she didn't bat an eyelid when told about her husband literally digging himself into a hole, or about the misplaced RSVP from Sebastian Reed – these two occurrences seemingly nothing more than commonplace in a house like Mydenhurst Place. Lady Fawcett was interested in the revelation about Marian and Walter Rook, though, but could shed no light on it as she was introduced to Lord Fawcett after his time at university and hadn't been in Mydenhurst during Sir James and Annie's courtship.

'How hard on the poor woman though, to be passed over due to her family losing its money. I shan't speak ill of the dead, but I do hope that James had other reasons. He never took a wife at all in the end, so perhaps he just preferred the bachelor lifestyle to marrying, and it was all just a coincidence.'

'There have been quite a few coincidences over the last couple of days,' Cressida said.

Dotty nodded. 'Coincidences are the first things sleuths in the books look out for,' she added. 'And here we have two poisoned men both found with a highly valuable gold coin on their person.'

'More than that,' added Cressida, 'there's a chance that they both knew where more of that gold was.'

'But were killed before they could unearth it, or reveal it,' concluded Dotty.

'Which means you still think one of the historical society is the murderer?' Lady Fawcett asked. 'Your papa would be so upset. He'd hate to think he shared historical titbits with a killer.' She picked up a shortbread biscuit from the tray that Molly had brought in and nibbled on it.

'I just don't know, Mama.' Cressida sighed and sank further down into the chintz sofa, feeling more than a little defeated. 'The gold and its allure... it has to be, doesn't it?'

'It's certainly a jolly good motive. From what you've told me almost everyone in the society, except that poor chap over in Willowmere, has a pressing need for more money. And not just the society. I know they would be the ones who knew more about it, but then there's Dr Catchpole, and,' she dropped her voice to a whisper, 'even a darling girl like Molly might have her head turned by that much money.' She looked at the half-eaten biscuit the maid had just brought in, pulled a face and put it down.

'And what a fortune that hoard would bring. Even finding one or two coins, as Mr Pringle did, would be life changing,' wondered Dotty.

'Gold...' said Cressida, resting her chin on her fist and looking over to the panels. The gold of their frames glinted in the glow from the fire. The framed paintings definitely needed a new colour behind them. 'Behind them...' whispered Cressida to herself, then got up from the sofa, causing Ruby to look up from her place on Dotty's lap, as her mistress crossed the room and stood in front of the panels.

'Oh, will you finally choose a colour for them?' begged Lady Fawcett, but Cressida wasn't listening. She placed her palms flat on the panel and looked at the golden frames of the pictures, still catching her eye with their glittering surrounds.

'The gold is on the outside,' she whispered, unhooking the catch that kept the panels closed shut. 'And they hide the goddess of truth within...'

'Yes, poor Aletheia, hidden behind there. I suppose we could put the Canaletto somewhere else as she so often gets hidden behind those panels.'

'The truth is literally hidden by the gold...' muttered Cressida again as she turned on her heel, energised, with the glint from the fire's flames now dancing behind her eyes too. 'Dotty, we've been looking at this all wrong. The deaths are *due* to the gold, but not *because* of the gold. The truth is under the gold, or behind it... well, you know, hidden by it. Gosh, Dotty, I've been so thick. It's all there in front of us. Just hidden by the gold. The birds by the stream, "that it should come to this", a shotgun wedding all those years ago, those pickle jars and the Turkish Delight known to be his favourite! And, of course, she's being framed...'

'Is she always like this Dorothy?' Lady Fawcett turned to Dotty, who nodded.

'Yes, but it's a good thing, Lady Fawcett. She's only gone and cracked it, I'll wager.'

Suddenly Cressida's face fell, and the thread she'd been pulling, that one she'd been trying to grasp to unravel the case, came loose and it was as if the whole tangled mess fell on her. She batted it off, mentally, though she did get odd looks from her mother and Dotty, and she realised she really had waved her hands in front of her face.

'Wasp,' she lied, trying to explain herself, then she looked out of the window, the realisation that the sun had long since set suddenly coming upon her. 'Where's Alf? And Papa? Could he have already gone to the Royal Oak?'

'Yes, dear. Alfred popped his head round the door when you were in the kitchen earlier and let me know that he had very kindly offered to drive your father there. I knew your father was keen to go. The society thought it best still to meet, to raise a glass to James and, of course, Bob too. No doubt they'll touch on the gold as well. Dear Alfred. I think it was just to show willing to your father, really. They had been holed up in his study again just beforehand. He is so dishy, isn't he, darling?'

Cressida rolled her eyes at her mother, but otherwise ignored her. 'And Andrews is in Willowmere do we think? Mama will you do me the most enormous favour?'

'Look after the puppies?' Lady Fawcett said, a look of resignation on her face.

'Yes. That. And put in a telephone call to Andrews at Willowmere police station. Ask him to meet me at the Royal Oak in the utmost haste.'

'Utmost haste? What on earth are you worried about, darling? You won't miss much at the meeting and I'm sure dear Andrews isn't that interested in charcoal manufacture in sixteenth-century Wealden towns.'

'Please, Mama, he'll understand. And, Dotty, good thing I have my little motor car. Which is fine for the two of us, as long as you don't mind holding Ruby?'

'What is the rush, darling?' Lady Fawcett went from exasperated to sounding quite parental. 'Tell me.'

Cressida took a breath. Time was of the utmost essence, but she owed it to her mother to explain. Or at least try to explain as quickly as possible.

'Mama, we need to get to the Royal Oak before something terrible happens.'

'Terrible?'

'Yes, terrible. Unless we can stop them, there's going to be another murder – I'd bet an entire hoard of Saxon gold on it!'

## 36

Cressida and Dotty found coats and hats and in a matter of minutes they were seated in the little red Bugatti that Cressida loved so much and valued above all things, saving perhaps her darling pup, her even more darling friends, her independence... And perhaps now Alfred. The pieces of the puzzle had come together in her mind like a decorating scheme fitting perfectly together.

However, despite Dotty's repeated requests to find out what was going on, Cressida couldn't explain it with the roar of the engine and the whoosh of the wind between them. But she had figured it all out. Marian wasn't the murderer, that was for sure, but because of her, someone else may well die this very night unless Cressida could get there quickly enough.

She pressed her foot down on the accelerator pedal and steered the car as best she could down the now dark and treacherous lanes that ran between Mydenhurst Place and the Royal Oak.

The route to the Royal Oak was quick, despite the darkness that had now settled across the county. Within a few minutes of first clambering into the car, the two friends and Ruby were fumbling with door handles and climbing out again, having arrived at the pub. The headlight bulbs and engine ticked as the car cooled and as Cressida closed the door of her car behind her, she was relieved that all seemed normal from out here. The oil lamps and fire burning in the old inglenook of the pub shone through the windows and Cressida could see the historical society sitting at their usual table, her father and Alfred with them. She reached for the latch handle of the pub's door, but felt a grasp to her arm.

'Cressy, please. Tell me what we're heading into?' Dotty pleaded with her and Cressida let her shoulders sag as she relented.

'I don't really know, Dot, and I don't know how dangerous it might be. You don't have to come in with me.' There was a snuffle at her feet. 'And neither do you, Rubes.'

'Don't be a booby, Cressy, of course I'm coming in. But who is it? And who do you think will be killed?'

Cressida was about to tell Dotty, when the door opened abruptly, pushing them both back into the pathway.

'Oof, sorry,' a man in his cups pushed past them, not someone they recognised, but as he staggered out into the night, they were left exposed by the open door. Alfred caught Cressida's eye and unaware of her suspicions, waved enthusiastically. She waved back. Then with a shrug of apology to Dotty, Cressida walked into the Royal Oak.

'What ho, Papa,' Cressida said, pulling off her gloves as she and Dotty walked towards the round table at which the historical society were sitting. She glanced towards the bar as Alfred stood up and pulled over a chair for her, and fetched another one for Dotty, too.

'Hello, poppet,' Lord Fawcett replied. 'How lovely to see you. Of course, I forgot, Dorothy, do forgive me. You're a history buff too, aren't you? Should have invited you first off, so sorry.'

'Not at all, my lord,' Dotty replied, still looking and no

doubt feeling a bit discombobulated by the whole situation she found herself in. Cressida sat next to her, and after one more glance over towards the bar, took in the faces around the table. Next to her father, in a clockwise direction, was Lilian Catchpole, with a pen and notebook in front of her, no doubt taking minutes, then Madge and Percy White, followed by Sebastian Reed, with his crutches propped up next to him and his hair as haywire as it was earlier, then Reverend Dunn, then Alfred and Dotty and finally Cressida herself. The whole historical society. The very reason for the murders that had happened over the last couple of days.

'Papa, and everyone, we're so sorry to interrupt,' Cressida started then whispered to her father, 'Papa, are Walter and Annie Rook here tonight?'

'Yes, they're out back, I should imagine. Quiet night tonight and they can trust us not to reach behind the bar and help ourselves.'

Cressida creased her brow.

'What is it, Cressy?' Dotty hissed over to her. 'Is it Annie? Was she cross at Sir James?'

'Shall we continue?' Lilian Catchpole said rather pointedly, opening her notebook. 'Madge, I believe you were telling us about some arrowheads you found in that newly tilled field behind you?'

'Yes, well—' Madge started talking when suddenly a crash of broken glass and crockery from the kitchen interrupted them all. Cressida stood up, her chair clattering to the ground behind her, much to the bemused look of the rest of the table. All except Dotty, who looked at her more quizzically.

'No need to panic, Miss Fawcett,' Percy White said. 'Walter's always knocking things over.'

'I'll... I'll just go and check...' Cressida said, gesturing towards the bar as she stepped away from her chair.

'Cressy?' Dotty asked, the tone of worry in her voice alerting Alfred.

'Cressy?' he added his own query to her as his sister scooped up Ruby and got up to go to Cressida's side.

'Come with me,' she whispered to her friends, and then smiled at her father and the others. 'Huge apologies!' She clasped her hands together in a prayer-like way, asking for their forgiveness, then edged towards the bar and the small door at the end of it that led to the back room.

She could hear muttering behind her from the society, and she hated embarrassing her father like this, but she was sure something untoward was going on in the room behind the bar.

'Chaps, I'm going back there, to see what the crash was,' Cressida said, opening the hinged part of the bar that usually kept the punters firmly on the other side.

'Us too then,' Alfred said and Dotty nodded, though she held Ruby tightly to her chest as they all edged along behind the bar.

'I hope no one thinks we're pilfering the sherry,' Dotty whispered, glancing back towards the historical society. Cressida looked too, darting her eyes over the society. Luckily her father and his friends seemed engaged again in discussing arrowheads from times gone by.

She turned back to the task in hand. They could only move in single file behind the bar, and having got to the door, it was up to her to carefully turn the knob and open it. She did so, and gesturing for quiet from her friends she hovered at the threshold, trying to take in what she could see. Not much, was the answer, for the back room – a kitchen, Cressida thought – was gloomy, the only light coming from the doorway in which she stood. She took a deep breath, but something felt off. She knew who she was looking for. The real person behind the deaths, but all of a sudden she couldn't think straight. She held onto the doorframe, needing the support of it, and turned to face her friends.

'What is it, Cressy?' Dotty whispered and Alfred raised an eyebrow too, while reaching into his pocket for his pipe. As he brought it out a box of Bryant & May matches fell from his pocket and Cressida watched as they seemed to tumble in slow motion to the damp floor of the pub. Alfred leaned down to pick them up and Cressida realised why she was feeling so woozy.

'Alfred, don't you dare light up. In fact, oh no...' Cressida looked around her at the oil lamps that were giving the pub such a warm glow, and the open fire that crackled and spat just behind the table where the whole historical society were sitting.

'Go back, both of you! Open every window and door you can and put out the lights. Dotty get everyone out, including you. I've got to go and turn off this gas!' She shoved her friends away from her and, covering her nose and mouth with her sleeve, she made her way as best she could into the dark of the kitchen.

'Cressy, no!' Alfred shouted, realising what she was doing, but before he could stop her, she was gone, slamming the door behind her.

Cressida knew her friends would try and stop her from being so hot-headed but if she didn't find out where this gas was coming from, they'd all be toast. Her darling papa and his friends included. She could feel the soft cashmere of her jumper clenched across her face as her eyes adjusted to the only light now in the Royal Oak's kitchen – that of the moon coming in through the small, cottage-like windows. She edged forward, hoping against hope that she could survive on her one breath until she could find the gas leak.

Her eyes adjusted to the soft silvery light and a motion outside the window caught her eye. She couldn't focus, the whole room was starting to spin but she was sure she recognised the figure caught in the moonlight – the figure holding up a key to the window, goading her, telling her that without doubt the back door that would have led her to life-giving fresh air, was locked. Cressida turned back to the kitchen, falling and bumping against the countertop as she lurched towards the oven. The door to it was open and Cressida could hear the hiss of the gas and even through her sleeve she could smell the sulphurous fumes of it. She moved closer, using the arm not flung across her face to help her find her way. She was almost there, the hissing getting louder and the room around her feeling more and more blurry, when her foot hit something soft yet solid. Gripping the counter to keep herself upright she peered down and through the swirling lights and fog on the brain she recognised the shape of a body lying on the ground.

*Oh no...* Cressida clenched her eyes shut, her sleeve still clamped over her mouth and nose. But this was no time for squeamishness. She had to save the others, the pub, herself too... with this resolve, she opened her eyes and picked her way carefully over the body, framed as it was by broken glasses and plates – the sound she must have heard only moments ago – and she reached inside the cold oven. Her fingers trembled as she felt for the switch. She had it, she was sure of it, her fingers on it... then nothing, and she fell to the floor as the room around her turned to black.

## 37

'Cressy! Cressy!'

The voice sounded like it was far away and then suddenly very close, but Cressida's head ached and she didn't want to open her eyes. It was so much nicer being sleepy and she was more than happy just—

'Cressy!' Her name was followed by a sharp sting to her cheek, which really did wake her up.

'Ow,' Cressida said, raising a hand to her face with what felt like the same effort needed to raise Tower Bridge. 'Whattedy-oudoatfor?'

'She's coming round,' the serious voice said, and Cressida recognised it. Gentle but firm, head-girl-like in its tone, the type of voice you'd like to listen to when you fell asleep... 'Cressy!'

'What?' Cressida finally opened her eyes to see what the fuss was about. A conker-coloured bob moved to one side and a benign, sandy-haired face appeared instead.

'Cressida?' Lord Fawcett placed a hand on her shoulder. 'You scared the life out of me.'

'And me,' Dotty said, coming back into focus next to Lord Fawcett.

Cressida started to put it all together. The historical society, the pub, the clatter of plates, the gas...

'Oh, Annie? Is she... alive?' Cressida knew who had been on the floor in front of the oven. She was *always* going to be the third death. She should have been the second... The memory of those last few moments of consciousness before she blacked out came back to her and she could picture the face of the figure in the window. And the rope that was around Annie's wrists and ankles. She must have pulled over the stack of plates and glasses to try and get help. That crashing sound had alerted them, and hopefully saved her life. Saved all their lives. If the gas had penetrated through that closed kitchen door through to the bar, the whole pub would have exploded like war-time ordnance.

'Dr Catchpole says you got there in the nick of time. She's inhaled quite a bit of gas, but she's going to be all right. But you put yourself in danger too, Cressy.' Dotty looked miffed.

'But I'm fine. I think.' Cressida yawned. Dotty put Ruby into Cressida's arms and Cressida hugged her close, enjoying the warmth of the small dog's solid little body. She could feel a large, woollen jacket over her shoulders too and realised it must be Alfred's tweed, given to her to fend off the sharp bite of cold in the air now the warmth of the sun was long gone. *So like him to be so thoughtful...* She breathed in the scent of it, and nuzzled Ruby closer, but as the cool of the spring night's air brought her mind more into focus she realised she still had a killer to catch. A killer who was very much still here, in the little group standing around outside the Royal Oak, watching her recover.

It only took a few moments longer for the pub to be declared well aired and gas-free. The fire was rekindled, the lamps relit and the historical society, with Cressida and her friends with them, were sitting around the table in front of the large inglenook fireplace.

Cressida was relieved that DCI Andrews was with them, and once she was settled, with Ruby on her lap, he came up to her.

'Miss Fawcett, am I to understand from your mother that you know who killed Bob Pringle and Sir James Colston?'

'Yes, I do.' Cressida sat up straight. She could still feel Alfred's jacket around her shoulders and her head, finally, was clear as crystal. 'The same person who tried to kill his wife tonight here at the Royal Oak.'

'Walter Rook?' Lilian Catchpole said, looked confused. 'He tried to kill Annie? His own wife?'

'If it's him, then he almost killed all of us!' Percy White sounded justifiably offended. 'And would have blown this whole place to smithereens in the process.'

'Talk about covering your tracks,' Sebastian Reed added, and Cressida noticed that he was still relying on his crutches and rather red in the face with the extra effort it had taken to evacuate so quickly.

'No evidence left after that,' Madge White agreed. 'This place would have looked like a burned-out dugout on the Somme if that gas had gone up.'

'Andrews?' Cressida nodded to where Walter Rook, who had been lurking behind the rest of the society, both outside during the evacuation and while they stoked the fires back up and lit the gas lamps, was now sidestepping his way towards the back door. In a moment, Sergeant Kirby was on him, a strong hand around his collar and another on the suspect's arm.

'Let go of me, you oaf.' Walter struggled with Kirby, but the young policeman was fit and soon, aided by Andrews who helped hold him still, lowered him onto a chair beside a table in the corner of the pub. 'Prove it!' Walter shouted over to the assembled villagers. After a sharp warning to not say anything else, DCI Andrews left him in Kirby's care and walked over to where Cressida was sitting.

'Can you prove it, Miss Fawcett?' he asked, and Cressida took a deep breath, this time not one poisoned with house gas.

'I think I can. But it might be easier if I explain it all – as I see it, anyway. How this all came about and why it happened *now*.'

'I'm just relieved it's nothing to do with the society,' said Lilian, looking about her, her hand gripping the pearl necklace around her neck.

'So am I,' Cressida agreed. 'Or indeed some Saxon curse. I can't believe that for a minute or two I genuinely believed that some ancient curse was killing off people who touched the coin.'

'I don't blame you, Cressy,' Dotty said, frowning. 'That rhyme has been local knowledge for centuries, it must have been in the back of your mind from your childhood.'

'Not that she ever remembered her history.' Lord Fawcett nudged his daughter from his seat next to her.

'Well,' Cressida said with a shrug, 'curse or not, I'm sorry I also suspected the society for so long.'

'I should think so. On behalf of all of us, I feel a little aggrieved.' Lilian Catchpole's voice had a haughtiness to it that Cressida had no time for after what had just happened.

'I'm sorry, Mrs Catchpole. And you're right, despite your naughty children and quite valid motive for needing money to pay for your sister's care home, it wasn't you. And Mr Reed, despite being wholly reprehensible about those less fortunate than yourself, and with no alibi to speak of, it wasn't you either.' Cressida drew breath as she turned to the Whites and Reverend Dunn. 'And I'm sorry I ever suspected you both, Mr and Mrs White. You only do good work with those horses and more than anyone here deserve help in doing that. And, Reverend, well, I hope the roof repair fund gets topped up somehow, though I know you didn't kill anyone for the gold that could do just that.'

'But you just said it wasn't about the gold,' snapped Lilian

Catchpole, still smarting from being told about her naughty children.

Cressida turned to look at her. 'Ah, well you see, it *is* all about the gold. In some ways it was the motive after all, even though it wasn't the original motive. Let's call it the catalyst.'

'But Walter hadn't found the hoard? Had he? He didn't know where it was, did he?' Lilian asked, looking to Cressida's father for confirmation. Lord Fawcett shook his head and shrugged, but Cressida had a more certain answer.

'No, he hadn't. And neither had Bob Pringle, despite his nods and winks alongside his generosity to you all with that round of drinks the other night.'

'But Bob *had* found a fortune, even with three coins,' Dotty clarified.

'Yes, but he hadn't found the hoard, and didn't dig those coins up. Do you remember earlier when we were talking about them with Andrews and Kirby in Papa's study? And that jay clattered against the window? It startled us all, but also startled something in the back of my mind, I think. Jays are like magpies, and other corvids; they love shiny things. And they nest in the trees by the stream. I think *they've* found the hoard.' Cressida paused – she had to, to let the historical society gasp in shock – then continued. 'And they dropped one or two, or I suppose three or four, into the stream. Bob sat there every day eating his sandwiches. Marian said he often shared a bit of his lunch with them, and gardeners are well known for their relationships with birds. Robins come and chat to them in the winter as worms are unearthed with each spade, and crows and jays have been known to bring gifts to people who help them. We even have the parable of the crow and the pebbles in the stained-glass window of Saint Barnabas, which I know is a little different, but shows how clever they are. I think the jays by Hell's Ditch were thanking Bob for feeding them. Luckily for them, what killed him, didn't harm them.'

'His sandwich?' Lord Fawcett asked.

'Yes. With *atropa belladonna*; deadly nightshade. And the natural leap is to suspect Marian, his wife, a cook. As surely a gardener would never accidentally eat deadly nightshade. So how had it got into his system?'

'How?' Lilian Catchpole asked.

'His cheese and pickle sandwich. And the pickle was made by Walter Rook.'

'He does, he makes them for the church porch.' The Reverend Dunn looked shocked. 'I eat them!'

'We all do!' Lilian gripped her pearls tighter.

'And I'm sure those ones are safe,' Cressida reassured the assembled group. 'But he brought one laced with deadly nightshade to Mydenhurst Place a few days ago.'

'Oh dear,' remarked Lord Fawcett. 'That was close then, wasn't it?'

'No,' the reassuring voice of DCI Andrews said to his old commanding officer. 'Dr North has worked miracles and already had the results back of the unopened jar we found in the pantry of Mydenhurst Place. It's not poisoned.'

'Aha, you see!' Walter Rook shouted from the corner, but was shushed by Kirby.

'But...' Andrews continued, 'we also got a bit more information out of Marian Pringle, who told us that Walter had actually brought two jars with him recently, the sealed one we've just tested and an open one, given to her under the guise of the recipe making too much for the amount of jars he'd sterilised and that this small amount – enough for just one sandwich – needed using and he thought Bob might like it for his next sandwich.'

There were gasps from around the room. But Cressida nodded thoughtfully.

'I'm glad that's clearer now. You see, I don't think Walter ever intended anyone else to get hurt, not before tonight anyway. And especially not Marian. He loved her. Always had since they were an item before Walter and Annie were married.'

'Gosh,' Lilian Catchpole said, loosening the grip on her pearls and leaning in. 'So why did Walter marry Annie?'

'That rings a bell, you know,' added Madge White, who nudged Percy who merely shrugged in the way that husbands do.

Cressida continued explaining. 'Duty and honour and that sort of thing. I don't want to cause blushes, but Annie did mention to me that her own daughter, Susan, who lives over in Petworth now with her children, had her first child rather soon after getting married. "Like mother like daughter," Annie told me. Implying—'

'Ah, yes, yes. Understood.' Lord Fawcett rested a hand on his daughter's shoulder. Cressida could feel the blush reach her cheeks and dared not look at Alfred in case she became quite pink all over. Instead, she patted her father's hand to reassure him and carried on.

'So, yes, Walter had been attached to Marian. In fact, I think he still was very attached to her. Something Molly, our maid, said to me made me wonder that perhaps Walter would visit Marian independently of him and Annie coming over. And that's when he must have brought the "extra" pickle.'

'I see, so you're saying Walter poisoned Bob? And then killed Sir James?' Lord Fawcett crossed his arms. 'Because of something to do with him and Annie in the past?'

'I can see why you'd think that Papa, as the Marchmont sisters are another link between the two men – just like finding that gold coin on both of them – but the truth is far more tragic. And it explains tonight's near miss of an explosion. Sir James was never meant to die you see. His death was a horrible, horrible thing for all who knew and loved Sir James, the venerable Saxon historian. But it was utterly confusing, too, and sent us off on the wildest of goose chases thinking that the murders must be linked by the gold. But they weren't. Sir James's death was a terrible, tragic accident. He was the wrong recipient of some very deadly Turkish Delight.'

## 38

'Turkish Delight?' Lord Fawcett said. 'We had that last night.'

'We did,' agreed Percy White, indicating most of the other men in the room. 'The five of us passed it around after dinner.'

'And Alfred told me that only Sir James was seen tucking into it, thank heavens for small mercies. If any of you had helped yourselves, you'd be dead too.' Cressida's words were stark and fell among gasps from the society members.

'Hate the bloody stuff,' muttered Cressida's father, 'but where did it come from?'

'That's the thing. I think Walter prepared it for Annie, probably here in the pub's kitchen, knowing her fondness for it. She even told me herself that she and Sir James used to tuck into it with "gusto"'. But with no inkling that it was poisoned, she added it to the gift basket she brought up to her sister last night.'

'Walter never meant for it to be at our house?' Lord Fawcett asked.

'No, he never meant for it to leave his own home, or be shared around. He meant for his wife to eat it, and die in the same way that Sir James did – by taxine poisoning.'

'The seeds of the yew tree,' said Reverend Dunn.

'Yes. There are, of course, yew trees all over the village. And every part of them is highly toxic; and with our minds focused on the gold being the motive, and poison being so freely available, it meant we wasted time suspecting the historical society.'

'They say it's why the pagans and early Christians planted them near their places of worship, not to kill, but because some say the tree itself gives off such noxious substances it can make men hallucinate and therefore see the gods, or God himself,' Reverend Dunn mused, lost in his own thoughts.

'A highly poisonous tree,' Cressida agreed. 'But it's the seeds in this case. The post-mortem found one lodged in one of Sir James's teeth. He ate almost the whole box of Turkish Delight, but only five or six seeds would have been enough to kill. And dare I say it, he was a large and rather unfit man. His heart couldn't take the poison.'

'This all fed into our belief that Marian was the murderer,' DCI Andrews admitted, scratching his beard. 'Poisonings are usually a woman's way of killing.'

'Yes, sorry. That was my fault. It's so often the case in the books I read,' Dotty apologised to him. 'But, Cressy, you never thought it was Mrs Pringle, did you?'

'No, I just couldn't believe that our lovely cook, Marian, could kill not one, but two people. It never sat right with me that she would kill over Bob's gold either, or indeed Sir James if she thought he knew where the hoard was too. The first thing she said when I comforted her the morning we found Bob was that she wasn't sure what was to become of her, where she'd live and all that. Those aren't the worries of someone who had just killed for a fortune.'

There was a murmur of agreement around the group, and once it had died down, Cressida carried on. 'So, yes, poison is usually a woman's weapon, but in this case it was just the easiest thing available to Mr Rook. You can't go round stabbing people without blood getting everywhere, and not everyone's got a gun. Strangling is a bit up close and personal and could lead to being overpowered yourself. But deadly nightshade and yew seeds are guaranteed to kill, from a safe distance and while you have an alibi. And what's more, they're free.'

'Free? What's that got to do with it?' DCI Andrews asked, turning over a new page of his notebook, which had now been out for quite some time as Kirby was occupied in restraining Walter Rook.

'Quite a lot really. You know I said this was about the gold in a way that wasn't the obvious way? That it was a catalyst of sorts?'

'Yes, and it was annoyingly oblique of you,' the older policeman grumbled.

'She's like that,' muttered Lord Fawcett. 'No idea where she gets it from.'

Cressida rolled her eyes at her father, then continued explaining. 'I got it from the panels, Papa—'

'That's not what I meant... oh never mind.' Lord Fawcett took a deep breath. 'Carry on, poppet.'

'The panels in the library at Mydenhurst Place. They open to reveal Aletheia, the goddess of truth. She's there in plain sight, but only when not hidden by these panels covered in gold-framed paintings. So, I wondered if the gold was blinding us, what with its associated talk of curses too and all that, and hiding the truth of what, and who, was behind these murders. And then little details fell into place.'

'Like in a very good decorating scheme,' Dotty said, proudly.

'Exactly, chum. I think I'm right in saying Walter loves Marian. He's always loved Marian and I think Marian's still fond of him. Not so much that she could bring herself to leave Bob; it was his house after all that they lived in after her parents had disinherited her. And Walter knew that. The pub is

Annie's too, so if he leaves Annie, where would he stand? Any money he'd brought with him to the marriage was sunk into this place, on running repairs and bad business decisions. It was common knowledge the pub wasn't doing too well. The debt collector we saw outside today is testament to that. Which is why if Marian and Walter left their partners, divorced them and ran away together, they'd have nothing. And as Marian said yesterday, when I thought she was talking about Bob, "Love can only get you so far."

'Last Thursday, Bob Pringle came and sat at that stool next to the bar and bought the whole village a round of drinks. He used to sit at the bar a lot, almost as if he was keeping tabs on Walter. Sebastian,' – she turned to the youngest member of the society – 'you told me that, saying it seemed as if Bob wanted to keep an eye on Walter. Making sure he wasn't popping down to the kitchen at Mydenhurst to visit his first love, Marian. But for one night, Bob put all that aside and relished buying a round of drinks for everyone in the Royal Oak. A night that was intended to taunt the historical society. He had found gold. Not all of it, but those friendly jays had scattered enough coins at his feet in the stream that he could happily retire with a tidy fortune. And, Walter,' – she looked over to the suspect in the corner – 'I have to assume that you eked this out of him. You then discovered the true value of Bob's coins, having telephoned the coin dealer in London pretending to be Bob. Then you decided that now was the time, after all these years, to get rid of Bob and marry Marian – who'd be a rich widow, rather than a poor divorcee. With Annie dead too, he could sell the freehold of this pub, adding more to their fortune and ridding himself of a business that was failing, but means too much to Annie to simply sell.'

'So that's why he did it?' DCI Andrews said, nodding, but Walter, who had been listening to it all from the other side of the room bellowed, 'Prove it!'

Cressida paused, but DCI Andrews replied for her. 'As you

said, Miss Fawcett, Walter put a call in to the coin dealers in London. A call that we've had verified from the colleague of Mr Denton. He said the man who telephoned from the Mydenhurst exchange didn't sound like the man who had visited them, which was why it raised their suspicions. He had a West Country accent, you see, whereas Bob was Sussex through and through.'

There were gasps from around the table, but Cressida grinned at Andrews. To think, after all the supposition and theories that she knew to be true but couldn't prove, it was the landlord's accent that gave him away.

'Do you have anything to say for yourself, Mr Rook?' Cressida asked.

'Just that I never meant for Marian to get involved. I didn't realise that she'd be up against the wall for Bob's death. It was meant to just look like natural causes, and it would have if you hadn't started meddling, looking into the pickle and all that. Annie too.' He shook his head. 'It was all planned out. Marian and I could have finally been together.' Walter Rook growled at Cressida.

'That explains that, at least, but I meant more an apology, perhaps, to the good folk here who you were willing to kill in order to get away with it all?'

'Apologise? I spent thirty years wishing I'd stayed true to Marian Marchmont. That one night, all those years ago, when a weeping Annie came to me. Marian and I had never... well, our courtship was chaste, but Annie got me drunk and lifted her skirt. I had to marry her, once Susan was on the way. It broke Marian's heart at the time' – his face softened – 'but the sort of person she is, she forgave us both.'

'And she made the best of her life with Bob,' continued Cressida. 'Despite being disinherited by her father for marrying so beneath her, in his eyes, in any case.'

'It was the least I could do,' Lord Fawcett said, stirring from his position by the fire next to Cressida. 'To help Marian. She'd been in our circle growing up and to see her laid so low... Rosamund and I offered her the job of cook to help out, and we hoped that when we were abroad for those spells she could somewhat make herself at home. Maybe linger in the library a little longer than usual. Play the piano and all that.'

'It's all too tragic,' Dotty muttered.

Cressida nodded as DCI Andrews made the arrest and, with Kirby's help, marched Walter Rook to the awaiting police car.

'I hope that's evidence enough to keep him under lock and key,' Alfred said, joining Cressida and Dotty by the fire. 'I don't doubt for one minute that you're spot on in your analysis, Cressy, but apart from a telephone call on a rusty exchange... Well, it would be a darned shame to see him freed if that's not enough to see it through.'

Cressida thought about it for a moment, then looked brighter. 'Annie. She'll testify, I should imagine. Once one's husband has tried to kill one twice – by Turkish Delight and gas suffocation – I should imagine one would be more open to telling a jury all about the financial problems of the pub, her husband's eye for her sister and, of course, how he tied her up and left her to die in the kitchen.'

'What a rotter,' Dotty said, tutting to herself.

Cressida crossed her arms and stared into the fire. 'Indeed. Walter Rook... a first-class crook.'

## 39

'So... two for you as a wedding present,' Cressida said pointing at Fortnum and Mason, 'and I owe that nice policeman from the Mayfair Hotel one, for his daughter, Beth. She can have Lulu, maybe. What am I going to do with the other three?'

Cressida and her friends were sitting at the white cast-iron table by the croquet lawn, watching Ruby's puppies as they once again ran around the hoops and pegs, rolling over balls and skipping over mallets. An actual game had lasted no more than a few minutes before it was called off as a bad job as Suki had become so attached to Alfred that she'd got in the way of every shot.

It was a beautiful morning though, and they had freshly brewed coffee and biscuits straight out of the oven, courtesy of Marian, who had been released from custody as soon as Walter had been arrested. Marian had decided that she *would* take a few days off after all, as the situation had all been rather taxing on her. But she insisted that she wouldn't leave until Cressida and her friends had returned to London and the ancient walls of Mydenhurst Place were no longer ringing with the sounds of puppies yapping and scrapping.

'You could keep one,' Dotty suggested. She looked over to Alfred, who had just put Suki down on the grass, having peeled her off his leg a moment ago. 'I know a certain puppy has become quite attached to a certain person.'

Cressida kicked Dotty under the table, not hard, but enough to elicit an 'ouch'.

Alfred, however, took the hint. 'Fancy a walk down to the stream, Cressy?' He stood up, straightened his jacket and dusted down his trousers, never once looking her in the eye, which suddenly gave Cressida more shivers than she'd experienced during any murder investigation.

'Yes, all right then, Alf,' she replied, getting up herself and joining him on his side of the table.

'Right,' he said.

'Right,' she said. And with a small wave to Dotty, who was grinning from pearl-earringed ear to pearl-earringed ear, Cressida joined Alfred as they walked towards the summer pavilion. Ruby did not take the hint, and joined them.


'It's been quite a couple of days,' Alfred said, having cleared his throat and for once, put his pipe away. 'Lovely, of course, to be here in glorious Sussex, but two deaths and more than that...' He paused, though they walked on, turning the corner behind the pavilion and heading into the little copse. 'You were very nearly almost killed. Again.'

'I know. And I'm sorry about that. I just sort of pieced things together in my head and knew it was Walter, and that Annie might be in danger. Then with the gas and knowing the pub might explode with some of my favourite people in it... I had to try and stop it. I know you think I'm a hothead, Alf, but—'

'You *are* a hothead, Cressy,' Alfred interrupted her. They were walking through the long grasses now and were almost at the bridge over Hell's Ditch. 'But you're also the most coura-geous, clever, clued-up person that I know.'

Cressida could feel the blush spreading across her cheeks. Did Alfred, who was pretty game for most things, as loyal as anything and as handsome as a matinee idol to boot, really think those things about her? She slipped an arm through his as they reached the old stone bridge.

Alfred turned to face her. 'You know, I had a chat with Sir James, may he rest in peace, over the port two nights ago.'

'Oh yes?' Cressida tried not to sound disappointed in the change of subject away from her many and varied virtues.

'Yes. And, as you know, he was a boffin about so much of the Saxon history of this county, but specifically Mydenhurst. I suppose it being close to his ancestral home and all that.'

'I was surprised when we found out he'd been a young lad here, careering around with Papa and the Marchmont sisters in open-top carriages and the like.'

'An image for the mind indeed.' Alfred chuckled. 'But he told me a thing or two about this specific place.'

'Hell's Ditch? I always wondered why it was called that.'

'It wasn't originally. Other towns have Hell Ditches or Hell's Ditches, most because the stream was the last crossing convicted felons would make before they were taken to the out-of-town gallows.'

'Oh.' Cressida looked into the crystal-clear water, seeing how it tumbled over the pebbles and stones. 'That's not very nice.'

'No. But this one is different.'

'Phew!' Cressida looked up from the water. She hadn't much liked the thought of there being a site of an ancient gallows anywhere near the beautiful grounds of Mydenhurst Place.

'Sir James said it was one of those times when words sound alike and get changed over the years. So originally it was never

Hell's Ditch, but Hæl Ditch. From the Anglo-Saxon word for feeling whole, or safe. I suppose it was a sort of moat around the old settlement, dug to keep them safe from marauders.' Alfred took Cressida in his arms and looked at her earnestly. 'And I feel whole when I'm with you, Cressy.'

Cressida let herself be pulled into his arms and allowed all the worries and fears of the last couple of days to wash away from her. Safe – that was the word. She felt safe in his arms and she never wanted to leave his embrace.

She looked up at him, the oh-so-familiar chestnut-brown eyes, with those handsome little crinkles at the corners. She closed her eyes and was waiting for his kiss when instead she felt his arms pull away from her. Had she read too much into it all? Had Alfred just had second thoughts? She cautiously opened her eyes to see... nothing. Alfred wasn't there. A small snort-snuffle from a certain pug made her look down and she gasped in surprise to see Alfred there, kneeling on the ground, a red leather box held in his hand as he looked up at her.

'Cressy, I know you'll say no, as you have said time and again that you never want a husband, but hear me out—'

'Alfred, I—' Cressida was speechless, yet she had to say something before Alfred carried on. But somehow the words were stuck in her throat and she was helpless as she looked down at his handsome face, his deep-brown eyes. He took one of her hands in his and carried on.

'Cressida Fawcett, I love you. I love your wildly independent ways, your hot-headedness, your brilliant mind. I love how fun you are, and how witty. And I love being by your side, whatever adventure comes next.' He paused. Then he stood up and pocketed the box. Cressida looked at him, her brow furrowed, her eyes inquisitive, until he carried on. 'But I don't want to stifle you, I don't want you to feel that you've lost any of your independence. You're the Honourable Cressida Fawcett, and as much as I'd adore you to be Lady Delafield, and one day, the

Countess of Chatterton, I can't ask that of you.' He took both of her hands in his and looked her square in the eye. 'So, Cressy, would you do me the honour of *not* marrying me? Not yet anyway. Not until you've lived every moment of the life you want to as a brilliant, independent woman.'

'Alfred, I...' Cressida gripped his hands in hers and pulled him close to her. His words had melted her heart. His assurances that he loved her, not for her money or her social standing – two things she'd always been cautious of when it came to suitors – made her wonder if perhaps marriage might not be so loathsome after all. Letting go of his hands, she raised hers to hold his face and pulled him down to her waiting lips.

After a blissful few moments, Cressida pulled away, lowering her hands, via a quick straightening of his lapels, to the pocket in which she'd seen the small red box disappear. Alfred let her delve in and when she pulled out the box he took it from her and opened the lid.

'Alfred, it's beautiful,' whispered Cressida as the sun glinted off the gold band with three diamonds set in a row, the middle one the largest of the three.

'What do you say then, old thing?' Alfred asked. 'To not marrying me?'

Cressida took the ring out of the box and slipped it onto her own finger as Alfred grinned at her. 'I think I could get used to being Lady Delafield,' she answered, resting her hand with its glinting new ring on it, against his lapel again. 'Not yet, but soon. Maybe sooner than you think.'

A yapping from the stream distracted them both and Cressida took a step back as Alfred glanced down, then pulled off his jacket and flung it to the ground.

'Be careful, Alfred!' Cressida exclaimed as he vaulted off the bridge and landed with a splash in the waters, inches from where Ruby was stranded on a half-submerged stone in the middle of the stream. Alfred bent down to rescue her and Cressida laughed as she leaned over the stony edge of the small bridge. Ruby was snorting and snuffling and Cressida stopped laughing and peered more closely instead to where Ruby had been standing. 'Alf, I think she's trying to tell us something.'

'Well, congratulations are in order—' Alfred said before he was interrupted by the flapping of wings, as a large, beautiful jay flew down to the water. A flash of turquoise from under the bird's wing caught Cressida's eye as it flew off, but she noticed something else too. As the bird flew back up into the boughs of one of the yew trees in the copse she saw the sun reflect off something in its beak.

Something small. Something gold.

A Saxon coin.

# A LETTER FROM FLISS

Dear reader,

I want to say a huge thank you for choosing to read *Death in an English Village*. If you did enjoy it, and want to keep up to date with all my latest releases, just sign up at the following link. Your email address will never be shared and you can unsubscribe at any time.

*www.bookouture.com/fliss-chester*

I really hope that you've enjoyed reading about Cressida Fawcett, and perhaps discovering a bit about Saxon coins (though I don't profess to be an expert!). I've loved delving into the medieval world and coming up with poems and curses – and I think Cressida enjoyed herself too, despite the murders! If you love our amateur sleuth – and Ruby too, of course – I would be very grateful if you could write a review of *Death in an English Village*. And I'd love to hear what you think, too. Reviews from readers like you can make such a difference helping new readers discover my books for the first time.

If you have any thoughts about this story – or tales of your own about mysterious hoards of gold – you can get in touch you can get in touch on social media or my website. I'd love to hear from you.

Thanks,

Fliss Chester

www.flisschester.co.uk

f facebook.com/flisschester
instagram.com/flisschester

# AUTHOR'S NOTE

It takes a certain amount of parental inspiration to come up with a family like the Fawcetts, and although mine aren't quite so aristocratic or eccentric, my step-father does say 'what ho' when he sees me and my mother and I were discussing colours for the dining room walls just this morning... So thank you to Mum, Rosalind, and Philip my step-father, for always being so fun and giving me so much support and inspiration as I've been writing these books.

Another inspiration, especially for the scenes in Mydenhurst's study between Cressida and her father, comes from conversations many years ago between me and a great family friend, Professor John Adair. Author of countless books himself, he always inspired me to write, even as a teenager, and I'm incredibly proud that he's seen me be published thirteen times now. Still not as many as him, but I'm catching up, John!

Thank you as ever to my literary agent, Emily Sweet, and the contracts team at Aevitas Creative Management. And also to both Rhianna Louise and Cerys Hadwin-Owen at Bookouture for your editorial input – it's always such a relief to know that I can ask your advice at any point during the writing process and not be judged on my half-baked ideas!

As I've noted before, being an author, though a huge privilege, is also a lonely trade, and I rely so much on my good friends in the industry – those in the Criminal Minds WhatsApp group and beyond. Thank you all for your support and help as we all tackle our characters and plots together.

And last, but never least, thank you to my darling husband Rupert for all of his support and encouragement. I couldn't have written these books, or introduced you all to Cressida and her wonderful world, without him.

# PUBLISHING TEAM

**Turning a manuscript into a book requires the efforts of many people. The publishing team at Bookouture would like to acknowledge everyone who contributed to this publication.**

### Audio
Alba Proko
Melissa Tran
Sinead O'Connor

### Commercial
Lauren Morrissette
Hannah Richmond
Imogen Allport

### Cover design
Debbie Clement

### Data and analysis
Mark Alder
Mohamed Bussuri

### Editorial
Cerys Hadwin-Owen
Charlotte Hegley

9 781836 183853